a real slice of life told in the verr
irvine welsl

CW00469759

talesofaggro

matteo sedazzari
author of a crafty cigarette

Published by ZANI

For information contact:
. info@zani.co.uk

Front Cover and Inside Cover design by Andy Catlin

Tales of Aggro is dedicated to my mother, Patricia.

A big thank you to everyone and anyone who bought and supported A Crafty Cigarette – Tales of a Teenage Mod, the list is fxxking endless, it means a lot and always will do, thank you again from the bottom of my heart.

I would like to thank my mother, Dean Cavanagh, Gavin Sanctis, Irvine Welsh, John Cooper Clarke, Loren Jenkins, Mahen Widyalankara, Tracey Dawn Wilmot, Nick Taylor, Laurence Parmiter, Danny Rampling, Eric Turner, Carla Brown, Rob Buckley, Jason Pearce, Alan McGee, Fiona Cartridge, Louise Davies, Paolo Sedazzari Christian Kernot, Martina Cole, Nick Philpin, James (Jimmy)Constantinou, Rick Buckler, Richard Knights & Trudi and the gang, for supporting me either professionally or personally, during the course of me writing Tales of Aggro. Your help, advice and encouragement helped me to reach the finishing line, nice one!

And thank you to you for holding a copy of this book, I hope you enjoy this collection of short stories all about love and unity with a little bit of aggro......

TALES OF AGGRO DISCLAIMER FROM MATTEO SEDAZZARI
—Please Read

Please detach yourself from everyday life and enjoy this modern-day collection of fantasy tales with a contemporary and realistic narrative.

There are characters within Tales of Aggro who are real people, alive or dead. In addition, I would like to state that their engagement within this collection of short stories is a work of complete fiction. Under no circumstances is any malice intended other than for the sole purpose to make this book more entertaining and engaging, in a nutshell it is satire.

Apart from one deceased disc jockey and broadcaster, who appears in latter part of book. I have no qualm about being unpleasant about them, as their traits outlined and highly criticised are true.

Moreover, some of the stories are written in the first person, where local dialogue and slang is used, as opposed to a detailed analysis of a situation. In short, the characters speak as if they are reminiscing an anecdote in a public situation. Similar to my debut novel, A Crafty Cigarette—Tales of a Teenage Mod, where the story was told by a boy, aged from 11 to 14 years old, throughout the book.

Some readers may find some of the language offensive in this book, this is not the aim. Furthermore, as an individual, I do not use offensive language to discredit race, religion, gender or sexuality in my everyday life. Yet some of the fictional characters in Tales of Aggro would, as some of the stories are set in an era where certain impolite words would be used more, regardless of whether they upset anyone. However I felt it was necessary to keep the dialogue as credible as possible in certain situations.

Matteo Sedazzari

Foreword
by Steve White

The Magnificent Six in Tales of Aggro evokes the memories of me growing up in South London. It captures the youth, the clothes, the music, and the camaraderie perfectly. In concurrent with all the factors that are vital to our 'salad days', the book focuses a great deal on the humour of youth, which gives the young unstoppable energy and lust for life in even the toughest of times.

With hints of Quadrophenia, a soupçon of Budgie and a with a taste of Minder, this novel is a vivid and enjoyable slice of London life in the 80s, with a wealth of detail and characters, that are full of richness and broadness. Like Detective Arthur Legg, a spiteful and corrupt policeman that bullied and blackmailed his way to the top, a new fictional villain to despise and fear.

The Magnificent Six in Tales of Aggro is a hidden gem of a novel and I keep telling my friends, this book is perfect for a pool and a beer combination, and I say the same to you my friends, happy reading!

Tales of Aggro Table of Content

tales of aggro: book one

matteo sedazzari

how can you live
when you don't exist
how can you smile
ain't been happy for a while

1

Prologue

Six teenagers—Eddie the Casual, Oscar De Paul, Honest Ron, Jamie Joe, Quicksilver and Dino—sharply dressed outside a chip shop in Shepherd's Bush. They have no agenda, no place to go, yet their need is to be together in the dark streets of London, where anything mad or bad can happen. These boys, locally known as The Magnificent Six, adore the darkness—to them it is their spiritual home, wandering the streets, meeting all kind of folks, some good, some bad, some insane, some lovely, but always an experience. They hit on girls in the local Wimpy, wind up drunks in the pubs, stand their ground and respect the local villains. While doing all this, they always check their reflections in the mirror, as looking good is so important to them, more important than love or work.

Eddie steps forward and faces the boys. They huddle round, with Oscar by his right-hand side. Many suggestions are put forward about what they should do tonight—it's a big decision for them, as none of them want to go home bored after an uneventful evening. The Magnificent Six want an encounter, something to talk about for years to come, something to boast about and tell the next girl they date.

Oscar breaks away from the group and walks round the back of the chip shop into a dark alleyway. The stray cats that feed every night from the thrown away fish and chips run away. Oscar relieves himself, then returns to his mates. He takes out a cigarette, lights it, inhales, and starts to think about his past, present and future. It makes no sense to him, but he doesn't want it to make sense. All Oscar wants to do, is to live a mad life.

2

Oscar De Paul in Another Day, Another Dollar

'You can bring tanks, bulldozers, even drop the bloody H-bomb, but you ain't knocking down me fish and chip shop, you hear me son?'

'Mr Pilcher, I do understand your annoyance. I know it is a slight inconvenience.'

'A bleeding slight inconvenience? I'll give you a slight inconvenience.'

'Mr Pilcher, Hammersmith and Fulham Council wrote to you 60 days ago, informing you that we wish to take our shop back. We requested that you vacate the premises no later than Wednesday 27th May 1987 at 09.00 hours on the dot. That is tomorrow. We are offering you and your family one month's accommodation in a bed and breakfast in Ealing and 50 per cent of the market value of your business, so you have been warned.'

'Listen, son. I never got the bleeding letter.'

My face breaks into a wry smile, as he is well and truly rattled. 'Mr Pilcher, please, there is no need to swear.' Oh, I do like to have authority—makes me feel good.

'Listen, you ponce, I will do more than swear, sonny Jim, you are taking away my livelihood.' He is going spare. Any second now he will crack.

'Well, Mr Pilcher, according to our records, you did receive the letter—it was sent recorded delivery.' A verbal left hook to the ribs. I can feel his legs starting to wobble.

'It must have been the bloody missus. Sheila? You daft cow. Bugger, she ain't in. You married son?'

Got him. He's punch-drunk, He doesn't know whether to fight or flight.

'Engaged, we haven't planned the big day yet,' I reply in a jovial manner.

'Do yourself a favour, young man—don't. My stupid cow of a wife just signed away me fish and chip shop. My granddad started this business in the 20s. Been part of Shepherd's Bush for generations.'

Well and truly KO-ed. I've broken him. Mr Pilcher starts to mutter to himself.

'Mr Pilcher are you OK?' I ask in a concerned manner.

'Here, son, you said the council are offering me 50 per cent of the market value. Give me 200 per cent in cash by 3.30. It's only ten now, so you've got plenty of time to get to the bank. Me and the missus will be out of here by opening time. I'll even buy you a drink.'

I must admit I like his fight back. I knew he had it in him.

'Mr Pilcher, thanks for the invitation for a drink. Maybe another day. No, fifty per cent is the highest we will go to. I do believe the council is being very generous, as I sampled your fish and chips before I made the decision, and I must say they are not up to scratch. Fat Ralph's fish and chips around the corner are of a much better standard.'

Any second now, he is going to lay into me over the telephone. 'Fat Ralph? He's a bleeding pikey, only been in the game for five minutes. Pilcher's have been serving the BBC and Thames Television for years. They drive all the way from Teddington to sample my grub. Got signed photos all over the place from Frank Bough to Angela Rippon. You must have seen them when you came in. All over the place.'

He is sparring again. Like it—a worthy opponent. 'Must have missed them,' I come back with a verbal uppercut.

'Missed them? I've got a great photo of Bernard Manning stuffing a saveloy down his throat and Mike Reid tucking into my famous chip butty.'

'Mike Read the TV presenter? I like him—Saturday Superstore.' This is a little nutcracker.

'Not that ponce who thinks he is Cliff Richard—Mike Reid the comedian.'

I reply with, 'What? "Runaround… now!"' in my over-the-top Mike Reid impression.

There is an eerie silence. I start to get nervous, as I may have blown my cover.

'I recognize your voice,' replies Mr Pilcher in a confident manner.

Well, he should, I live nearby. I have been going to Pilcher's since I was about eight. I'm now a young adult. Seen all the photos, seen the stars in person as well. Seen Mike Reid many a time there. Let's just say we don't get on—we always have a dig and I take the piss by mimicking his old catch-phrase, 'Runaround… now!' Most of the stars that pop into Pilcher's are OK, apart from Mike Reid and Jimmy Tarbuck. We had a run in with him when we were kids—long story—and there is still a feud. As for the grub, it is excellent, better than Fat Ralph's, but I do like a wind-up.

'Mr Pilcher, we possibly spoke when I came to your food emporium. Other than that, I can assure you we haven't met before. I'm George Elliott, town planner of Hammersmith and Fulham Council. Anyway, I think Mike Reid is a bit of a steamer.' Hopefully, this verbal jab will sway him.

'Come again, son?' replies Mr Pilcher in an aggressive manner.

Now for a verbal right cross. 'He is a steamer—he's never made me laugh.' I close my eyes, waiting for the abuse.

'Bit of a steamer? I'll give you bit of a steamer. I will tear your lungs out. Knock your teeth out. No one calls Mike Reid a steamer.'

I put the telephone down, catch my breath. Usually, I am laughing, but this time I nearly got caught. Funny—Mr Pilcher lost his temper more when I insulted Mike Reid than when I tried to evict him from his fish and chip shop.

I suppose it's the boredom of the day job that has made me resort to making prank calls. I'm Oscar De Paul, Shepherd's Bush boy, 20 years old, 21 on the 23rd November, please do drop me a card. Been doing telesales, display and classified ads for Hammersmith & Shepherd's Bush Gazette for about eight months now. First two months were hard, really hard, arguing with people from florists to funeral directors, then got my first order—Mr Grahame, a hardware shop in Acton. Once I broke my duck, my confidence soared, and I've been selling ever since.

It's the longest I have ever kept a job, which pleases my mother no end. I've no idea, what I want to do, I really don't. Don't get me wrong, I am not stupid, far from it. Got two A-Levels last year, night classes, sociology and psychology, both grade Es, but I left school along with all my mates with no qualifications. We were Casuals—still are, I suppose—known around town as The Magnificent Six, a nickname given to us when we were at Christopher Wren School by some snotty nosed girl in pigtails, two years below us, who shouted out 'It's The Magnificent Six,' as we were bowling around the school, giving it the big one. The name stuck. We like it, I must say.

The cheeky girl was Stephanie Clarke. I've been going out with her for a year now. Took us yonks before we got together, a few false starts. A beautiful girl in body, spirit, soul and mind. Great dress sense and boy can she move—seen her turn many heads when she struts on the dance floor—and what a beautiful singing voice.

So, as you can tell, there's six of us: me, Eddie the Casual, Honest Ron, Quicksilver, Jamie Joe and Dino. Eddie isn't called Eddie the Casual because he was the first to become a Casual—it's because we had two Eddies in our year, Eddie, my mate, and the other Eddie, Eddie Green, a top footballer when we were at school (last I heard, he was playing for Brentford's reserve team), so it was Eddie the Casual or Eddie the footballer. But Eddie, my Eddie, makes out he's called Eddie the Casual because he was the sharpest. He wasn't—I was.

Anyway, we, The Magnificent Six, just thought our swagger, boyish good looks, thieving, cheeky charm, dress sense, and proficiency at music, street fights and gallows humour were all we needed to get on. But we have all learnt a harsh lesson—it isn't. Well, not yet. But I tell you something: these skills are genuine, all from the heart. No bleeding teacher, no textbook, no educational film can teach you these. You have to learn them for yourself. But we're just biding our time, making and waiting for the breaks. So, in the meantime we are all earning. As the Dire Straits sing, 'I shoulda learned to play the guitar.' So true, but I bloody hate that band.

I've been job-jumping for yonks. Couldn't seem to keep a job down—either I got fired or walked out—and before that, no one took me seriously when I was looking for work. My father died three years ago. I am not making excuses, but it did throw me off course, as it did my mother and my older sister Olivia. Some bastard was driving down the Uxbridge Road like Mad Max.

Didn't see my old man crossing the road. Bang, he died on impact. The fella got three years—three bloody years for dangerous driving. Only done 18 months. He's moved out of the area—he's a wanted man. One day, oh yes, one day.

Nearly broke us. I became angry. But it was Olivia who kept us together. She was the one that made me go to night classes. Otherwise, I would have been drowning my sorrows every night, and my sorrows are strong swimmers. But a year ago, after she landed a well-paid posh job in some Sloane Ranger public relations firm down the King's Road, the brother/sister love we once had turned into hate. I have no idea how or why. I used to adore her—still do. Perhaps it's just a phase she is going through.

I moved to the Bush when I was seven in the summer of 1974. I was born up the road in Chiswick. Don't really remember too much about it, apart from we had a big house and my father was doing well. But it wasn't due to his salary, oh no. He was a chief accountant or something at Shell on the Embankment and was skimming off some of the profits. Don't know the ins and outs—he would never tell me. Trust me, I did ask. I just remember one evening after It's A Knockout, there was a knock at the door from the Old Bill. They took him away.

He got bail, but life was bad after that. A sort of darkness hung over the family, there were no smiles, no laughter. I think my mother knew my old man was on the take because she was always dressing up like Raquel Welch and spoiling herself, Olivia and me.

He went on trial, Old Bailey, straight up, he was sentenced, got six years. Well, we lost the house—my mother couldn't afford the mortgage. The three of us, broken-hearted, moved to some flea-bitten bed and breakfast. Then three months later my mother managed to get us into a three-bedroomed house, 51 Bloemfontein Avenue, right in the heart of White City, and I went to Bentworth Primary School to make some new friends.

Which was easier said than done, as I was scared. I was the posh kid, I really was. Bullied and teased for about a year, mainly by Dino and Honest Ron. Then one day I fought back. I have no idea where the strength came from, possibly from watching Henry Cooper on Sportsnight, but I floored Dino and Ron ran off crying. We were about eight, nine maybe. My self-taught fighting skills won me the admiration of Eddie. We became mates and have been ever since.

I didn't meet Quicksilver and Jamie Joe until we started at Christopher Wren. Quicksilver (real name Simon)—he's got a silver streak in his hair, which he got when he was about 12, poor sod. Jamie became part of the gang after he had a good old-fashioned school fight with Eddie. Fighting can win you enemies and friends. Who says love conquers all? Hippy shit. I mean if I hadn't fought back, my life would have been Hell, bullied every day. I became part of a gang, grew with them, that old cliché 'we are family'.

I feel at home at the Bush, and I know why I do, because my father was born here. After a few dead-end jobs and a bit of petty crime, my father found out he had a good head for figures. He went to college in the evenings, became an accountant and got a job at Shell. Don't know when he started to 'fiddle the books', as he never told me. Quite secretive was my father. He came out of prison in 1979, after his second parole hearing—failed his first one.

The summer of 1979 was the summer when me, Ron and Eddie became Mods—well, Dino was a Rude Boy for a while—but I was the first to become a Mod, don't let Eddie tell you different. The Who, Shepherd's Bush boys, made an LP about the original Mods from here, Quadrophenia, in the early seventies. The film came out the same year my father was released from prison. I remember us seeing the cameras, the scooters, the actors, but it didn't really sink in then, what it was all about. What mugs we were. The Sex Pistols' Steve Jones and Paul Cook are from around here—went to the same school as me, Christopher Wren—so the Bush certainly has a lot of soul.

My father, Malcolm Paul, changed the surname to De Paul by deed poll before I was born. I think that was my mother's idea. When he was released, he settled in well, he was happy, an old boy returning to the roost if you like. He was respected for being an ex-con, not out of fear or anything like that, but because he stole for his family, went to the Old Bailey and done his bird like a man. My mother, who you could visualize at Abigail's Party, and my sister Olivia, the missing Charlie's Angel, wanted to move back to Chiswick, but I think my father missed and loved the Bush. And as for me, this is my destiny.

I landed this job via my good friend, Honest Ron—you know, my one-time bully, now my partner in crime. Ron went down last year, only three months, shoplifting, that's been on the cards for years, and possession, as he had a little bit of personal puff on him. Ron's been serving up for the local loon Rooster, but Ron is savvy enough never to carry too much puff. He's still works for Rooster—let's just say, he's a junior partner, as Ron has got the school leavers as his foot soldiers. Dig the new breed—ah. As for the nicking, the lad will never change. Ron was born a tea leaf.

When Ron came out, he was assigned to one of those loving and caring hippy chick probation officers or social workers—can't remember which—Susanna Oakes. Met her a few times with Ron, out and about. A real throwback from the 60s. Good-looking woman though.

Old Oakes has got a real soft spot for Ron. Loads of girls do, especially the posh ones. Has a bag of chisels as a face, about the size of a dwarf with a Kevin Keegan perm, but he's got the gift of the gab and, I hate to say it, he is funny, a real class clown.

Oakes is friends with Kelvin Crooke—he's the sales director here. Anyway, she says to Crooke that one of her probationers, Ron, is a natural salesman and he should give Ron a chance. Then Oakes says to Ron he could make an honest living for a change. I was shocked, we all were, when Ron agreed to an interview, and nearly fainted when he was offered the job and accepted it.

I reckon Oakes is having an affair with Crooke. Ron's grilled her a few times, but like a seasoned criminal, Oakes' didn't crack under the pressure.

Within a few weeks, Honest Ron was doing all right. Saw him most evenings, telling me about his sales, the girls and the money he was making. I was either signing on or in some shit job. I was jealous—everyone had something going, apart from me. So, after hearing about his success for a few months, I asked if he could get me a job. He didn't exactly say yes straight away. No, he just started laughing, as did the rest of The Magnificent Six. I lost my temper and stormed out of The Queen Adelaide. I can still hear the laughter today.

A week or so later, Ron gave me a call, said some fella on his table had resigned. So, I got my best suit dry-cleaned. Three-button, dark blue mohair—guess I am still a Mod, deep down. I can't stand these new double-breasted, wing-collar suits. Awful, absolutely awful.

Like Honest Ron, Crooke took a shine to me. I was offered the job on the spot. Been here ever since. As you know, it took me some time to get my head around sales, getting the orders, earning the commission, but now I am a master. If it wasn't for Ron I would be top at telesales, but I can't beat him.

Come close. Boy, have I come close. Ron loves it. Doesn't muck about. He just hits the phones hard in the day and, in the night, he's a naughty boy again, a real Jekyll and Hyde.

Then a few months ago, on the way home from work, it struck me that if I, a 20-year-old kid, can get a total stranger to buy off me in less than ten minutes then I could get them to do something else. Anything. So, one afternoon when the office was noisy, I decided to call Mick Palmer, a greengrocer on Hammersmith Broadway. Used to nick apples and all that, years ago. Dino used to work there. In fact, all the Magnificent Six have worked there.

Well, apart from me. I turned up, asked for a Saturday job. Dino was working there that day. Palmer spat out his coffee, started to laugh, as did Dino and the two old ladies he was serving. I had never seen these old biddies in my life before, one of them even shouts out, 'This is a man's job, not for mincers,' which was met by more laughter. As I turned my back to walk out, the other one shouts out, 'Shut that door!' My face went bright red as the laughter grew louder. I was only bleeding 14. How humiliating. Ended up doing two paper rounds, one in the morning, one in the evening, for shirt buttons.

So, I called the git Palmer in my most authoritative and well-spoken voice. I said to him that I'm from the Food Council. Asked where he got his tomatoes from. He said Nine Elms. I said he had to destroy them as they were contaminated. We argued for a bit, then he said he would.

After work I walked to Palmer's. It was about six, so the shop was closed. Underneath the closed sign was a white bit of A4 paper, stuck on with blue tack and 'No Tomatoes' written in black marker pen. I cried with laughter, also felt a little bit of revenge, so I went over the road to a pub for a celebration drink.

The following day I called Bransdon News Agent. Mr Bransdon Jr. was another one who wouldn't give me a job, but he gave my sister a job. Again, same scenario, went in, asked for a job, he along with his new Saturday girl, Louise—she's going out with Eddie now—started to laugh, along with old Mr Yates, who was buying his Racing Post. In fact, he laughed so much, he nearly had a heart attack. I felt like a cross between Yosser Hughes—you know, 'Gis us a Job' from Boys from The Blackstuff—and Norman Wisdom. But, I

Matteo Sedazzari

did nick a few packets of fags, as they both took the old boy round the back for some water. Kept a few of the packets for myself and the rest I sold that evening around the estate.

I believed this was a sign that I was to become a criminal like my father. After I left school, me, Eddie, Dino and Quicksilver earnt a living from shoplifting, breaking into warehouses and ransacking hotel rooms, thanks to Eddie's uncle Rockin' Wilf, who taught us the art of thieving. Wilf was fitted up by the Old Bill the year I moved to the Bush. Done a bit of bird as well. Honest Ron and Jamie Joe weren't up for nicking, so they decided to knock out puff instead.

Then, towards the end of 83, start of 84, it got too much. Old Bill on our case, living hand to mouth, seeing other kids from White City going to Feltham Borstal, boredom. We started to get proper jobs. But we still dabble—of course we do.

I phoned Mr Bransdon Jr and said I was from the government, that an Emergency Bill had been passed, that the selling of all pornographic magazines was now illegal, so he must remove them at once. He argued, but eventually he gave in. The following day on the way to work, I go in to pick up my ten Bensons for the day and ask for a copy of Mayfair. Mr Bransdon Jr, who was serving, says that it was illegal to sell them. I walked out with a smile and a sense of vengeance.

After I got reprisal on all those that had chuckled at me when I was a school boy looking for work, I moved onto new targets. I've had hotels remove beds as there was a new epidemic of bed bugs, removal companies burning all their cardboard boxes as they were now illegal, florists getting rid of their red roses, as Margaret Thatcher had banned them as she views them as a symbol of the Labour party—the list is endless, and the number of gullible victims grows. Ron has sussed. He's a bit disappointed, but he's more gutted that he hadn't thought of the scam first. He's a rogue and always will be. The Magnificent Six is in his blood.

I sit in a group of four: me, Ron, Lisa Lee—she's all right is Lisa (well, she laughs at my jokes anyway)—and the new lad, Billy Harris, 17. Wet behind the ears, good kid, learning the ropes, but he is always asking for permission. I helped him get his first sale—I did feel proud. Now he's doing all right. Every now and then, Ron and I take him for a quick drink after work.

On the other table are two fellas who think they are from Miami Vice. I am telling ya, they do. Boast about 'some babe' in South Ken they are seeing, a new wine bar, VIP party they've been invited to, trips to South France, and they even dress like Crockett and Tubbs, Tim Maxwell and Denzel Cooper.

It nearly kicked off a few months ago between us. Crockett and Tubbs nicked Billy's homemade sandwiches. We squared up ready for a fight, only to be broken up by Matthew Prior, our manager. We all got a verbal warning from Crooke, shook hands and had to go for a curry to show no hard feelings. It was OK, but we are worlds apart. Now it's just civil between Honest Ron, me, Crockett and Tubbs.

On their table are the queens of Benidorm, Tracey Jones and Lorna Hughes. That is all they talk about—their holiday in bloody Benidorm. I have never set foot there, but thanks to them, I know it like the back of my hand, where to eat, where to sleep, where to shag. Though this year, they said they are going somewhere different, not Australia, America, Italy, France or Greece but bloody Ibiza, a boat ride away. In saying that, I've heard some of the older lads from the manor talking about Ibiza. Even Eddie was talking about it the other day, as he was speaking to some of the lads from the Special Branch—no, not the Old Bill but the fellas that do club nights around London. The Magnificent Six started going last year. According to Eddie, two of the DJs, Johnny Walker—yes, that's his real name—and Danny Rampling, invited Eddie to go over this summer. Didn't invite me, well not yet.

Then there's the girls in personnel, Debbie and Harriett. Loads of fun and, like me and Ron, love life. I've seen Debbie down The Wag with her boyfriend. She's on the ball.

Everyone else is soulless and non-descript, but I have been speaking to the journalists here. They're OK. Not as exciting as I thought they would be, but there is one young journo, Tim Ryan, who's a bit lively. Tim loves The Red Skins, as I do. Seen them a few times. He's told me to have a look at the National School of Journalism at the Elephant and Castle. Steph, the love of my life, says she could easily see me becoming a writer. I do fancy writing a book one day—read a lot. The others used to take the piss, now I'm respected for being a book worm. My mother got me into reading, well before my father went inside. But before I write the book, there's cash to be made from my pranks.

Today, by accident I stumbled across Stavros the Greek's restaurant in the Bush. I've forgotten about him. Yes, you guessed it, I went in there when I was a schoolboy, asking for a job, only to be laughed at by him, his staff, customers and his beautiful daughter Saina, meaning princess in Greek. I really fancied her up until that moment. I went home, looked in the mirror for ages. I couldn't—still can't—see why people laughed every time I asked for a job. I was half expecting Crooke to laugh at me when I turned up for my interview. Forgot to say—never bothered to ask at Pilcher's, my confidence by the age of 14 looking for part-time work, was shattered. But I thought old Terence Pilcher would be ideal for a wind-up.

Anyway, done my usual spiel to old Stavros. You know the routine by now—you've got to move out, had a letter from the council. Then I roll the dice, my first big step into extortion. If I can pull this off, then I can give up the day job, rent an office and make a fortune from conning people out of their money.

'Mr Stavros, of course paperwork, court orders, eviction notices can go missing.' I use the pregnant pause to build up the tension.

'So, you're saying if I contribute something, then this could go away? A present for a present?'

My heart skips a beat, my first but certainly not my last victim. I delay the silence. 'Yes, look at it like exchanging Christmas presents.' I wait with eagerness.

'How much?', he asks in desperation.

I calmly reply, 'Two grand and this will all go away.'

'Two grand? You bastard. You should read the papers. Everyone knows about some little yuppie prick making hoax calls. You little sod. Think you can get one over on Stavros? I will cut your balls off.'

I put the telephone down. I've been tumbled before I've earnt a bleeding penny. Maybe it's a sign from my father that the life of major crime is not for me.

I rush down to reception to pick up this week's paper. How did I miss the headlines? 'Police warn of hoax calls to traders.' I thank God that Stavros cracked or I would have been nicked.

I am going to get my head down for the rest of the day. No more prank calls, I promise.

■ ■ ■

Now I am standing in Pilcher's with Steph. I did suggest Italian or a curry, but she insisted: fish and chips. My baby can be pretty persuasive.

I've been too scared to come here, since the wind-up. I order plaice and small chips for my beautiful girlfriend and large cod and chips for me.

'All right, Oscar? Haven't seen you for a while. Food coming right up. Please, you and your lovely lady take a seat. Here, had some nutjob phone me the other week. It's in this week's paper. Nearly got taken in, telling me my fish and chip shop was shit, being pulled down. He even slagged off Mike Reid.'

'Never! Not "Runaround… now!" Mike Reid?' I say, doing my terrible Mike Reid impression. Oh shit. An impression I have done numerous times in front of him and Reid. I've blown it.

Pilcher looks straight at me and his mind starts to tick. 'You little shit,' he screams.

'Now come on, Terence. It was just a laugh,' I reply in a feeble fashion.

But I can see he isn't laughing. I make a dash for the entrance, grabbing Steph by the hand as I do. Confused, she starts to run with me. As we sprint down the road, she screams out between breaths, 'What the Hell have you done, Oscar?'

'Just having a laugh, sweetheart.'

3

Those Summer Nights—Part One

'I've just nicked a bike and a nice bit of grub. 'Ere, 'ave a butcher's,' pronounces a boastful Honest Ron, hoping that his latest misdemeanour will impress his sharply dressed teenage friends, who are sporting a range of multicoloured Lacoste, Ellesse and Fila polo shirts, in a range of Lois cords and Fiorucci and Levi's jeans, with a collection of Adidas trainers and Clarks desert boots as footwear. Looking good is important to Ron and his friends Eddie, Oscar, Jamie Joe, Dino and Quicksilver.

Yet, to Ron's disappointment, they are more interested in eating their chips from Pilcher's than what their acquaintance is saying. In between bites, they are chuckling and reminiscing about their recent and amusing encounter with BBC Breakfast Time presenter Frank Bough, who had been picking up some much-needed food after a long day at the Beeb. The lads had heard via the Bush grapevine that the image Bough portrayed of being clean-cut and a family man was a myth—in fact, he liked wine, women and song. Dino openly asked in front of Pilcher's customers if Bough wanted to partake in smoking a sly spliff on Bush Green. Outraged, Bough threw down his cod and chips, offering them out one at a time or all at the same time, which amused the lads no end. The proprietor, Terence Pilcher, who has banned the lads on numerous occasions mainly for 'winding up' television personalities, along with his assistant manager Jordan Hill chased the cheeky Casuals out of the chip shop. A ritual that had been performed on numerous occasions and will continue to do so.

'Did you hear what I said?' snaps Ron.

With a sigh, Eddie replies in a patronising manner, 'Yes, loud and clear, Ron. You've nicked a bike, I can see that, and a bit of grub. So what? We've just wound up The Bough.'

Eddie's remarks are met with sniggers by the rest of The Magnificent Six, who left Christopher Wren School three weeks ago and are now enjoying the summer with mucking about, fighting, wind-ups, gate-crashing parties, chatting up girls, smoking the odd spliff and dressing well, before they think about their future.

Edward Savage—aka Eddie the Casual—Dino, Honest Ron and Oscar have been good friends since Bentworth Primary School, with Oscar joining the school later when there was a change in family circumstances. Simon Moran—soon to be known as Quicksilver due to the natural white streak in his jet-black hair he got when he turned 12—became part of the gang when all five of them started Christopher Wren School in September 1979. Simon, a confident and cocky kid from Acton, and his family were rehoused to White City in August 1979. A month later, he was put in form group 2 RG with Ronald Reynolds, aka Honest Ron. Their new form teacher, Miss Rose Green, decided Simon would sit next to Ron in their first registration.

The moment Simon sat down next to Ron, he joked, 'Bugger me, it's Quicksilver.' The joke was really a test, to see if this boy could be a victim or not, as Ron enjoyed manipulating kids outside the gang.

Simon fiercely replied, 'Bugger me, it's one of the seven dwarfs, Grumpy.' They both started to laugh and by the final bell, Honest Ron and Simon, now enjoying the nickname Quicksilver, were the best of friends.

They both had a shared interest in QPR, The Jam, Madness, Debbie Harry from Blondie and similar dress attire: cheap Millet parkas, covered in Mod-related badges and patches, from The Who to Union Jacks. After school, Ron invited Quicksilver for a kick-about at Wormholt Park with Eddie, Dino and Oscar, who were also young Mods—well, apart from Dino, who called himself a Rude Boy. After a few games of three-and-in, the lads accepted Quicksilver as one of their own—even Oscar, who hated anyone outside of their circle. Yet Jamie Joe's inclusion in the gang was one that was literally fought for.

By September 1981, Eddie, Oscar, Honest Ron and Quicksilver had come a long way from four snotty nosed kids in cheap Mod clothing. Now they were the best-dressed kids in the school, top Mods, with Dino swapping the black Harrington for a green trench coat. One more year to go and the lads would officially be the 'top boys'. However, Eddie's standing as a 'hard nut' had made the boys in the top year, especially Stephen George and his mates, wary of Eddie and his friends. That coupled with Eddie and George having a fight that summer round the back of Pilcher's, with Eddie coming out on top with ease. Therefore, these boys were the unofficial 'top boys', with many outspoken admirers and a few silent enemies throughout the school.

Starting that term at Christopher Wren School was a troublesome, gum-chewing, well-dressed Soul Boy, James Joseph (aka Jamie Joe), who waltzed into the school with black suede pointed shoes, black sta press, a small-collared white button-down shirt and a one-button burgundy leather jacket. Upon his first step on the cracked tarmac of the schoolyard, Eddie and the boys noticed him straight away, as they stood next to the schoolyard wall thirty feet to the left of the main gate, where they wanted to see all the kids coming in. Most of them would say hello, apart from Stephen George and his cronies, the usual evil glares from both parties.

As Jamie Joe headed to the school office to report to the headmaster, Mr White, he walked past the boys with an arrogant swagger and equally arrogant stare.

'What you looking at?' snapped Quicksilver. Jamie Joe just smiled and emphasised the fact that he was chewing gum.

'Who's he? Thinks he's bloody Fonz from Happy Days,' snapped a defensive Oscar, who didn't like the new kid's attitude one bit.

'More like Richie. I don't know Oscar who he is. Full of himself, ain't he?' replies Eddie, who felt an immediate threat when his and Jamie Joe's eyes made contact.

'Just give him a smack, Eddie. That will stop him giving it the big one on our patch,' added Honest Ron.

'In time, Ron, in time,' Eddie says with a degree of reluctance, as deep down he feels a little fearful of this new boy.

Jamie Joe is put in 4RP, the same form group as Dino. Dino agrees to look after the 'new boy', hoping to get a full SP on him, so he can report back to the lads by morning break. Dino, who is the least aggressive of the boys, asks Jamie Joe as they are sitting down during registration which football team he supports. Dino states he is a QPR supporter, to which Jamie Joe replies Chelsea, following it with a right hook that not only knocks Dino off his chair but also knocks him out.

Their form tutor, Mrs Pearson, who has her back to the class as the commotion occurs, turns around to see a young Dino sparked out on the floor. Mrs Pearson starts to yearn for a vodka to calm her nerves. Roberta Pearson is 21 days into her Alcoholics Anonymous 12 Step programme. Her husband told her to change jobs to something less stressful, but Roberta stated she could handle the pressure—in fact, she relished it. Yet, as she observes one of her least favourite pupils on the floor, with the new boy clearly the culprit, all young Roberta Pearson wants is a drink and a cigarette.

'What happened?' she yells out, hoping her desire for a drink will pass.

'He fell off, Miss,' says Jamie Joe, accustomed to teachers, foster parents, social workers and policemen's accusations.

'Yes, I did, Miss. Sorry, Miss,' a feeble voice utters. All the class, including Mrs Pearson and Jamie Joe, look at the floor, and see Dino pick himself up, dazed and confused. Dino returns to his plastic chair. 'Been 'aving these blackouts since the summer. Ain't seen a doctor, Miss,' says Dino, playing the victim.

Dino, like most of the kids at Christopher Wren, would never grass on a pupil to a teacher—a golden rule in the unwritten book for school kids is the pupils sort the matter out themselves.

Mrs Pearson, annoyed that Dino is lying yet relieved that she doesn't have to enforce any discipline on her first day back, firmly says, 'OK, Dino Salvador. Go to the medical office and see what they suggest… Well, off you go boy.'

'But Miss, I've got maths after registration,' pleads Dino.

'Well, that will have to wait. We can't have you blacking out, can we?' Mrs Pearson knows Dino is covering up, but she must follow procedures. If a pupil falls ill—or supposedly falls ill—in her class, then they must go to the medical office straight away.

'No, Miss. OK, better get going,' says Dino. He turns to Jamie Joe and whispers, 'Cushy. A morning off.'

Jamie Joe chuckles.

Eddie was fuming when he heard at morning break about Jamie Joe hitting Dino.

'Give him a good hiding, Eddie,' suggests Quicksilver.

'I'll have a word with the little toerag at dinner time,' replies Eddie, deep down fearing the new kid.

'It's lunch, not dinner,' snaps Oscar.

'Is that really fucking important right now, Oscar?' yells a rather irritated Eddie.

In the queue in the dining hall, Eddie and Jamie's eyes meet again in the same aggressive manner as they did this morning. As Jamie Joe and Eddie scrutinise each other, they wait for today's special: mincemeat and mash. Eddie decides to throw the gauntlet down, believing—well, more hoping—that the new boy will apologise and back down. Eddie looks to the heavens, as he approaches Jamie Joe, who smiles as Eddie walks towards him.

'Here, mate, you knocked out my good friend today. What's that all about?' delivers Eddie in a calm manner.

Jamie Joe, looking Eddie up and down, hostilely replies, 'What it's about? It's about me not liking you, that's what it's about. Now piss off, I'm hungry.'

Eddie can't recall the last time, if ever, he was spoken to like this. 'After school, me and you,' says Eddie as he pushes Jamie Joe on the chest.

'Fuck after school, that's passé. How about now?' says Jamie Joe as he hits Eddie square on the jaw, hoping one punch will knock Eddie out.

Eddie, who has been boxing since age seven, can sustain punches, as well as having a powerful attack of his own with his fists. His status as a 'hard nut' is not a fabrication. Eddie sways and throws a left hook at Jamie Joe's lower ribs followed by an uppercut, but Jamie weaves and bobs like a seasoned pro. Like Eddie, Jamie Joe knows how to box, too.

Suddenly, all the kids yell out in unison, 'Fight, fight, fight,' clearing the way to give Eddie and Jamie Joe space. As the teachers approach Eddie and Jamie Joe, the other pupils deliberately prevent them from getting access to the 'pop up' boxing match, allowing the competitors to fight it out. Blows are exchanged at a speedy and vigorous rate, making the battle a proper fight between two equal rivals. A fight of such high standard has not been witnessed for many years at Christopher Wren School, as most fights start with the quick exchange of blows, but end with the contenders wrestling on the ground. This is Christopher Wren School's 'Rumble in the Jungle'.

As the battle continues, Eddie and Jamie Joe are looking for that one punch that could bring them everlasting glory. Eddie, thinking quickly, tries to fool Jamie Joe by moving backwards, as if he is retreating from the fight. The plan works, Jamie Joe drops his guard, leaving his face open. Eddie thinks to himself it's now or never. Within ten seconds, he double jabs, followed by a right cross and a left hook, with each punch making contact, resulting in Jamie Joe losing balance and hitting the ground. Everyone, apart from a handful—mainly Stephen George and his gang—cheer to see their 'local champion' keep his title.

The kids, seeing that the fight is over, move out of the way, allowing the teachers to approach Eddie and Jamie Joe, who is starting to get to his feet. Eddie stands back, for it is too soon after the fight for him to show his opponent any form of support. The teachers pounce on them, with PE teacher Mr Burke screaming, 'Right, it's Mr White for you two. You're for the high jump.' The two battle-torn teenagers, Eddie and Jamie Joe are frogmarched by Mr Burke and two other teachers, Mr Davies and Mr Garrett, to the headmaster's office.

Eddie and Jamie Joe sit outside Mr White's office, with Mr Burke between them in case there is more trouble. Yet fighting is the furthest thing on these boys' minds, as they start to reflect on a brutal yet rewarding contest. Eddie is pleased that his reputation remains intact, whilst admiring a worthy opponent, whereas Jamie Joe is pleased with the outcome, even though he lost by a whisker, as he now knows he will be accepted by the boys.

For that was his aim—Jamie Joe wanted to be friends with them when he first saw them three months ago, just after he moved to White City with his mother, after years of being apart. When Jamie saw Eddie and the boys mucking about, he wanted to be their friend. However, Jamie Joe thought a smile and a flash of the ash would make him vulnerable and a victim. Jamie Joe thought the only way in was to fight the leader—win or lose, he knew he would be accepted. So, Jamie Joe kept a low profile, watching and studying from afar, working out who was who and what was what. To Eddie and the boys, he was invisible, as Jamie Joe planned the whole manoeuvre. Little did he know that the lads would probably have accepted him anyway.

Mr White abruptly opens the doors. 'Savage and Joseph—in here now. Mr Burke, you can go now.'

'Sir, I feel I should be present.'

'Mr Burke, I am more than capable of talking to two misbehaving boys. Or are you saying I am not capable of being headmaster, hmm?' asks Mr White in an abrasive manner.

'Sorry, Sir,' meekly replies Mr Burke. Mr White just grunts, and walks back into his office, with Eddie and Jamie cheekily waving to Mr Burke. 'Mr White, the boys are being rude,' he says hoping that Mr White will admire his discipline with the boys.

'Mr Burke, please go,' he shouts without turning around. Mr Burke goes red in the face with humiliation, bows his head and returns to the mayhem of the school, while Eddie and Jamie try their best not to laugh.

Mr White takes his seat, while Eddie and Jamie stand in front of his desk, hands by their side, trying to show remorse, as neither wants to be expelled. Eddie loves the social life and laughter that school brings, even enjoys the odd lesson or two, whilst Jamie Joe wants to settle and get to know his mother. Jamie Joe wished he had waited for the traditional after-school fight, but his adrenaline got the better of him as Eddie confronted him.

Mr White, a seasoned and sometimes unorthodox headmaster, knows that it is the classic case of a new kid trying to get a reputation by fighting the established tough kid. He has seen it so many times during his 25-year career, a profession that ends in two years' time when he turns 65. For his final years, Mr White wants a quiet life, which is easier said than done at Christopher Wren School.

He is faced with a dilemma. He knows if he expels Edward Savage then Stephen George will step up and out of the two, Savage is the lesser of the two evils. As for Jamie Joe, the last thing he needs is a liberal social worker stating that Mr White expelled an unwanted child on his first day as a pupil, as he couldn't provide the support he needs. He would have to attend meeting after meeting when he would rather be at the Hanwell Conservative Club. A devoted Tory, who has been overlooked by private education all his working life, he is a man who deep down resents the working class yet oversees their education. Of late, Mr White has been reflecting on his life and how things could have been so different if he hadn't attended those 'life changing' social events under the influence of one too many gin and tonics. Now he is full of regret and remorse.

Studying the weary teenagers, Mr White contemplates their punishment. 'Savage, Joseph, I understand in youth, as well as in adulthood, reputations amongst peers is important. I was young, too, and by no means was I bullied or pushed around at school. I, too, had to fight, believe it or not. Usually, on something as serious as this, it would be immediate expulsion. Savage, I would not go so far as to say you are a model pupil. However, you are seldom in my office. Maybe you are well behaved or you don't get caught. Either way, on record, you are not regarded as troublesome.'

As Mr White speaks to them, Eddie and Jamie Joe start to feel at ease, sensing a lecture as opposed to a punishment. 'Thank you, Sir,' quips Eddie.

'I was not after your approval. I can still expel you,' says Mr White, wanting to stamp his authority.

'Sorry, Sir.'

'As for you, James Joseph—or, as you like to be called, Jamie Joe—I see that trouble follows you around like a bad smell. However, I know that you have not had an easy life, moving from foster home to foster home, so I do appreciate, you have had it tough from an early age. Yet I understand you and your mother are recently reunited, so I want to give you one final chance. But I must make myself clear, I will not tolerate fighting. Understand, Joseph?'

'Yes, Sir. Sorry, Sir,' mutters Jamie Joe.

'An apology. So many men and women have gone through life believing an apology will resolve self-created problems, myself included. Ha! If we, as human beings, thought about the consequences before an action, so many prisons would be empty, hospital beds free and such like, but that is easier said than done. As humans, we are driven by emotion, not logic. I suppose that is what makes the world a colourful place.'

'Yes, Sir,' say Eddie and Jamie Joe, as they turn sideways, looking at each other with confusion.

Mr White looks out of his window to the grey buildings that has been his universe before John, Paul, George and Ringo became household names. For years, Mr White believed being brutal was the only way to teach children, but now he wants to leave a legacy for these kids, not a bad reputation.

'Now, I believe this to be an unlicensed boxing match between two willing competitors, with no malice intended. For a few terms, I have discussed with Mr Burke about running a boxing club for the pupils to learn the noble art, like you two. Now you two, along with Mr Burke, will run a boxing club in the gym after school, every Tuesday and Thursday for an hour and Saturday mornings. Savage, you alone will bring many kids, and as for you, Joseph, I can see this, as a step in the right direction.'

Eddie replies, 'Thank you, Sir, but can we run it without Mr Burke?'

'Savage, you are not in a position to make demands. Or shall I change my mind and expel you?'

'No, Sir,' replies Eddie, realising he is onto a good thing.

'This afternoon, I will call an assembly, to announce the new boxing club. Savage and Joseph, do we have a deal?'

'Yes, Sir, we will support the boxing club with all our heart and soul,' says Jamie Joe, who is genuinely enthralled by the concept.

'That's the spirit. I will see both of you back here at three o'clock on the dot. Now go—I have much work to do.'

'Thank you, Sir,' both boys say as they leave.

Mr White smiles, stands up, walks towards the window and says to himself, 'God, I am trying to be a better man.'

Eddie and Jamie Joe walk out of Mr White's office with an element of surprise and delight. Eddie turns around, offers his hand to Jamie Joe, who responds straight away.

As they shake, Eddie says, 'That was a good fight.'

'Oh, yeah,' replies a cheerful Jamie Joe.

'After school, fancy coming for a bite down the Wimpy?'

Jamie smiles and replies, 'All right, Eddie,' whilst thinking, 'Job done.'

■ ■ ■

'Sorry about this morning, Dino, I really am,' says a rather sheepish Jamie Joe as he bites into a quarter pounder with cheese while the lads are sitting down in the Wimpy.

Dino smiles. 'Apology accepted, mate, you bloody Chelsea hooligan.'

'Piss off! You ain't Chelsea,' says Oscar, hostile as ever to outsiders.

'If you cut me open, I will bleed blue blood,' retorts Jamie Joe.

Oscar tuts, then asks, 'How come you're a Soul Boy?'

'I think you are trying to size me up?' replies Jamie Joe.

'Ignore him, Jamie. We all do,' adds Quicksilver.

'Shut up, Q. No, I ain't sizing you up. I just want to know how come you're a Soul Boy?' cracks Oscar.

'I was a Mod for a while, then a Skin.'

'Bloody knew it,' says Oscar in an arrogant manner.

'Yeah, a right little shit. Then I got moved to these foster parents—the Knights in Ealing. Nice people, first ones to treat me like family. Next door were two lads, living with their parents, Nigel and Jack Cobb, older than me. They were wearing you know baggy jeans, granddad shirts, karate slippers, wedge haircuts—real Soul Patrol. The oldest, Nigel, had one of these purple Cortina's—Mark Three, I fink, with the furry dice, and his and his bird's name, Perrie, you know with the white lettering on a green sticker across the windscreen.'

'Yeah, we've got a few of them around White City,' adds Honest Ron, who is successfully stealing chips off Quicksilver's plate.

'So that's what made you a Soul Boy—the Saturday Kid's funkmobile?' says Oscar in an offhand manner.

'What the Hell are you talking about?' asks Quicksilver, still failing to see that half of his chips have been stolen by Honest Ron.

'It's from The Jam, Saturday Kids. "Drive Cortina's, fur-trimmed dashboards, stains on the seats—in the back, of course."'

'Jesus Christ, Oscar! I don't think you can go a day without reciting The Jam,' jokes Eddie.

'Love The Jam,' says Jamie Joe.

'Do ya?' asks an intrigued Oscar.

'Yeah, I do. But Oscar, it wasn't the motor. I kept hearing his music, either blaring out of his car or from his bedroom. We got talking, as you do, became mates I

25

suppose. Nigel would tell me about do's at Canvey Island, clubs like The Wag, Beat Route and a DJ, Chris Hill. I started to nick blank cassettes from Woolworths, so he could do me tapes—Yank stuff like Chuck Brown, Chic, Funkadelic, Parliament, loads of it, and British stuff, Hi-Tension, Light of The World, Linx. Oscar, I'll bring a few tapes in tomorrow, you will love it, all of ya will.'

'Cheers. Jamie, we do know about funk 'ere in the Bush,' says Oscar coldly.

'Yeah, but listen again to the beat, the trumpets, the bass, the guitars, those beautiful voices. Changed me. Like the Mods in the 60s listening to soul from America, the Soul Boys of the 80s are listening to funk from America and England, of course. Mods and Soul Boys are cousins.'

'You reckon?' says Oscar, thinking about what Jamie is saying.

'Yeah, I do.'

■ ■ ■

'OK, you've nicked a bike, but it's a rust bucket. Take it back, we can't sell that. It's BMXs, we want,' says Eddie in his annoying fashion.

'Eddie, I never said anything about selling it. My bike is knackered, bent forks,' Ron snaps back.

'Bent like the owner,' jokes Dino, which is met by a few giggles.

Ron, shaking his head whilst smiling, replies, 'The wit of the kid, you should get a job writing jokes for The Two Ronnies. 'Ere, remember that time I nicked Ronnie Corbett's battered sausage when we were at Pilcher's?'

'Oh yes, Corbett went mental. He knocked you out,' says Oscar in a joyful manner.

'Piss off, O. Corbett didn't knock me out. We exchanged blows, remember?' states Ron, as if he was being interviewed by the police.

'Slow down, Ron. No need to get touchy, just cos you got slapped by someone bigger than you,' says Oscar, relishing the fact that his friend is now getting annoyed.

'Shut up you two. Ron, you know, I know, Corbett knows, we all know, in fact, that Corbett knocked you out,' confirms Eddie.

Ron bows his head in shame, then looks up. 'OK, how come none of you slapped him?'

'Piss off, Ron. All the football hooligans and villains round 'ere love The Two Ronnies. We would have had to leave White City in the middle of the night,' states Oscar.

Ron nods his head, starts to laugh and says with a chuckle, 'True, Oscar. The other one is all right. Barker, he gives as good as he gets.'

'Yeah, Barker he can handle it, cos he knows we are just kids having a laugh. I mean Frank Bough offering us out—must be drugs withdrawal or somefink,' says Oscar.

'Fuck, you should have seen it, Ron. Old Bough went bright red like a Pringle jumper, screaming, "Come on then! All of ya or one at a time!",' says Jamie Joe, picking up the growing ecstatic mood of the lads.

'Would have loved to have seen that. So, old Frank Bough is really a nutter? Bloody knew it,' says an excited Ron.

'Oh yes, don't be fooled by that Mr Nice Guy,' adds Quicksilver, also enjoying the vibe.

'They are all nutters at the BBC. I'm telling ya some creepy shit goes on there,' says Oscar breaking the mood.

'Osc, you sound like bloody Shaggy from Scooby Doo. Anyway, Ron, if you wanted a new bike, why nick that one?' asks Eddie, who is now genuinely interested in Honest Ron's latest spot of petty crime.

'Cos some knob left it unlocked outside the pub, along with his shopping. Look, eggs, bacon, beans, Mother's Pride bread and four cans of Double Diamond. Give the beers to me brother Lee, the rest have as munchies,' says a proud Ron.

'Here, split the grub,' snaps Quicksilver.

'Finders keepers and all that. Listen I've got to split. I promised the old gal I'll give her a hand putting up some shelves,' says Honest Ron, as he starts to slowly walk away with the stolen bike and food.

'What about the old man?' asks Eddie as Ron starts to mount the bike and peddle off.

'Got a new job. He's doing a drop off in Italy, back on Friday. See ya,' says Ron.

'See ya, wanker,' shouts out Jamie Joe.

'Yeah, a wanker with a new bike and some grub,' Ron shouts backs as he rides off with a smile.

'Shit. Didn't know his old man was doing Europe on a lorry. Just thought he went to Hull and back. If I had known, I would have rustled some cash together to get some clobber,' says Eddie in a contemplative mood.

'Yeah, Ron told me the other week his old man has got a new job. Loads of runs to Europe, better basic with loads of overtime,' says Oscar.

'Why didn't you tell me?' says Eddie severely.

'Well, I didn't really think it was that interesting Ron's old man got a new job,' says Oscar, rather taken back by his friend's aggressive reply.

'He's going to Italy, Oscar, through France. Think of the clothes he could buy, even nick. I've got to have a word with his old man,' says Eddie.

'Save your breath—his old man is as straight as they come, unlike his son,' says Dino.

'Every man's got a price. I reckon we should do a stowaway on his next trip. Come on, let's pop down Wormholt Park, see if those birds are practising their gymnastics again. What was that blonde one's name?' asks Eddie.

'Claire. Good-looking girl. I like her mate Suzanna. Anyone got any puff? Smoked me last spliff,' states Dino.

'Ron has. Never mind. Might be able to ponce a smoke en route,' suggests Eddie, as they turn off Bloemfontein Road onto Bryony Road towards the Park. The Magnificent Six minus Ron see marching towards them a well-built man in his early 20s, over six feet tall, with a small Mohican haircut, wearing light green combat trousers with dark black jackboots and no top so he can show off his tattoos.

'Oh shit, it's Rooster,' says Quicksilver.

4

Those Summer Nights—Part Two

John Roost aka Rooster was born 9th Nov 1959 at Chiswick Maternity Hospital to George and Irena Roost, a bricklayer and a secretary respectively. George and Irena showered their first born with love, devotion and toys. A happy and yet quiet child, he showed no interest in anything particular until Christmas Day 1964, when his grandparents gave John an Action Man as a present. That evening, while Irena put John, along with his younger brother Malcolm— born 21st March 1961—to bed after a joyful and affectionate celebration, John declared his purpose in life.

'Mummy, I want to be a soldier.'

A delirious Irena ran down the stairs to the living room in Australia Road, Shepherd's Bush, to tell George and her parents, who were polishing off a crate of light ale in-between bites of cold turkey sandwiches, 'Our Johnny wants to fight for Queen and Country.' Irena's announcement was greeted by loud drunken cheers that woke the children, much to her annoyance, as she had to go back and put them both back to sleep.

After that eventful Christmas, every toy, book or game that was war- or soldier-related the hard-working Roosts bought for their John. When John Roost turned 12, he joined the army cadets. He took up boxing a year later. He was a natural and excelled in his out-of-school activities.

At Christopher Wren School, John wasn't a popular pupil with his peers nor teachers, due to his reserved nature. Nevertheless, John was left alone by the bullies as they knew he could fight back. He left school in the summer of

1976, aged 16. Through his father, George, John Roost got a job with Barratt Homes. John knew he could join the army with his parents' consent, yet he wanted to build himself up, experience a bit of life on civvy street as well as have money in the bank. John Roost also knew the 16-year-old recruits were easy targets in the barracks.

John Roost turned 18 on 9th Nov 1977, the year former Christopher Wren School pupils Steve Jones and Paul Cook were causing chaos in the world of music and fashion with their Punk band, The Sex Pistols. John Roost couldn't abide Punk, yet this was little concern to him on this day, as he was travelling to Army Careers Information Office, 76A Rochester Row, Westminster, London SW1, to enlist. Due to his impeccable record as an army cadet, John was offered two days training at Aldershot Barracks on the spot. John Roost ran all the six miles home from Victoria to Shepherd's Bush in less than an hour, as he was so excited and unable to sit still, let alone wait for the bus.

Overjoyed and proud, too, George and Irena took their beloved John and his younger brother Malcom, now aged 16, to Aberdeen Steak House in Soho, to celebrate his birthday and his first step in joining the army. John Roost, who throughout school and after had resisted the temptation of alcohol, bowed to the pressure of his parents, who by 1977 were both heavy drinkers, and had a beer. John Roost thought one beer wouldn't hurt him. Yet the moment the hops and yeast touched his tongue, John felt a new sensation that he rather enjoyed. John downed his first pint and ordered another one straight away. His parents were delighted to see their son enjoying his first drink. John Roost started to wonder why he hadn't drunk before. The more he drank, the happier he became. Then the merriment turned to rage when a waiter, a young Maltese lad named Elias, refused to serve John Roost any more beer, as his behaviour and language were upsetting the other customers.

Outraged, John Roost stood up, grabbed an empty wine bottle that his mother had just polished off and smashed it over Elias's head. Elias screamed out in pain. The sound of his agony delighted John Roost, who followed up with a punch to the stomach, winding Elias as he fell to the ground. On the table next to the Roosts sat Ron and Beth Schaefer, a thirty-something couple from Brooklyn, New York, on their first ever trip to London. Ron, a former

American college football player and now a New York yellow cab driver, yelled out as Elias lay on the floor, 'This is worse than the Bronx.'

The sound of an American accent made John Roost irate. 'Fuck off, Yankee Doodle Dandy.'

Ron, a man never to bow down to an insult, was left with no alternative but to challenge the aggressive teenager.

'So, you're a wise guy, you Limey bastard,' stated Schaefer, as he ran towards a drunk John Roost. Schaefer believed that this intoxicated youth would be a push over, one punch and down. Schaefer didn't consider John Roost was an experienced boxer. But Schaefer acknowledged the fact, when John Roost hit Schaefer in the throat, with a well-placed and powerful punch. Schaefer fell to the floor, gasping for air and in severe pain.

Beth Schaefer screamed out, 'Ron!'

John Roost, equally annoyed by the sound of an American female, ran over and slapped Beth hard across the face, knocking her out in the process. The melee was in full progress, with many of the customers and staff heading for the main entrance, causing a major commotion as they feared for their lives.

'John, for the love of God, please stop,' screamed a heartbroken Irena, while a shocked George begged, 'John, please listen to your mother,' as the 16-year-old Malcolm bowed his head down in shame.

John Roost, enjoying the pleasure and power he had caused from mayhem, turned to his loving yet shocked family, glared at them insanely, and proceeded to tear off all his clothes, proclaiming, 'John is dead. I am Rooster, I am the Rooster.' It was a nickname given to him at Bentworth Road Middle School that followed John Roost to Christopher Wren School. He hated the nickname, yet pretended that it didn't bother him, to avoid any bullying. But today, during John's baptism of fire in alcohol and violence, he felt reborn—a new teenager and that teenager was Rooster.

As Rooster stood in his birthday suit, the remaining terrified staff and customers cowered underneath the tables. Fifteen Metropolitan Police's wooden tops came smashing through the main entrance with their truncheons. Upon seeing the wild and stripped teenager, the police advanced towards Rooster, hitting him hard with their batons when they got within touching distance.

The fast and furious onslaught knocked out Rooster upon impact. Five of the police dragged a beaten, bruised and naked Rooster through the streets of Soho to Vine Street Police Station, while the remaining ten coppers carried on with their truncheon attack on his family, staff and customers, knowing full well that the Metropolitan Police would get away with it by declaring it was a riot and they had to use necessary force to stop it. Sergeant Marshall of Vine Street will chuck a few quid to his crime-reporting drinking friends down Fleet Street, to write articles corroborating the police's version of events.

A well beaten and now clothed Rooster was taken to the Vine Street Magistrates Court the following morning, 10th November 1977, charged with GBH with intent, criminal damage and threatening behaviour. Rooster was remanded in custody, as the Metropolitan Police believed him to be a danger to the public and himself.

Rooster was sent to HMP Wandsworth to await trial. The heartbroken Roosts, via a solicitor who was getting wealthy from their life savings, debated whether John Roost should be charged as a juvenile not an adult as this was his first offence. However, due to the magnitude and madness of his first crime, coupled with John Roost attacking an American couple, the Metropolitan Police and the British Government were under severe pressure from the US government, for John Roost to be charged and to stand trial as an adult. The Prime Minister James Callaghan wanted to maintain a positive transatlantic relationship.

For the first few weeks at Wandsworth, Rooster was nervous and scared. Yet after winning a fight with a hard nut, where the prison guards turned a blind eye, Rooster was accepted and respected by prisoners and staff alike. Furthermore, word got across the wings that it took fifteen coppers to arrest him—a slight variation of the events, yet Rooster wasn't going to dispute them.

Rooster stood trial on 10th April 1978 at Southwark Crown Court. The charge of GBH with intent was changed to ABH, the charge of threatening behaviour remained, whilst the charge for criminal damage was dropped. Rooster was found guilty and sentenced to four years and four months, with time taken off from his period in remand, on 21st April 1978.

From his arrest to the trial, Rooster became a media sensation. With the

Sex Pistols splitting up in January 1978, the press needed and yearned for a scapegoat to scare the British public and portray the youths of Great Britain as devils. Rooster fitted the bill perfectly. Coined by The Sun 'The Naked Punk Rocker', the tabloids loved him. Soon, Rooster was front-page news, with former pupils whom Rooster had never spoken to and neighbours who had never swapped Christmas cards with his parents stepping forward to state he was a hooligan from an early age, beating and bullying them, stealing, drinking and taking drugs. All lies, but with Rooster behind bars and his family shattered, they were unable to tell the truth that it was just one bad evening.

Yet Rooster was enjoying his newly-found notoriety and his status was heightened further when ex-Sex Pistols Steve Jones and Paul Cook jokingly said in an interview with the New Musical Express they wanted Rooster to be their new front man upon his release. The NME overlooked the humour and the following week, Rooster was on the cover of the NME with the headline 'Rooster, the new Johnny Rotten?', which was picked up by the other music papers and the tabloids alike. Even John Peel on his Radio One show joined in with the debate.

Rooster was now, in the eyes of the media and the British public, a Sex Pistol—even though Rooster had never recorded or performed with them and had never really spoken to Jones or Cook while at Christopher Wren School or even around Shepherd's Bush.

So, when Rooster, a category B prisoner, set foot in A Wing HMP Brixton, one afternoon in late April 1978, the excited young inmates started to sing The Sex Pistols' 'Anarchy in the UK' at full belt, resulting in the prison guards screaming at them to 'Shut it!' Their order fell on deaf ears, as the older inmates, thrilled by the commotion, joined in with the chorus. Anything to upset the system. Rooster was given a hero's welcome and he was moved to tears.

After slapping the 'daddy' of A Wing in full view of the inmates and guards, who always looked the other way when there was a challenge to the hierarchy, Rooster became the youngest inmate to run the wing. He took a cut, with the help of the former daddy's henchmen, from the pill-peddling, dope-dealing, protection rackets and other misdemeanours that brought in revenue. Rooster was well and truly loving life, as he felt this was his true calling, not the army.

Evenings were spent smoking weed and occasionally sipping hooch with his cellmate and best friend Winston Walker—a Notting Hill lad, tall and strong, with a natural flair for illustrations and cartoons, all self-taught after reading DC and Marvel comics at an early age. Winston's parents came to England from the West Indies in 1956 and Winston was born the following year, 4th August 1957. Not a rogue, Winston was just a lively, mischievous and intelligent child, who found himself incarcerated for six months at the age of 16 at Feltham Borstal, when he drove off in a Job's milk float for a laugh with his friends, early one morning in September 1973. His parents, hard-working and law-abiding, pleaded with the police and Job's Dairy that it was a schoolboy prank, but the Metropolitan Police saw it as an unemployed black teenager stealing. Yet Winston wasn't unemployed—after leaving school, he was working part-time at a local greengrocer's while he worked on his port-folio, as he dreamt of going to art school, a dream that was shattered by the establishment.

After his release, periods of unemployment and low-paid jobs followed, so Winston returned to crime as a full-time occupation, this time as a small-time car thief. He was arrested when by chance, Winston accidently went into the back of a police car down Portobello Road on 2nd February 1978, in a nicked Datsun 120Y that had been reported stolen that morning. After his arrest, the police, without a search warrant, ransacked his bedroom at his parent's house. The police found £100 in used notes (which they reported as £1,000), two log books (increased to twenty by the boys in blue) and Winston's personal audit of cars he had stolen and to whom he had sold. This documentation never existed, so WPC Pryce was given the task of creating it, so Notting Hill Gate Police could clear up their car theft figures for 1977. The police knew the judge and jury would never believe a young unemployed black man telling the court he was fitted up. Winston Walker was sentenced to three years and six months in May 1978, a month after Rooster was sentenced.

By April 1980, things are looking up at last for Winston. 'Got me first parole hearing next month, fingers crossed,' says Winston smoking a spliff that Rooster has just passed to him.

'You'll walk it—you've got A-level art. The Board love that, the reformed character,' says Rooster, in a rare moment of dropping his guard and his new persona of Foghorn Leghorn, an identity Rooster created after watching the famous Warner Bros character one evening during association. Rooster was mesmerised how the cartoon rooster controlled his yard, by his cunning and brave ways. Within days, Rooster was mimicking the actions of Foghorn Leghorn and started to use the character's catchphrase, 'I say, I say,' as his battle cry, a warning he would give before he hit them. Soon after, Rooster went to Sailor Morgan in his wing, a former merchant seaman who was inside for breaking and entering and a master of Indian-ink tattoos, inspired by American tattoo artist Sailor Jerry. Rooster requested that Sailor Morgan tattoo the name Rooster across his chest and a huge image of Foghorn Leghorn on his back, which Sailor Morgan happily obliged for half an ounce of Old Holborn.

'Thanks, Rooster, I know I was fitted up, but I was on the rob. Can't deny that. I would've just carried on until I got caught. I am going straight. Should have gone straight after my time at Feltham, really should of done. I don't want to come back here. Fuck, we lead the best life we can in a shit hole. A few joints, the odd hooch, a handful of dirty mags, soft toilet paper, extra snout, double rations if we want them. But fuck that Rooster. We're young men, there ain't no crumpet, no discos, no beer, nothing but the sound of locking doors and geezers snoring. I miss the sound of a letter coming through the letterbox, the whistle of a kettle, me mother yelling at me to get up, the theme tune to Match of the Day, the sound of bacon sizzling,' says Winston in a positive and reflective mood, as he knows he could be a free man soon.

'I hear you—a bacon sarnie, crispy bacon melting the butter,' says Rooster, showing his vulnerable side.

Winston, sensing this in his friend, tries to offer him some support. 'What you going to do when you get out, Rooster?'

Rooster ponders, as since the day he was arrested, his mind has been a whirlwind of mayhem and violence and he hasn't really thought about his future. 'Don't know. Thought I was going to join The Sex Pistols—those fucking rotters, Jones and Cook, ain't never replied to me letters. Got a few mates, site work, ain't bothered if you done a bit of bird, as long as you can graft. But I don't know Winston, really don't know. Still got to pass me first parole hearing.'

Winston smiles and reassures his friend. 'Rooster, you've got about six to twelve months to go, you ain't never been on report, even got a trustee's job in the library. You are on the right road.'

Rooster laughs out loud, knowing his excellent record wasn't due to his good behaviour or reform, but the fact that Governor Jasper Rawlings was receiving generous kickbacks from A Wing's daddy. With a forbidden business association formed, Rooster was given what or who he wanted. This was the only part of Rooster's criminalities Winston didn't know about.

Rooster was given early release in November 1980 due to 'good behaviour', as Winston had predicted, and time served on remand. First thing Rooster did was go to Hackney via public transport to see Sailor Morgan, who was released September 1980, at his and his brother Jacob's tattoo parlour, Tattoo Ahoy. This time, Sailor Morgan tattooed white feathers up to Rooster's elbow and Foghorn Leghorn's cartoon claws on the top of Rooster's real feet. Rooster returned to his parents' house in Australia Road, Shepherd's Bush, where he called his mother by her first name, Irena, and his father by his surname, Mr Roost.

As Rooster truly believed he was the bastard son of Foghorn Leghorn, by now Rooster was totally and utterly insane.

■ ■ ■

'The geezer is a loony tune,' quips Dino.

'I agree, Dino. Shhh. All right, Rooster? Off down the pub?' asks Eddie, hoping Rooster will just say yes and carry on walking.

'Off down the pub? You taking the piss, boy? I was down the pub until some muppet nicked me bike and me tea.' Eddie and the lads exchange anxious glances. 'You lot know anything? Seen a mincer on a bike with a shopping bag?' demands Rooster.

'Ain't seen a thing, Rooster. We'll keep our peelers open,' says Jamie Joe, hoping his false clarification will make Rooster go away.

Rooster looks Jamie Joe up and down in a suspicious manner then utters, 'Rooster is hungry, Rooster wants eggs and chips, Rooster likes eggs and chips,' referring to himself in the third person, as so often Rooster does.

'What about your Lambretta?' asks Oscar, who can never resist the temptation to wind up Rooster.

Rooster starts to flap his arms and screeching like a rooster, if they were able to talk, 'Boy, what do you know about me lamby? You ain't nicked that? I don't want, "I say", you I really don't.'

'No, no. Just thought you could pop down Paolo's Café on your scooter to get some eggs and chips, they are still open,' says Oscar in a sardonic fashion, as Rooster starts to move his neck forwards and backwards like a farmyard rooster.

Rooster recently purchased a Lambretta SX200, as he longs to be a Scooter Boy after seeing several West London scooter clubs riding through Shepherd's Bush—inspired by their army-cum-rockabilly-cum-Punk look, bombing around town on their colourful and unique scooters. After purchasing his Lambretta SX200, Rooster went to Louie the mechanic down Latimer Rd, a Hell's Angel who is well known for his dodgy MOTs, car-rigging and his expertise in customising motorbikes. Louie is now earning with a nice cash-in-hand number, due to so many of London's scooter boys requesting his skills to make their scooter exclusive. Rooster got fork extensions, a Taffspeed engine, leg panels cut down and an image of Foghorn Leghorn painted on the side panels. It looks and sounds like a Harley Davidson.

Rooster believes he will be welcomed with open arms by the West London scooter clubs. He is still waiting to hear back.

Rooster spits on the floor, walks towards Oscar and lightly presses his forehead to Oscar's. 'Listen, you muppet. Some muppet nicked Rooster's bike, Rooster's tea, Rooster's beer. That muppet is a dead muppet.'

Oscar pulls his head slightly back and steps to Rooster's left. Eddie pushes him fully out of the way and resumes his role as the lads' spokesman. 'That's out of order Rooster, I'll put the word out.'

'Put the word out. You mincers are going to help me find the little shit that nicked it. Popped in for a quick pint before it closed at three. Been hodding bricks all morning. Rooster was thirsty, come out, it's gone, so you little mincers are going to help the Rooster find his bike. Aren't ya?' says Rooster getting more irritated by the second.

'Yes, you can go that way and we'll go this way,' suggests Eddie.

'Good idea. OK, see ya,' says a pleased Rooster.

The lads breathe a sigh of relief, smile and turn back towards Ron's house.

'Better tell him to lose the bike sharpest. Knob—he had to nick Rooster's bike,' says Quicksilver.

'Fucking Hell, Q. Never thought of that—go to the top of the class,' says Oscar in a sarcastic tone.

Before Quicksilver can reply, they hear a familiar unfriendly voice yell out, 'Here, there's more of you than of me. Two of ya are coming with me.' The lads turn around to see Rooster marching towards them.

'Rooster, we've got to get home for our teas. We'll come after, promise,' pleads Dino.

'You taking the piss boy? I ain't had me tea,' says Rooster in a sinister low tone, as he approaches the lads.

'No, we are not taking the piss, Rooster. We would love to help ya… but…' As Dino desperately tries to a plea to Rooster's better nature, Rooster reaches down into his left black jackboot and pulls out a seven-inch commando knife.

'Say hello to me mate, Slicey.' The lads all step back fearing their safety, in particular their faces. Jamie Joe reaches into his Lois jeans' back pocket and touches the handle of his Stanley knife, just in case. 'I said say hello to Slicey,' says Rooster, enjoying the trepidation he is imposing upon these recent school leavers.

The lads, standing well back, reply with hesitation and unison, 'Hello… Slicey.'

Rooster smiles, then puts the spine of the knife to his ear, like a puppeteer would do with a glove puppet. 'What's that, Slicey…? Yes, Slicey… OK, Slicey.'

The lads exchange more concerned glances. Oscar puts his head down and whispers to Eddie, 'He's a fucking loon.'

Eddie whispers back, 'I think I can work that out for myself.'

Rooster then smiles at them and says with a slight laugh, 'Slicey says no slicing today. Ain't you going to thank Slicey?'

Eddie looks at the lads, egging them on to thank the knife and the madman standing before them. Again, in unison but with an element of bemusement, they all say, 'Thank you, Slicey.'

'OK, Rooster. Oscar and Jamie will go with you,' says Eddie. Oscar gives Eddie a hard punch in the ribs.

Rooster starts to flap his arms, then squeals, 'Jamie, yes, but not the mincer,' as he points aggressively towards Oscar.

Oscar smiles and says, 'You sure Rooster?'

'Of course I'm bloody sure. But first, Rooster is going to have a smoke. What is Rooster going to do?'

'Fucking Hell, it's like Hammer House of Horror meets Playschool,' mutters Oscar to Dino, who smiles, just out of Rooster's sight.

The lads, now accustomed to his insane ways, jointly reply, 'Have a smoke Rooster.'

'Good lads. Here, Jamie, do the honours?' As Rooster says this, he pulls out a big lump of black hash, a packet of green Rizlas and a gold Zippo lighter from the left leg of his combat trousers' pocket, which he throws with caution to Jamie Joe. Jamie catches the gear and starts the ritual of making a joint, a skill he is renowned for across the Bush, even by Rooster.

After leaving prison, Rooster became a drug dealer. Despite his persona of a mad man, Rooster has a good head for figures and business, which he acquired from his prison sentence, and within one month, he was making a small profit. However, Rooster knew the police were keeping an eye on him, so he decided to return to the building sites as a hod carrier, so the police and his probation officer would believe he is a reformed character. Yet Rooster loves the work, the money and the banter of the building game.

This summer, Rooster's profits from selling puff have trebled, as many of the local teenagers, from the Mods to the Casuals and especially the Magnificent Six, have started to enjoy smoking dope, from solids to weed. The Magnificent Six nominated Jamie Joe to go and purchase their 'puff' from Rooster, as he and Rooster seem to be kindred spirits.

Jamie Joe finishes rolling the joint, lights it and passes it, along with the dope, lighter and Rizlas, back to Rooster.

'Cheers Jamie… (cough)… you packed that good boy… Rooster… is going to get high… Yee -haw.'

Jamie Joe winks at the others. Oscar smiles back, then nods for Jamie Joe to talk to Rooster. Jamie Joe understands his motion. 'Nice one, Rooster. Look, we'll find your bike. Expensive is it?' asks Jamie Joe, knowing full well it is a rust bucket.

'Nay, shitty Puch, but it was me brother's. Gave it to me on his death bed. Malcolm said, "Rooster, I know we ain't been friends for ages, have me bike, to remember me. Every time you peddle, remember our holidays in Selsey Bill."' Rooster starts to wipe away the tears.

Oscar is holding back the laughter. Eddie and Jamie Joe look at him, shaking their heads, as the lads all know that Rooster's brother is alive and well and living in Milton Keynes.

The atmosphere suddenly takes a turn for the worse, as Rooster throws down the joint, stares at the lads then yells, 'Here, there's usually six of ya, the Magnificent Six or some ponce name like that. The six mincers, if you ask me. Where's the ugly dwarf? Heigh fucking ho, the mouthy one.'

'Ron, he's at home, helping his mother out,' says a nervous and annoyed Quicksilver.

'Helping his mother out? Tosser. OK, let's go round there. She can knock me up some egg and chips, then we find me bike,' demands Rooster.

The lads all know once Ron's mother or even Ron himself opens the front door, Rooster's bike is bound to be in the hallway, Slicey is bound to come out again and this time, Slicey will be less sympathetic.

'Rooster, I don't think she will have enough food to go round. Let's go to Pilcher's. I'll shout you a bag of chips,' says Oscar, now seriously concerned for their safety.

'I didn't say nothing about you lot. Rooster wants egg and chips. Rooster will get egg and chips. Listen, boy… Oh, fuck it. I say… I…'

Before Rooster can complete his legendary war cry, a familiar husky voice shouts out, 'Rooster! Found your bike! Saw some little shit on it, gave him a slap. Then he legged it like a bleeding rabbit.' The lads turn around and see Honest Ron, wheeling the bike, minus the food and with a football under his arm. All the lads look to the heavens.

Rooster runs to the bike like it is his long-lost lover. 'Thanks. Ron, isn't it?'

'That's right, Rooster—Ron.'

'What about the grub?' Rooster asks.

'Sorry, didn't see that. I just saw some kid riding the bike towards Hammersmith Park. Me brother, Lee, came home from his early shift, told me you had seen him, asking after a nicked Puch racer. So, after I heard that, I came out looking for the bike,' says a confident Ron, with his years of talking to the police with fabricated stories coming into full effect.

'You're Lee Reynold's kid brother?' asks Rooster.

'That's right,' answers Ron in his usual cocky manner.

'He's all right is Lee. Good boy. Here, have a smoke on me, Ron.' With that Rooster pulls out the big lump of black that Jamie Joe had given back to him and passes it to Ron.

Ron smiles and winks at the others, 'Oh, thank you, Rooster, but I was just looking out for the White City lads.'

'Too right,' replies Rooster, as he reaches down to his left jackboot, pulls out Slicey, then slowly walks towards Jamie Joe and passes the knife to him handle first.

'Here, son. Have this. Got a feeling you're going to need Slicey.'

Jamie Joe slowly nods, warming to Rooster's respect.

'You're good lads. See ya,' says Rooster, as he takes his bike back from Ron, mounts it, rides off and lets out a rooster crow. Honest Ron swaggers towards the lads, just like the cat who has got the cream.

'Ron, you jammy git. Skin up, son,' says Dino.

Ron chucks the black to Dino, who catches the puff with ease and enthusiasm. 'Yeah, Lee came back, walking through the door, looking like a ghost, telling me about Rooster and his bike, saw the bike, told me. I was like, "Oh fuck… act the good Samaritan." But he owes us now,' says Ron, as if he was bringing a murder-mystery play to a close.

Eddie starts to laugh, then enquires, 'But what about the food?'

'In the fridge. Having it later, after football.'

As the reunited Magnificent Six head back towards Wormholt Park, Eddie gently pulls Honest Ron back and whispers in his ear, 'Here, does your old man fancy doing a bit of importing?'

'Don't start, Eddie. Not now.'

5

The Confessions of PC
Graham Legg—Part One

Graham Legg—an enthusiastic yet nervous young man who recently gradu-
ated from the Police Staff College, Bramshill, and is soon to be stationed at
Shepherd's Bush Police Station, Uxbridge Road. His father, retired Detective
Sergeant Arthur Legg, was also stationed there, so he pulled in a favour with
former colleague Sergeant Duncan McDonald to give his naïve son a helping
hand.

Sergeant McDonald—a huge brute of a man, 6'2", 16 stone, with jet
black hair, pasty skin and a huge beer gut due to his love of takeaways, lager
and general lack of exercise. Both he and Detective Sergeant Legg loved to use
their fists and other forms of abuse to get a suspect to confess or become their
'snout', regardless of whether they were innocent or not. Their reign of terror
peaked in the 70s and ran right through to 1979 when Detective Sergeant
Legg retired from the police force. Few were sad to see the back of Detective
Sergeant Legg, especially the Savage brothers: Kenny, Ronnie and Wilfred
(known locally as Rockin' Wilf due to his passion for rock 'n' roll). The three
brothers, together or separately, never succumbed to Sergeant McDonald's
and Detective Sergeant Legg's methods. For years, Detective Sergeant Legg
held resentment, frustration and jealousy towards the Savage brothers as they
didn't fear him—they would mock Detective Sergeant Legg openly and were
well loved around the Bush.

When Rockin' Wilf was arrested and charged, stood trial and sent to prison by the Metropolitan Police at New Scotland Yard in late 1974, Detective Sergeant Legg was furious that he was not included in the operation. Legg heard via his 'sources' that he was not to be informed, as New Scotland Yard felt he was incompetent and could hinder the entire process. After that, his love for the job dwindled tremendously and when he could take early retirement at the age of 55 in April 1979, he took it.

With his 'nest egg'—which neither the Inland Revenue nor the police knew about—pension and sale of the family home in Ealing, Detective Sergeant Legg, along with his long-suffering and loyal wife Beverly, moved to a nice bungalow in Horsham, East Sussex, leaving their two sons, Gerald and Graham, to survive in the big wide world on their own. Gerald had thought about joining the police, but he wanted to see the world, so he joined the army in 1978 and is now doing his third tour of duty in Northern Ireland. Gerald had never needed a helping hand from his parents—unlike Graham, who was yet to find his true self and occasionally relied upon his father and mother. His mother doted on him, whilst Detective Sergeant Legg reluctantly did what he could.

■ ■ ■

With Graham Legg's seven O-levels looming in the summer of 1974, Detective Sergeant Legg decided to visit his son's school, Ealing Mead County School in mid-May of that year. Detective Sergeant Legg gave the two glamorous school secretaries, Dorothy Hart and Sharon Roberts, a fiver each and the afternoon off, saying he had cleared it with the headmaster, Mr Eric Griffiths. As 'the girls about town' were heading towards the door to ''ave a laugh' down the King's Road, Detective Sergeant Legg gently pulled Sharon back and whispered in her ear, 'I think you and me should have a nice chat tonight.'

Sharon, aroused by his strong smell of Hai Karate aftershave, giggled and replied, 'I fink we should.'

Detective Sergeant Legg started to laugh like his idol Sid James, 'Yak, yak, yak,' smacked her gently on the backside whilst staying in character as Sid James and said 'Get up there, girl'—making Sharon and Dorothy laugh in a saucy fashion.

Mr Griffiths was not that receptive towards Detective Sergeant Legg's request to let him copy the exam papers, but in return, Mr Griffiths' recent driving offence would be forgotten. Mr Griffiths was equally annoyed that he had given his two secretaries the afternoon off, when there was a backlog of work. Detective Sergeant Legg heartily listened to Mr Griffiths concerns. As a connoisseur of violence and a master of manipulation, Detective Sergeant Legg proceeded to hit Mr Griffiths' head hard against his oak desk in his office, with Mr Griffiths pleading, 'For the love of God, stop, please.'

'There is no God. I am the devil. I am the things your nightmares are made of. Now give me the keys to the cupboard with the papers and the pain stops, or do you want me to carry on with this pain?' whispered Detective Sergeant Legg in a voice like that of Boris Karloff.

Reluctantly and knowing he was no match for Detective Sergeant Legg, Mr Griffiths pulled the keys to the cupboard from his left trouser pocket. Detective Sergeant Legg snatched the keys from him and smacked his head on the desk one last time, resulting in the headmaster being knocked out. Detective Sergeant Legg loved pain and humiliation.

With Mr Griffiths unconscious and covered in blood, Detective Sergeant Legg whistled the theme tune to Dad's Army as he copied the exam papers, knowing that Mr Griffiths would live the rest of his life in fear, wondering if he would be fitted up by the vicious Detective Sergeant Legg.

Detective Sergeant Legg hit the roof when Graham only got five grade Cs, one grade E and one grade B. Yet his wife, not knowing about her husband's recent visit to the school, thought her lovely Graham was a star pupil. Detective Sergeant Legg, when his wife and Gerald were out, went into his son Graham's room and demonstrated his police interview techniques, with Graham as the suspect. Graham stayed in bed for a week after their 'role playing'.

A few weeks later, Eric Griffiths was arrested on Clapham Common while walking his dog for soliciting in a public place, thanks to Detective Sergeant Legg's brass friend, Doris Greene.

Graham Legg went on to find a job as an apprentice draughtsman at Smiths Industries Ltd, which resulted in Graham moving out. Detective Sergeant Legg was happy to see him go, but Graham's mother was heartbroken. Detective Sergeant Legg and Graham rarely spoke after his departure, even when Graham came home for Christmas. The exchanges between father and son were just civil.

Then in the summer of 1981, the now-retired Detective Sergeant Legg got wind that Wilfred Savage was soon to be released from HMP Isle of Wight, thanks to an ongoing public campaign led by investigative journalist Peter Hill and the British comedian, Mike Reid. To add insult to injury in the eyes of Detective Sergeant Legg—now known as Arthur Legg since giving up work—he heard on the grapevine that Wilf's older brothers, Kenny and Ronnie Savage, had left the Bush, but Kenny's only son, 14-year-old Edward Savage, was leading his own gang into the world of petty crime.

Arthur Legg felt it was his calling to stop the Savages, so he requested reinstatement, which was denied. He asked his favourite son Gerald to join the police, but he refused. Arthur Legg's only option was to make his less favourite son, Graham, join the police force. After visiting his son at his flat in Battersea, Arthur Legg laid into Graham hard with a rubber hose until he agreed to resign from Smiths Industries Ltd and sign up with the police.

Graham Legg excelled at his police training course and was fast-tracked, not because he had improved as a student but because Arthur Legg had photos, documents and such like that could put many of his former colleagues away for a few years, even destroy their lives. Arthur Legg learnt about the art of blackmailing after reading The Adventure of Charles Augustus Milverton in The Return of Sherlock Holmes, during his time at Bramshill. One of the many strangleholds Arthur Legg had was on Duncan McDonald, as he possessed a collection of photographs of a rather drunk and drugged up McDonald in a bear suit (without the bear's head), three high society madams and a rather jolly pig in a Mayfair Hotel from 1975.

■ ■ ■

'It's a different game now, Arthur. All these bleeding Perry Mason wannabees giving the villains rights. They reckon by the end of the decade interviews will be recorded. Bloody recorded!' says Sergeant McDonald to his former friend, now blackmailer.

'I've heard, Duncan. It's getting by the book. I mean we got results, villains behind bars, grasses on the street,' states Arthur Legg in a proud manner.

'So, your lad starts tomorrow. Going to give him White City, as no other fucker wants it, bloody no other fucker wants it,' says Sergeant McDonald, thinking the lad could be of some use.

'Make sure you give him the full SP on the Savages, OK? Duncan, Graham is a turd, you've got to toughen him up.'

'OK to give him a few slaps? Bloody a few slaps?' asks Sergeant McDonald with enthusiasm.

'Yes, the more, the better,' orders Arthur Legg from his study in his cosy bungalow as he puffs on a Cuban cigar—luxury items purchased from Arthur Legg's former colleagues making sure his 'information' on them stays safely locked away.

Sergeant McDonald, believing there is a warmth between him and Arthur that he hadn't felt for many years, asks his former colleague, 'After tomorrow, you'll give me the photos, so I can burn them? Bloody burn them?'

'Duncan, if you ever ask me that again, I will kick your lungs out, kill your dog, and send the photos to all the police stations and the papers in Great Britain. You're the one that crossed the line that night, not me. As Kodak say, "For the times of your life." Now, piss off—my wife is doing cauliflower cheese.'

Arthur Legg slams the telephone down, leaving Sergeant McDonald feeling rather annoyed and stupid, as he stands in the hallway holding his trim phone, with the dead tone piercing his ear—in his favourite fancy-dress bear costume, as his wife Mavis and the two girls are away visiting Mavis's sister.

■ ■ ■

'OK, Legg, these are the little herberts. I want you to nick, knee and book. NKB, bloody NKB,' orders an annoyed and anxious Sergeant McDonald, knowing that PC Legg's father has power over him. PC Legg was hoping to be shown round the station and meet all the staff. Instead, he was instructed to go to interview room number one upon his arrival, for a private introductory meeting with the sergeant.

'Yes, Sir,' says PC Legg, standing to attention, as commanded by Sergeant McDonald, who looks to the heavens, breathes a heavy sigh then slaps Legg round the face for good measure.

'Now listen, son. It's Sarge or Sergeant, not Sir. You need to listen, son—I haven't told you their names. In this game, you need to listen to your elders and betters, bloody your elders and betters.'

Shocked, sore around the face and wondering why Sergeant McDonald must repeat his final sentence with a prefixed bloody, PC Legg replies, 'Yes, Sergeant.'

'That's better. Your beat is going to be White City. Now I want you to keep your peelers open for Edward Savage aka Eddie The Casual, Oscar De Paul (no alias—got a stupid name already), Ronald Reynolds aka Honest Ron, James Joseph aka Jamie Joe, Simon Moran aka Quicksilver, and Dino Salvador aka Dino—bloody original that one. These little shits have just left Christopher Wren. Fancy themselves as football hooligans. All tea leaves—clothes, bikes, anything. Edward Savage's uncle, Wilfred Savage, aka Rockin' Wilf, is their Fagin—he got out from stir two years ago. His brothers, Kenny and Ronnie, moved out of the manor a while back, so we ain't bothered about them, but Kenny's son Edward is living with Wilfred at 14 Hudson Close—the council gave him his flat back when he came out, bastards. Apart from Wilfred Savage, they all go about by the gang name of The Magnificent Six. Don't think for one second you are dealing with nursery school kids, these are horrible little shits that terrorise the neighbourhood. Bloody terrorise the neighbourhood.'

Sergeant McDonald is right about their endeavour into theft, but The Magnificent Six love White City and all who dwell there. These lads are just lively school leavers that belong to the Casuals subculture. The Magnificent Six are the least menacing and dangerous out of all the criminal cultures that thrive in and around the estate.

'Any questions, Legg? Bloody any questions, Legg?' asks Sergeant McDonald.

'Sergeant, you gave me their names—do we have any photographs?'

The second the word photographs leaves PC Legg's innocent and inquisitive mouth, Sergeant McDonald goes red as his mind switches to the photographs of him with the happy pig that Arthur Legg is holding to ransom.

Sergeant McDonald punches PC Legg hard in the stomach who falls to the floor. Badly winded, he tries to get up, but the sole of Sergeant McDonald's size ten boot pushes down hard on PC Legg's face.

'Stay down, little Legg. Bloody little Legg,' orders an aggressive Sergeant McDonald, as he unzips his flies as if he is going to urinate all over the youthful PC Legg. Then Sergeant McDonald steps back, leans against the cold wall and slowly starts to slide down, sobbing, 'Just go. Bloody just go.'

■ ■ ■

PC Legg confused and in pain after his 'prep talk' with Sergeant McDonald, descends towards White City, hoping the interaction with the outside world will help him to forget this morning's events. 'Got to tell me old man,' PC Legg thinks, as he says hello to passers-by and shopkeepers standing in their doorways. PC Legg is taken back by how friendly everyone is, as his father and Sergeant McDonald had painted this picture that the estate was a no-go zone.

With his mood lifting, PC Legg notices a thirty-something man in a bright white T-shirt, black jeans and boots, with a slicked back DA, just like John Travolta from Grease, walking down Australia Road. Either side of the rocker are two teenage boys: one in a white polo shirt, light faded blue jeans and light brown desert boots, with raven hair cut into a wedge; the other, bearing similar facial features to the John Travolta wannabe, sporting a short-sleeved, light green, button-down shirt, dark jeans and bright blue suede trainers with his blond hair cut short.

PC Legg, never an expert in fashion, is taken aback how striking they all look in this concrete jungle. Then the penny drops for PC Legg—it's Rockin' Wilf, his nephew and a member of The Magnificent Six.

'Piss off, Wilf, you're telling me that you got banned for life from seeing Showaddywaddy, cos you out-bobbed Dave Bartram?' laughs Eddie.

'Who the fuck is Dave Bartram?' asks Oscar as he smokes a cigarette.

'Who the fuck is Dave Bartram? He's the singer of Showaddywaddy. A real singer, not like that arse bandit you like, Paul 'fucking' Weller,' snaps Wilf.

'Piss off! Heard it all now—'Showaddywaddy are better than The Style

Council.' Showaddywaddy are a covers band, nothing more, nothing less. Weller has got style and class,' snaps Oscar.

'If you say so, Oscar. Anyway, before I was rudely interrupted I was at the Hammersmith Odeon with my girlfriend, Sheila—right dirty sort from Hackney. I tell ya, what we used to get up to in the sack,' boasts Wilf.

'Please, Wilf. Just about to grab some grub. Ain't interested in your made-up sex life,' quips Oscar.

Wilf, not rising to the occasion, just smiles and carries on with his anecdote. 'It was 1974, Showaddywaddy were just starting to make it. I was a fan and a mate before they hit the big time. Knew them all. Always on the guest list, had a laugh, a few beers.'

'Chat up the girls—they dig it,' cuts in Oscar, who can't resist reciting The Jam or Style Council lyrics at any given opportunity.

'Jesus Christ, it's like telling a yarn to the bloody Muppet Show. Anyway, at the encore, I'm invited on stage by Bartram, as he could see I was bopping like a goodun with Sheila at the front. So, I get up and start to 'shake me money-maker'. Bartram goes over to the drums to grab a quick beer.

'He was fucked. Leaving me on me Jack Jones to give it me all. I am going potty, the crowd are going bonkers, a few chaps who knew me start shouting out 'Rockin' Wilf! Rockin' Wilf!' Soon all the bleeding Odeon are chanting me name. I felt like a bloody rock star. I don't think Bartram expected me to steal the show, as he throws down his beer and joins me.

'But, by now, I am knackered, so I goes over to see if I can pinch a can of beer by the drums. Then I hear all these boos, look over and see Bartram fucking it up big time. He kept missing the beat, couldn't flip his feet in time. Then the crowd start to chuck their plastic pint glasses full of beer, hot dogs, fag-ends, whatever they could get their mitts on, whilst shouting out, "We want Wilf! We want Wilf!"

'Bartram storms off stage, with Showaddywaddy following him. I decide to do the same, hoping old Dave would see the funny side of it all. When I get into their changing room, Bartram points at me and says to his heavies, "Chuck him out." Suddenly, these three bloody massive geezers grab me, march me out and chuck me out at the fire exit, just like when you see Tom getting slung out in Tom and Jerry. As I land, Bartram comes out and shouts out, "You, Rockin' Wilf, are banned for life. No one and I mean no one out-bops the Bartram, not even me mother."

'Well, I wouldn't have said a word until he mentioned his mother, so I shout back, "I've had your mother!" That was it. Bartram came out with his heavies. I ain't a coward, Eddie, Oscar, but I ain't no mug neither. I knew I could take him, but his minders, nay. And I didn't have me lads with me, Tommy, Larry, Ian. So, I had it on me toes, shouting out more jokes about his mother. I look round—Bartram is doing the wanker sign. Lucky for me, Sheila, good girl, was hanging around for me. Shame—should have married her.'

'Two months later or so, Showaddywaddy played The Rainbow, but I got no further than the foyer. Must have had a poster or something, as I was asked to leave. Pity, as I still love Showaddywaddy, but old Bartram never had a sense of humour. Wanker,' says Wilf, as he brings his recollection to a close, with a slight element of regret and a smile.

Eddie and Oscar look at each other for a second, then both start to laugh. Wilf chuckles to himself. He loves to entertain, as he is a natural showman and genuinely funny—character traits that have helped him in life from the school playground to his recent incarceration at Her Majesty's pleasure.

'That's what I like to see—happy people,' cuts in an attempted authoritative voice. Wilf, Eddie and Oscar stop laughing, turn, and see a new bobby on the beat.

'It's bleeding Dixon of Dock Green. Evening all,' says an annoyed Wilf.

PC Legg smiles a dry smile and replies drolly, 'The legendary wit of Rockin' Wilf. My old man told me all about you. Arthur Legg—he remembers you well.'

Wilf's face breaks into a wide smile and chuckles, 'You're Half a Leg's little boy? Yeah, I remember your old man.' Wilf turns to Eddie and Oscar. 'Right bastard—fitted up a lot of fellas, liked a bung and hassled any girl round 'ere, from the Saturday girl to the vicar's wife. How's he's doing?'

PC Legg was hoping the name Arthur Legg would paralyse his father's adversary with fear. 'He sends his regards, Rockin Wilf',' states an aggravated PC Legg.

'Yeah, sure he does. We used to wind him right up. Half a Leg—he bleeding hated that. Trouble with your old man—apart from being a bent copper—he never had a sense of humour,' Wilf says as a matter of fact.

'We remember Half a Leg. We were just kids, but I remember the bastard, trying to nick us for eating chips the wrong way. Wanker,' recalls Eddie, with Oscar nodding in support.

PC Legg, expecting a little distance but not this hostility, decides to try to control the situation. Noticing Oscar is smoking, he says, 'You old enough to smoke, son?'

'First day on the job, trying to nick a 16-year-old for having a crafty cigarette? Course I'm old enough. Nick me, take me down the station. Sure old Mac bloody Mac would love your first collar to be a waste of time,' says Oscar in an arrogant manner.

PC Legg, snarling, retorts, 'Bet I would find a bit of hash in your pocket.'

Wilf, Eddie and Oscar smile at each other, as they know any copper will make a mountain out of a molehill over a bit of personal puff, so they agree to never carry any gear.

'That's slander, PC Legg. Search me, search me nephew, search Oscar— you'll find nothing. Now either nick us or let us get our fish and chips, cos you ain't got sweet Fanny Adams on us,' says Wilf, who is now bored of the situation and is craving for scampi.

PC Legg glares at Wilf, knowing that the John Travolta lookalike is correct. 'OK, on your way. Nice to have met you,' mocks PC Legg.

'Tsk. Come on, lads—let's get some fodder. My shout,' says Wilf walking off, with Eddie and Oscar following him.

As PC Legg, starts to walk down Bloemfontein Road, he notices a nervous lad in white shorts and a white polo shirt with bright white trainers on a racing bike with the handlebars turned up, heading towards him.

Toby Brown, former pupil of Christopher Wren School, and like The Magnificent Six enjoying a cheery summer, working on an ad hoc basis around West London with his older brother Thomas, who owns a small yet profitable gardening business. With money in his pocket from work and his parents' allowance, Toby is trying his best to be a Casual and be accepted by The Magnificent Six, yet to no avail, as Toby Brown is a sneak and a coward. The only things in Toby's favour are his looks and his superficial charm, which has helped him to kiss and tell with many girls from his ex-school and around the Bush. When The Magnificent Six have let him into a scam after he had conned his way in,

Toby was always the one that sung like a canary when they were caught. Now Eddie and the boys snub Toby Brown as he is not to be trusted. When Toby became a Casual, he thought the lads would welcome him, yet Toby wears items that are going out of style as he is never innovative in his appearance.

Like many teenagers around the Bush and beyond, Toby had smoked puff for the first time this summer after bumping into Honest Ron and Quicksilver, who were smoking a joint in Wormholt Park. As Ron and Quicksilver were both very stoned, they succumbed to Toby's snake-like charm, gave him a few tokes and told him they could sort out some gear for him from Rooster.

Yet after much exhilaration about meeting the Kingpin of White City, Toby is disappointed that he purchased his first eighth of Lebanese Hashish from Honest Ron on the corner of Commonwealth Avenue, rather than from Rooster directly. After Ron had found Rooster's 'stolen bike' a few weeks earlier, Rooster had set him and Jamie Joe up as his distribution around White City, as demand was high with the kids and Rooster needed people he could trust. Unlike Wilf, Eddie and Oscar, Honest Ron and Jamie Joe had no qualms about carrying puff around the Bush.

Toby races home to roll his first ever joint. Pedalling with a combination of excitement and fear, he sees PC Legg heading towards him. Overcome with anxiety, Toby pulls hard on his front brakes—so hard, in fact, that he somersaults over the handlebars and lands on his head in front of PC Legg. As Toby is coming around, he looks up to see PC Legg standing over him, holding his paraphernalia.

'Get yer trousers on, you're nicked,' says PC Legg, in his best impersonation of Regan from The Sweeny, to which Toby meekly replies, 'Sir, I've got shorts on.'

After a morning of stomach punches and odd behaviour from his sergeant and receiving abuse from a few local legends, PC Legg is in no mood for any back chat, so he pulls out his truncheon, hits Toby hard across the chest, taking out all of his frustration on the lad.

■ ■ ■

Toby sits alone in fear in interview room number one, waiting for Sergeant McDonald and PC Legg to come in, as they are whispering outside. PC Legg is trying to point out the correct procedure for informing Toby Brown's parents or a suitable adult of his arrest, to which Sergeant McDonald replies in a muffled voice, 'Little Legg, if you ever tell me how to do my job again, I will knock your teeth out and wear them as a necklace. Now let's get in there. Watch and learn—let me do all the talking, bloody let me do all the talking.'

As Sergeant McDonald opens the door with brute force, he gets a sensation on seeing the trembling teenager. Sergeant McDonald walks over to Toby and slaps him hard across the face, knocking him off the chair. 'Don't back chat a police officer, son. Bloody, don't back chat a police officer, son.'

Toby, getting up from the ground for the second time in a day, replies in some pain, 'I never said a word, Sir.'

Sergeant McDonald walks over to Toby, treading hard on his foot, causing the youngster much discomfort. 'That's good, son. Now sit down and speak only when spoken to. Bloody, speak only when spoken to.'

'Yes, Sir,' cries Toby, while PC Legg scratches his head, believing that Sergeant McDonald should see someone about his repeat final sentence and the prefixed 'bloody'.

'OK. Now, you've been caught red-handed with class B drugs with the intent to supply. How long have you been selling drugs on the White City Estate? Bloody, how long have you been selling drugs on the White City Estate?' asks Sergeant McDonald, looking sideways to PC Legg with a knowing smile.

'Sir, I am not a dealer. I bought the hash off Honest Ron, who gets it off Rooster,' screams Toby hoping to pass the blame.

'Ah, Ronald Reynolds, aka Honest Ron, and John Roost aka Rooster. Now, you are telling me that these boys are selling drugs, are you, son? Or do you want another slap for being cheeky to a policeman? Tell me the truth or a slap—choice is yours. Bloody, tell me the truth or a slap—choice is yours.'

Toby Brown, spineless and untrustworthy since birth, readily tells all, hoping Sergeant McDonald and PC Legg will let him off with his honesty.

'OK, son, you've done good. Bloody, you've done good,' says Sergeant McDonald, who can go from good to bad copper in a second. 'Now, I believe you, I really do, but my governor won't. He wants results, dangerous kids taken off the streets. I mean a kid with a pocket full of drugs—doesn't look good and it will break your parents' heart seeing you in the dock. Bloody, break your parents' heart seeing you in the dock.'

Sergeant McDonald pauses, letting the paranoia set into the inexperienced mind of Toby Brown.

Toby Brown, visualising a packed court room with his heart-broken parents and shamed brother looking on, desperately turns to the only friend he has at this moment in time, Sergeant McDonald, and cries out, 'Please, I can't go to court! I can't go to prison! Please, Sir!'

Sergeant McDonald relishes his fear. 'OK, son, now wait here. Me and PC Legg are going to have a little chat. Come on, PC Legg. Bloody come on, PC Legg.'

With this Sergeant McDonald stands up, pulling PC Legg up as he gets up, leaving Toby Brown more scared than before.

As Sergeant McDonald and PC Legg get out of earshot of the interview room, Sergeant McDonald pulls out his wallet, gets out a tenner and passes it to PC Legg. 'Pop down the Wimpy. Pilcher's will be closed. Get me a quarter pounder with cheese, French fries and a strawberry milkshake, and whatever you want. Oh, and I want the change. Bloody, I want the change.'

'Thank you, Sarge, but what about Toby?'

'What about him? Bloody what about him?'

'Sarge, are you going to charge him?'

'Little Legg, of course not. I am going to do some paperwork, wait for you, eat me burger, have a cat nap, then in an hour or so, tell him the deal is become a grass or go to court. We've got our way in with The Magnificent Six. This wouldn't make court—he ain't got no previous. He doesn't know that, but we do. Bloody, doesn't know that, but we do.'

PC Legg, not surprised by the outcome as he could see what was developing, asks one more question. 'What about the evidence? Will you destroy it, Sarge?'

Sergeant McDonald lets out a hearty laugh and affectionately puts his right hand on PC Legg's left shoulder. 'Don't be silly. I am going to have a smoke tonight. That's the beauty of nicking kids with puff—ain't worth the paperwork, but sure worth the puff. Bloody sure worth the puff.'

54

6

The Confessions of PC Graham Legg—Part Two

'Half a Leg's boy looks a right wally, don't he?' says Wilf as he, Eddie and Oscar head towards Pilcher's.

'They all are, Wilf. I have never met a copper that I've liked or trusted. Never,' adds Oscar.

'Met a few that play a fair game—straight up blokes, looking out for the neighbourhood, turning the odd blind eye. It's the boys at the top—they're the real bastards. Trust me—I should know. But Half's lad looks like a little boy lost, doesn't seem on his game, too nervous. PC Legg don't gel with Joe Public,' says Wilf, as he analyses Shepherd's Bush's newest boy in blue.

'What, like Mac bloody Mac? Yeah, he's a real people person. You of all people should hate coppers—they fitted you up,' says Eddie, disbelieving his uncle's sudden compassion for the police.

'That was political. Duncan McDonald was alright back in the day when he was a bobby on the beat. He liked a laugh, a few beers with what the papers would call villains. It's when Half a Leg got stationed here in the late 60s everything changed for the worst,' Wilf debates.

'But Legg is going to have his peelers on us. I say you two give the five fingers discount a breather, put the bike shop in Tooting on ice, until he gets his first collar. This Friday, you lads get rid of the last "duty free" fags. I know it's pin money. Tide you over, until…' Wilf pauses knowing his announcement might shock Eddie and Oscar.

'Until what, Wilf? You've got a better scam in the pipeline?' asks an enthusiastic Oscar.

'Well, not so much a scam.'

'Well, what then? Come on, Wilf, spill the beans,' says Oscar, anxious to know what Wilf is plotting.

Wilf looks at the lads and clears his throat. 'You will…'

'What, Uncle Wilf?' says Eddie, who only calls Wilf uncle when he is annoyed or mocking him.

'You two will have to get a job,' says Wilf, punching out his last word as if he was sentencing Eddie and Oscar to a year at Feltham Borstal.

'Piss off a job! It took me a year to get a part-time one. I was laughed at every time I asked for a bit of work,' snarls Oscar.

'Hold your horses, Oscar. It ain't the end of the world. Summer's over in a few months—a bit of graft will be all right. I ain't bothered,' says Eddie, who deep down couldn't see a long-term future in stealing and selling stolen goods, unlike Oscar who loved the romantic notion.

Wilf, pleased with his nephew's support, now knows Oscar will be easier to sway. 'I've got one sorted—four days on the books, one day cash in hand.'

'Oh, I bloody see. You are pimping us out, selling me and Eddie like slaves,' says an infuriated Oscar.

'No, helping you out, Oscar.'

''Ere, you and Legg planned this? You know, put the wind up us?'

'Shut up, Oscar. I know you are taking the piss. It's just bumping into him reminded me that I had something to tell ya. Me side with a copper? Idiot,' says Wilf, offended by Oscar's implication.

'Yeah, right,' snaps Oscar.

'Button it, O. OK, Wilf, tell us about the work you've got lined up for us,' Eddie asks, warming more to the idea of working by the second.

'It's me mate Raj. Remember him? Mate of mine from Maidstone. Streatham lad, he's got a building firm. They do decent work. Me and him priced up a few jobs round 'ere, got the go-ahead last week. Raj needs a few more hands on the labouring side. He's got his sons on board, they like a joint or two, a few beers,' says Wilf.

'Nice one, Wilf. Raj—good boy. I know one of his sons, Deepak—likes a laugh and the ladies. Oscar, it will be a giggle, a bit of honest cash. No more looking over your shoulder.'

Oscar, disgruntled yet knowing that their carefree days may be temporarily over, nods his head in agreement.

■ ■ ■

Oscar De Paul's day couldn't get any worse. As he walks into Pilcher's, he notices regular punter and British comedian Mike Reid tucking into a plate of large fish and chips. Mike Reid looks up and greets Wilf and Eddie. 'All right, Wilf? 'Ello, Eddie. Bet you are fighting off the ladies. Take after your uncle—always got a lady on the go, ain't ya, Wilf?'

Wilf and Eddie chuckle, then Mike Reid looks at Oscar and sniggers, as their dispute is none the closer to resolving since the fateful day in April 1976 at Bentworth Primary School.

When the headmistress, Mrs Joan Duke, announced that Bentworth Primary School had been selected by Southern Television to audition pupils for ITV's hit children's show, Runaround with Mike Reid, the children erupted into a state of euphoria, especially a young Oscar as Runaround was the highlight of Oscar's week. He would run around the house, shouting out the answers and drooling over the prizes, from the portable TV sets to the dartboards.

Mrs Duke, along with raven-haired beauty Miss Ingrid Early—who bore an uncanny resemblance to the British sex symbol Caroline Munro—and deputy head master Mr Patrick Neal, were to run several heats for the pupils, with fifteen pupils making it to the final heat in the assembly hall with Mike Reid, where five were to be chosen for Runaround. Oscar, Eddie and Ron made it to the final heat, with Toby and Dino failing. Oscar, so delighted and proud with his achievement, decided to swap his slip-on plimsolls for his brand-new lace-up ones for the final heat, even though Oscar still had trouble tying up his shoelaces. Yet he believed Mike Reid would be impressed by his choice of footwear. It was a choice that will haunt Oscar for the rest of his life.

When Mike Reid, along with his entourage, arrived at the School during the lunch hour, he was mobbed. Miss Early remarked to Mr Neal that it was like Beatlemania—something that Miss Early had witnessed first-hand at the London Palladium. After lunch, the final heat for Runaround commenced in a packed assembly hall. The final heat, like the heats beforehand, was more of a sports day event than the actual show. Southern Television, ITV's broadcasting licence holder for the south and south-east of England, wanted to see how sporting these children were and not so interested in their general knowledge. Maybe if it had been a general knowledge test, Oscar would have won hands down, but as he tried to run, jump and skip, Oscar kept tripping over his laces, much to the delight of his peers and teachers.

Eventually, Mike Reid shouted out when Oscar fell over for the umpteenth time, 'Get Charlie Chaplin out of here.'

Oscar, enraged, got up, tore off his brand-new plimsolls and threw them at Mike Reid, screaming, 'Why don't you just fuck off?'

The whole school gasped, Mike Reid snarled, but he knew his career would be over if he hit Oscar. Mrs Duke went over to spank Oscar on Mike Reid's behalf. As she approached, Oscar turned around, spat in her face and yelled, 'You can fuck off as well!'

With that, he ran out of the hall, barefoot, while being pursued by Miss Early and Mr Neal. They eventually caught up with him before he made it to the school gate. Mr Neal wanted to rough him up a bit, whilst Miss Early, a disciple of Love Not War from the late 60s, felt a hug would help a sad Oscar.

Oscar wasn't expelled, as Miss Early defended him to Mrs Duke, stating the boy was lost due to his father being in prison and being raised by his mother and sister, which was bound to put any boy under pressure. Mrs Duke reluctantly agreed, so Oscar was sent to a counsellor, which Oscar enjoyed, as he got every Tuesday morning off school. His popularity increased with his peers as they thought he was a total loon, yet Mrs Duke put on his school file that Oscar was mentally ill and was likely to be a danger to society in later life. Mrs Duke overlooked the simple fact that Oscar was broken-hearted.

Oscar's pain was heightened further when he heard before the show was aired that Eddie won Runaround, coming away with a dartboard. Oscar's only consolation was that Ron came last. After Runaround, Eddie and Mike Reid became friends, as Eddie told Mike Reid during the recording of the show about the wrongful imprisonment of his uncle, Rockin' Wilf. Mike Reid listened to the kid's concerns, spoke to his investigative journalist friend Peter Hill, and together they started a campaign to free Wilfred Savage, resulting with Mike Reid visiting the Bush to speak to Eddie, Kenny and Ronnie. Due to the recommendation from Mike Reid's friends at the BBC, he started going to Pilcher's for his lunch and dinner and has been coming ever since, as he has become good friends with Terence Pilcher.

'I see the loon is with ya,' says Mike Reid.

'Oh, look, it's Runaround Now Mike,' replies Oscar.

'You're just gutted, cos you never got on Runaround.'

'Gutted? I never heard of Runaround, until you turned up to Bentworth,' says Oscar, lying through his teeth.

'You should audition for Pinocchio, son, cos that nose ain't half growing,' jests Mike Reid, as he tucks into a forkful of cod.

'You're just gutted, cos the BBC never cast you as Del Boy.'

Mike Reid lets out a loud laugh, 'Oh, look, your shoelace is untied.'

'Wilf, Eddie, I'm off. I ain't sitting down with him.'

'Never invited you, son. By the way, Terry—lovely bit of cod. Lovely,' says Mike Reid now uninterested in Oscar.

Eddie walks over to his best friend, holding back the laughter. 'He's only winding you up, it's just banter, Oscar.'

'Oh, piss off. I'm off to Fat Ralph's,' says Oscar, storming off as he often does when things don't go his way, leaving Wilf and Eddie to enjoy their lunch with Mike Reid in peace.

■ ■ ■

Oscar lights up a cigarette as he heads to Fat Ralph's to get some fishcake and chips. Oscar is feeling quite flush from the tenner he has stolen in new pound coins, old pound notes and fifty pence pieces from the charity box in the Church of St Stephen and St Thomas—a swoop he has kept quiet from the rest of The Magnificent Six.

As Oscar steps into South Africa Road, heading towards Fat Ralph's, he notices Stephanie Clarke the snotty nosed kid who, a while back, coined the name The Magnificent Six—heading towards Hammersmith Park with a tennis racket under her arm. Oscar admires Stephanie in her white Fred Perry tennis top and matching skirt, even though Oscar associates Fred Perry with Mods and skinheads. Yet Oscar adores the white pair of Nike canvas with a light blue tick Stephanie is sporting. As Stephanie gets closer, Oscar is taken aback by how pretty she has become since he left Christopher Wren School.

'Anyone for tennis?' he lightly shouts out as they make eye contact.

Stephanie smiles and is touched, as it's the first time any of The Magnificent Six have spoken to her. Hiding her shyness, Stephanie says, composed, 'Yeah, off to play Lucy. Joined a tennis club at the park for the summer.'

Oscar, slightly bewitched by her beauty but trying to stay cool, nods with a smile. 'So you don't fancy joining me for lunch?'

Stephanie's heart skips a beat, as for a while and from a distance, she starts to see how beautiful Oscar is. Following her older sister's advice not to be too keen but to show some interest, she replies with zest, 'Sorry, I can't.'

Oscar shrugs his shoulders, ready to walk off, but Stephanie adds, 'But I can meet you this Saturday.'

Oscar feels the butterflies in his stomach, but remembering Eddie telling him, 'Don't be a prat in front of girls,' coolly says, 'Saturday? Yeah, should be OK. One-ish? Here?'

'OK, see you then.'

'See you then.'

Both Oscar and Stephanie go their separate ways, feeling an attraction, they didn't have ten minutes ago.

■ ■ ■

'You want a kilo? Bloody Hell, Toby. Seriously, mate, you don't want to be setting up shop round 'ere. You really don't,' says Honest Ron, surprised at Toby's request for puff in Wormholt Park, as the sun is setting.

Toby stupidly replies, 'Nay, I ain't setting up shop. It's for me brother, Thomas. He's going to an orgy.'

'An orgy?' Ron's face brightens up.

'Yeah, he's knocking off some stripper from Kensington. He does her gardening. She's having an orgy.'

Ron tilts his head to one side, looking at Toby, trying to work out if he's telling him the truth, as he knows his brother, Thomas—a non-descript lad, who drinks with Ron's old-before-his-time brother, Lee. 'I can't see your brother going to an orgy. I just see him coming home from work in his rust-bucket green Morris Minor van. Seriously, mate, who's it for?'

Toby, under severe pressure from Sergeant McDonald after his arrest two days ago to set up Honest Ron and the rest of The Magnificent Six, elaborates upon his lie. 'That's all a front, Ron. Thomas is at it non-stop. All those bored posh housewives with their fat and balding husbands, missing the feel of a working man. Thomas goes there, mows the lawn, pulls out a few weeds, then wham bam, thank you, ma'am.'

'Hold on a second. You work for him sometimes. How come you ain't never said anything before? You're at it at work with him as well?' says Ron, still disbelieving Toby.

'I wish, I really do. The bastard only brings me in when he's got a real job on with no bunk up at the end. I wanted to tell ya ages ago, but Thomas said he would stripe me if I said a dickie bird to anyone,' says Toby, playing the role of victim—a ploy he has used many times to gain the trust of people, especially girls.

'What a sod. No wonder Thomas looks knackered when I see him driving back. What man wouldn't after a day on the job?'

Toby, sensing that he is winning Ron over, turns the screw of deceit a little more. 'Yeah, he crashes straight out when he gets in from work. He's doing it three, sometime four times a day and, when he does the stripper's garden, he's at it all day.'

'What a lucky bastard,' says an envious Ron.

'So, can you sort out some puff for the orgy?' says Toby, thinking 'job done'.

'Hold on—if she's a stripper from Kenny way, she knows a dealer or two. How come she ain't sorting some puff out?'

Toby, thinking on his feet, turns the screw one final time. 'Their dealer, Leroy, got busted. It's not this Saturday, but next Saturday. Heard all her suppliers are dry or scared. That's why Thomas turned to me as we had a smoke the other day at work.'

Ron, knowing that one dealer nicked is another dealer's gain, says, 'Maybe. You going to the orgy?'

'Yeah. Just to drop the puff off.'

'Bullshit to drop the puff off. I am coming with ya. Ain't having you getting laid on my dope.'

Toby, now under pressure and without thinking, replies, 'Yes, but not the others.'

'Why not the others? We could hear about the orgy up the road.' Toby and Ron both turn around to see Eddie, Oscar, Quicksilver and Dino standing behind them.

'Oh fuck,' Toby thinks to himself.

■ ■ ■

'You promised them an orgy? Jesus Christ, what is it with you teenagers today? Sex mad! Bloody sex mad!' screams Sergeant McDonald, as he slams the receiver down to a trembling Toby in a telephone box on the corner of Goldhawk Road.

PC Legg looks on at his sergeant, while singing in his head Gilbert and Sullivan's 'When constabulary duty's to be done, to be done, A policeman's lot is not a happy one, happy one.'

Sergeant McDonald turns around to his newest PC. 'We will have to do our own orgy. Little Legg, go to Ken Market. Always some posh girl nicked for lifting. Bring her here. I'll do a deal—have an orgy or go to court. Toby can say he got the address wrong, as long as there's an orgy. The Magnificent Six turn up with the puff, then they are nicked, bloody they are nicked.'

PC Legg is dumbfounded that all of his and Sergeant McDonald's attention is on these Casual tearaways. Yet PC Legg doesn't realise that his father has been putting the pressure upon McDonald, saying, 'No arrest in a month then the photos go public,' giving the brutal Sergeant sleepless nights.

'But Sarge, Kensington is not our district,' states PC Legg.

Sergeant McDonald, snarling, says, 'Listen, son, I know how this works.

I've got mates at stations all around London. I'll slip them a few quid or owe them a favour. You've got a lot to learn. Now go out and nick me a girl—we've got an orgy to arrange, bloody orgy to arrange.'

■ ■ ■

'So how come, you ain't inviting me to the orgy?' asks Wilf, as Ron, Oscar, Dino, Jamie and Quicksilver wait for Eddie, who is getting changed before they go out to sell their last batch of 'duty free' cigarettes around the manor on a Friday evening.

'What orgy is that Wilf?' asks Oscar, as all The Magnificent Six, including Eddie, agreed not to invite Wilf, for one reason or another.

'The one Ron told me about,' Wilf says, as he points to Ron.

With all eyes fixed on Honest Ron, he nervously says, 'Well, Wilf caught me off guard. I couldn't help it lads, sorry.'

'What did he use? Thumbscrews or something?' snaps Jamie Joe.

'Well, Wilf just asked me if I had anything on the horizon. Just slipped out we're off to an orgy next weekend. Simple mistake. Anyone could have done it. It's Wilf—he's one of us, ain't he lads?' replies Honest Ron, who's been too nervous to ask Rooster for a kilo, as he doesn't want to invite him.

'Yeah, who got you the bloody fags to sell, let you smoke weed and doss round 'ere, kip 'ere sometimes? How many times you lot been round for a Sunday roast, cooked by muggins here?' says Wilf.

'Wilf, mate, it just looks a little odd, us turning up with the randy uncle in tow,' says Eddie, as he enters the room, looking as sharp as ever.

Wilf lights up a cigarette as he cracks open a small can of Colt 45. 'I know, Eddie. Just winding you up. Anyway, taking Rita out that night. Now piss off—got Debbie coming around later.'

'Jesus, Wilf—how many girls you got on the go?' asks an amazed Dino.

'Dino, when a man has been away for a few years, he's got a lot of catching up to do. I just hope it never happens to any of you. Now, please, piss off.'

For The Magnificent Six, it wouldn't be a Friday evening without their customary bag of chips from Pilcher's, a ritual the lads have been performing for many years—when they are not banned that is. As they queue for a takeaway bag of small chips and a can of coke, Terence Pilcher surprises them by saying, 'On the house, lads. Anyone fancy a saveloy?'

'On the house, too?' asks a confused Oscar.

'Of course, for my favourite youngest customers.'

All The Magnificent Six look at each other with some surprise, then the reason behind Terence's generosity comes to light. 'Heard you boys are going to an orgy next Saturday. Mind if I tag along?'

Eddie pulls out a five-pound note. 'We'll pay for the chips, if you don't mind.'

As The Magnificent Six head to Wormholt Park to eat their chips, followed by a quick spliff before they go to work selling their cigarettes, Rockin' Wilf's upstairs well-to-do and God-fearing neighbour Mrs Day walks past the lads, giving them a more disapproving stare than usual. 'You boys will go to Hell! An orgy? May the Lord have mercy on your souls. You boys are Satan's spawn, evil to the core,' Mrs Day spits out as if she is preaching at a sermon. The Magnificent Six's only reaction is to laugh in Mrs Day's face, who crosses herself, looks to the heavens and prays, 'Please save these poor creatures.' Then she walks off to pick her dinner up from Pilcher's.

Once the laughter subsides, Eddie turns to his troops and says, 'Bloody Hell, I think the whole of White City knows. Nice one, Ron.'

Ron is about to answer, when two top older Casuals, QPR, home and away, Alan Harvey and Ben Wright walk past with Ben saying, 'Nice bit of solid, Ron. Same again tomorrow?'

'Yeah, course, Ben,' replies Ron, pleased they have saved him from a grilling.

''Ere, lads, don't forget to invite us to the orgy,' adds Alan as they head towards the Tube for a night of fun in Soho.

Oscar laughs, then he sees Stephanie and Lucy over the road. Oscar starts to feel butterflies in his stomach. Looking forward to their date tomorrow, he waves at the two girls.

Stephanie glares at him, then shouts out, 'You're sick in the head, Oscar. A boy your age going to an orgy? Don't ever speak to me again.'

Oscar's dream of love is shattered, then he hears the familiar voice of Rooster, 'All right, lads. What's this about an orgy? Rooster likes an orgy.'

''Ello, Rooster. Was on my way to tell you about it. Need some puff,' says a stressed Honest Ron.

■ ■ ■

'You're barmy,' screams Pauline Wyle, arrested on suspicion of shoplifting in Boots, Kensington High Street.

'That's the deal—either have an orgy or go to court, bloody go to court,' orders Sergeant McDonald.

'Well, I will bloody go to court. You are a nutter.'

Sergeant McDonald steps forward to hit Pauline. PC Legg annoyed he didn't fight back when Sergeant McDonald slapped him, ashamed that he took out his frustration on Toby Brown, disappointed that he allowed Sergeant McDonald to bully Toby Brown, intervenes by hitting the sergeant firmly on the jaw, knocking him out in one punch.

PC Legg turns to Pauline Wyle. 'Come on, love. I'll see you out.'

Pauline follows PC Legg as he walks out of interview room number one into the foyer then into the main entrance. Bewildered from the strangest arrest she has ever experienced, she turns to PC Legg and says, 'This place is a madhouse. Get out before you go nuts.'

'I know love, bloody I know love,' he says, shocked that he has picked up Sergeant McDonald's habit.

■ ■ ■

'I ain't a police informer anymore?' cries a relieved Toby.

'Yes, Toby, but you'll have to stop buying puff.'

'Yes, I will, I promise. But PC Legg—what about the orgy? What am I going to tell The Magnificent Six?' says Toby, trying to hold back the tears as he sits in his parent's hallway after receiving a surprise yet welcome telephone call from PC Legg.

'Just say it was a fib. Better to be a fibber than a grass. You don't belong with them. They are not bad lads—some will turn a corner, some won't. You're just different, that's all. Listen, son, I've got to go. Bye.'

'Bye.'

With that, PC Legg puts down the telephone in the office in the duty room and returns to interview room one, to speak to a now-conscious yet broken Sergeant McDonald, sitting down and slumped up against the wall.

Through sobs and with a sore jaw, Sergeant McDonald mutters, 'It's your old man. Arthur. He's got photos of me with a few hookers in a bear outfit and a pig.'

'Stop! I don't want to know the details. No, I really don't,' cuts in PC Legg before Sergeant McDonald can close his sentence with his bloody prefix. Sergeant McDonald just nods. 'You will have to resign, take early retirement due to being bonkers and you are. You fail me now, today, right this second, on my probation, cos I am out of here. As for the photos, I don't know what me old man will do. But you bullied a school leaver, nearly hit a young woman, gave a bunch of teenagers a hard time, all cos of one bad night. Nay, no one suffers no more. You take what's coming to you. But you can't be a copper anymore. Deal, sergeant?'

Sergeant McDonald, knowing the game is up, looks at PC Legg for the first time with respect. 'Deal. It's not just me he's been blackmailing, bloody he's been blackmailing.'

Graham Legg always knew his father was a cheat. When Arthur Legg came home with the exam papers before his O-levels, Graham said thanks, put them in his drawer and took the exams without ever looking at them. However they were the exam papers from 1973. Ealing Mead County School hadn't received the exam papers for 1974 in mid-May of that year, something his father had overlooked.

Nevertheless Graham Legg wanted to pass or fail on his own merit, without his father controlling him. The beating he took was worth it, as it gave Graham an excuse to leave home. Yet the hiding Graham received a few years later was so brutal that he submitted to join the police force, knowing deep down it was more for his father's benefit than his. Graham doesn't care whether his father or brother speaks to him again, but he wants to make sure his loving and caring mother, Beverly, leaves his father for a better life.

PC Legg goes to his locker, hangs up his uniform for the last time and leaves the police station without saying goodbye. Feeling free, as he is Graham again, he heads off to White City for one final look.

Graham sees Rockin' Wilf casually walking along without a care in the world. Graham waves at Wilf, who waves back and says, 'Finished for the day?'

'Finished for good.'

'Couldn't hack it?'

'Something like that. Let's just say I want something different. I don't want you or The Magnificent Six living in my head any more cos of my father. I want to live my own life.'

'Hallelujah, you've found God or something?' jokes Wilf.

Graham Legg, now understanding the warmth that so many feel for Wilf, says, 'Yeah, seen the light. See you, Wilf.'

'See ya. Be lucky, mate.'

∎ ∎ ∎

Arthur Legg is reading the Sunday papers in his study one morning, still disappointed, but not surprised that Graham had failed at the police six months ago. Arthur Legg was equally annoyed that Sergeant McDonald had a breakdown and, like him, took early retirement. Even though Sergeant McDonald's services were rendered useless to him now, Arthur will taunt Duane McDonald until the day he dies with the photographs he possesses. It is the simple and cruel things in life that give Arthur Legg pleasure.

Yet Arthur Legg was taken aback by his wife Beverly's decision to disown her younger son. 'He's a failure, Arthur. I never want to set eyes on his wretched soul again,' whispered Beverly late one night as they lay on the bed, naked after making love for the first time in five years. Graham's let-down had been the catalyst they needed to kick-start their rocky and unloving marriage.

At last, Arthur felt a bond and one night during pillow talk, he revealed his second and lucrative income as a master and vicious blackmailer. Beverly aroused and enlightened by her husband's revelations, suggested she should become his bookkeeper and Arthur should start demanding more hush money and look for more victims. Arthur hugged Beverly tightly and agreed to a husband and wife partnership in extortion.

Lost in his thoughts a few days later, Arthur failed to hear two cars pulling into the gravel driveway, followed by the sound of car doors opening and closing and the heavy footsteps of men approaching the dark blue door with a brass knocker. Only when Arthur Legg heard a loud knock did he realise he had company.

'Expecting anyone dear?'

'No, Arthur. Shall I answer it?'

'No, love. Carry on making my breakfast. It's probably some hawkers on a Sunday. I'll invite them in, give them a few slaps.'

'Oh, Arthur, that would be lovely.'

Arthur Legg, approaching the door ready for some brutal fun on a Sunday, is taken aback to see two men in sharp suits, with two uniformed policemen standing behind them.

'I am DS Turner, and this is DC Foy. We have a warrant to search your home and other dwellings that you own, as we believe that you possess material used for intent to cause loss to another and making unwarranted demand with menaces.'

Arthur Legg is scared in his life for the first time, as only last week Beverly had suggested he got his ledger, all the documentation and photos from his hideaway—a lock-up garage rented under a different name in Surrey—and put them in the study for her to start a new filing system. Arthur knew they would find all the incriminating evidence within ten minutes of searching his home.

Arthur turns around to see Beverly standing in the hall of their bungalow in her apron, with a knowing smile. 'You fucking bitch! You set me up!' Arthur screams as he runs to her, putting his thick hands around her neck.' As Arthur attempts to strangle her, he yells, 'I'm going to kill you, kill you.'

DS Turner, DC Foy and the two policemen have no trouble in overpowering Arthur Legg, taking him to the Panda car outside and driving off with all his blackmail paraphernalia while witnessing the attempted murder of his wife.

■ ■ ■

'Hello, mother. Been a while—well, a week. I take it everything went well?' asks Graham, sitting in his new flat in Hampstead that he shares with his fiancée Diana, as he speaks to his mother on the telephone.

'Yes, Graham. Went to plan. Will you and your beautiful wife-to-be be coming here for Christmas?'

'Yes. Look forward to it. Love you, mother.'

'Love you, too, Graham.'

7

The Adventures of Rockin' Wilf—Part One

'Let's see 1974 in with a bang,' whispers Sue seductively, as she pours Rockin' Wilf a pint of Double Diamond at the start of the New Year's Eve celebrations in the Queen Adelaide pub.

'Oh, my Peggy Sue, my Peggy Sue, I'm off to The Palais with the lads in a bit. Just popped in for a quick one,' replies a cocky Wilf.

'It's always a quick one with you, Wilf. Never mind. Maybe next year, eh?' quips Sue, whose relationship with Wilf is purely no strings attached.

'Yeah, maybe next year, Sue,' says Wilf as he blows her a kiss. Sue theatrically clutches her heart while giving Wilf a cheeky wink.

Wilf returns to his friends Ian Potter, Tommy James and Larry Jenkins. The four are local and well-respected men in their mid- to late-20s. Ian and Tommy are wearing the current terrace look—cropped hair at the top, allowing the sides to grow, both in plain-coloured, tight rugby tops, cheap half-masted flared jeans while sporting a pair of 12-hole ox-blood DM boots. They both love the look of the aggro lad. Larry likes what he perceives as sophistication, as he sips his Brandy Alexander while wearing a tight white bright shirt with a long collar, three buttons undone to show off his treasured gold medallion, tight blue trousers flared at the bottom and a pair of fake black crocodile loafers, his long sandy blond hair parted on the right. Wilf is dressed in a tight light-blue denim shirt, his trusted dark-blue boot-cut Levi's 517 jeans and his prized brown leather cowboy boots.

The lads are feeling fine and dandy. 'Sue's a nice bit of crumpet,' says Larry.

'You're a married man, mate. You should be at home with Rita and the kids,' replies Wilf.

'I know, but a night out with the lads is what the doctor ordered.'

'You just want to get your leg over, you dirty old man,' says Tommy, trying his best to sound like Harry H Corbett from Steptoe and Son.

'Love Steptoe and Son. Did you see it on Christmas Eve where Harold wants to go to Majorca for Christmas? Me and the missus pissed ourselves laughing,' says Ian, married to Dawn, yet unlike Larry doesn't like to play around.

'Of course. You asked me that on Christmas morning,' jokes Wilf, who is pleased that one of the BBC's hit comedies, Steptoe and Son, is set in their manor, Shepherd's Bush.

In between curry houses, pubs, gigs, night clubs and football, Wilf, Ian, Larry and Tommy steal for a living. But they haven't hit the big league yet, much to their annoyance and frustration. However, Tommy has planned a little heist to tide them over until their 'ship comes in'. All four, like the rest of Great Britain, know that 1974 is going to be tougher than this year. As from tomorrow, Prime Minister Edward Heath is introducing power cuts, due to a dispute with the coal miners. Therefore, commercial properties and residential dwellings will be forced to turn off their electricity on set nights, as a cost-saving measure, and to make matters worse, there will be no television after 10.30pm. Yet according to Ian, he believes that he and his friends could make a profit from the country's misery, as he has been casing out Wickers—'Makers of West London's Finest Candles'—in Ealing.

'Wilf, it's a stroll in the park. No alarm. Nothing. Just a wall. An easy ladder job—in and out, just like Larry on a Saturday night,' says a proud and jovial Ian.

Wilf raises a smile and says, 'Me mother told me my old man made a small fortune with the blackouts during the war. I suppose I am following the family tradition.'

'How are Winston and Elsie? See them over Christmas?' asks Larry.

'Course. Staying at my Kenny's. You know that. My old man was here on Christmas Eve.'

'Oh yeah. Too much party seven and puff.'

'If I don't see them, give them my best,' says Ian.

'Will do. Cheers, Ian.'

■ ■ ■

14th Oct 1940, just after 8.00 pm. A young and dashing Winston Savage comes running through the back door of his house at 41 Braybrook Street like he is being pursued by the devil himself. His wife Elsie, in her favourite black and cream polka dot Madden dress, her hair in tight ring-curls and some waves forming around her pretty face, a beauty spot just above the left side of her lip, is startled by her husband's dramatic entrance, yet pleased to see him alive and well during a brutal air raid by the German Luftwaffe.

Elsie notices huge bulges in both pockets of Winston's dark brown Rain Man's trench coat. 'Aye, aye. Pleased to see me or had a touch?'

'Oh Elsie, you've got a one-track mind, dear. How come you ain't down the Tube station? Bleeding Jerry is bombing again.'

'I ain't deaf, I can hear, but you know I don't like going there without you. Men fink I am all lonesome, trying to have a quick grope behind their wife's back. Yuk.'

'Just say you're Winston Savage's girl.'

'I do, dear.'

'And?'

'They run rabbit, run, run, run.'

'Good girl. 'Ere, Elsie, feast your peelers on these,' says Winston, as bangles, bracelets, beaded necklaces and vermeil gold splash like a sea of jewellery out of his coat pockets and onto the Savages' wooden kitchen table.

The flashes of gold, red and silver light up Elsie's beautiful face. 'Oh gosh, what lovely trinkets. I do love you so much, Winston.'

Whilst many Londoners feared the loud screeching sirens, knowing an air raid from Nazi Germany was inevitable, Winston embraced the chaos and would venture out into the dark and dangerous streets of London to fill his pockets with ill-gotten gains. Not an opportunist racketeer, Winston would plan days, if not weeks in advance which jewellers or watchmakers to rob.

On this evening, Winston decided to do a smash and grab from Glovers the Jewellers, Old Oak Common Lane, as it had sentimental meaning to Winston and Elsie, which was where he purchased their wedding rings in March 1939—they married 31st August 1939, the day before war broke out.

In January 1940, Winston avoided conscription by paying Jack Brack, of Brick Lane, £10 and a tin of Lyle's Golden Syrup to impersonate him at the medical board, after Winston received his call-up papers. After Brack was examined at Whipps Cross, he had been declared unfit for duty due to an enlarged heart and was now offering his services to men like Winston who didn't want to go to war, so they could stay home and follow other pursuits. In Winston's case, it was thieving, as he saw the war with Germany could be a lucrative one for him and his bride.

Winston Savage was born 2nd October 1916 to Bernard and Doris Savage—both travelling fairground workers until they came to the Bush in 1912, when they decided to set up home and start a family in London. Bernard and Doris found it hard to make ends meet, so Bernard turned to thieving to put food on the table—skills and a belief he passed on to his two sons, Winston and Bert Savage, born two years apart.

Winston's and Elsie's first son, Kenny, was born 5th September 1940, then Ronnie was born two years later on 4th March 1942. The youngest, Wilfred, was born 3rd April 1948. Unlike Kenny and Ronnie, Wilfred was not planned but was conceived during a night of passion between Winston and Elsie, after Winston was released from HMP Wandsworth for burglary. During the war, most of the bobbies on the beat turned a blind eye to Winston's activities, thanks to cash, a nicked ration book or a bit of jewellery for the wife. But after the war, the alliance Winston Savage had with the local constabulary ceased, resulting in his first spell at His Majesty's pleasure.

By the time Wilf was seven, he was in awe of his two older brothers. Like their father, Kenny and Ronnie took to thieving, were top Teddy Boys around the Bush with a reputation as local hard nuts, loved American music and adored the local team, QPR. So Wilf was engulfed by crime, fashion, violence, rock 'n' roll and football at an early age.

When Wilf was 17 in 1965, he was already a thief, a ton-up boy riding a Triumph Thunderbird motorcycle and known locally as a tasty street fighter. It was a reputation established two years earlier when he was a pupil at Christopher Wren School in his final year. One afternoon, two local Mods, Mark Jones and Terry Hayes, tried to steal Wilf's satchel at Bransdon Newsagent, Goldhawk Road. Mark and Terry didn't expect this schoolboy to pull out a cosh from his shorts—a present from his father on his thirteenth birthday—and to beat them senseless while singing Bobby Day's Rockin' Robin. The proprietor, Mr Bransdon, didn't try to break it up. In fact, he was mesmerised by the whole event unfolding before his eyes, to the point he was doing backing vocals and hand claps to Wilf's violent a cappella take on a rock 'n' roll hit. The local legend of Rockin' Wilf was born.

Local Mod Ace face Larry Jenkins didn't respect Mark or Terry for picking on a schoolboy, as Larry saw schoolboys as civilians, so there was to be no revenge attack on Wilf. Larry also knew it was not wise to touch the kid brother of Kenny and Ronnie Savage. Two Shepherd's Bush Mods a year older than Wilf, Ian Potter and Tommy James, took a shine to Wilf and a 'secret' friendship grew. When away from the pressure of being in a tribe, Wilf, Ian and Tommy would ransack posh hotel rooms in Mayfair or break into warehouses around Hammersmith. When Larry heard about their escapades and the money they were making, he wanted in.

By 1968, after a few years of many capers, Wilf, Larry, Ian and Tommy were smoking dope, taking LSD, listening to Jimi Hendrix, The Who and new band Led Zeppelin, hanging out at the 100 Club or the Marquee, or going on the pull around Soho. Wilf felt he had a new family, as Ronnie was moving up to Manchester with some new girlfriend and Kenny, now married to Sheila, was looking after his first-born son, Edward Winston Savage, born 6th April 1967.

■ ■ ■

'Go away you sex maniac before I call the police. This is England, not Wales,' screams Mrs Day, Wilf's neighbour above his flat in Hudson Close. Mrs Day's screams, followed by the brutal slamming of her front door, awake Wilf after his New Year's Eve celebration at The Palais.

Hungover, Wilf looks at the clock. It's just gone eleven. He thinks to himself, 'Have breakfast, a bath, change of clothing, then pop round to Kenny's at 41 Braybrook Street to say goodbye to mum and dad before they head back to Bournemouth. Play with Eddie and his new toys, whilst Sheila makes some nice grub.'

As Wilf enters the kitchen, still dressed in last night's clothes, to make himself a bacon sandwich, he hears a knock on the front door, which gets louder and more demanding with each knock. Wilf goes straight to the pantry and pulls out his trusty leather cosh from his school days, wondering who he might have upset last night.

Then the letterbox flap opens. Wilf clutches his cosh, walks towards the door, ready for aggro. No man alive is going to take him out on the first day of 1974.

A Welsh voice shouts out, 'Hello?'

Wilf doesn't reply. He wants to size up who's knocking on his front door.

'Hello, sorry to bother you. I live upstairs, next to Mrs Day. David, David Hughes. I moved down from Cardiff about two months ago.'

Wilf recognises the Welsh voice coming through the letterbox, as he has spoken to him and his ten-ton Tessie of a wife, Beryl, a few times. Slightly relieved, yet annoyed to be disturbed, Wilf puts his cosh in the back pocket of his jeans and opens the front door. The sun beaming down on him warms him, but not the sight of a dishevelled overweight man in his forties, with a dirty dressing gown wrapped around him.

'Happy New Year, David,' greets Wilf.

'Happy New...' a nervous David replies, as he has forgotten his neighbour's name.

'Wilf.'

'Oh yes, Wilf. Thank you. I am sorry to bother you on New Year's Day. No one seems to be up. Well, Mrs Day is, but she slammed the door in my face,' says a bewildered David.

Wilf laughs out loud, knowing the well-to-do Mrs Day would not appreciate a semi-naked man knocking on her door, especially with her hatred for the Welsh, which no one in Hudson Close can understand.

'Well, that's Mrs Day for you. Anyway, what can I do for you? Locked out or somefink?' says Wilf smiling as he speaks.

David, sensing Wilf's friendly manner, is now at ease. 'Just want to borrow some teabags. I'll give you a quid for them. It's the missus. We haven't got any teabags for our tea. Went to a party. Just got up. All the bloody shops are shut.'

'David, you can have some teabags. Just buy me a pint down the Queen's one evening—when it ain't blacked out, that is.'

'Would love to buy you a pint. Forgot about the power cuts. That bloody Heath—I didn't vote for him. Ta for the tea. Heard you were a good man.'

'I didn't vote for him either. It's nice to know people speak highly of me. Hair of the dog? Got loads of Double Diamonds.'

'Better not. The missus is going spare. If she doesn't get her tea, I don't get me New Year's Day bunk up. Always like them bed springs to bounce like Zebedee at the start of the year, if you know what I mean?'

'Not really interested mate,' utters Wilf coldly.

'Wilf, she's a good bunk up is me missus. We can go at it for hours and hours, non-stop. I am dying to get me leg over. But she said no tea, no leg over. What a cow. Been thinking about it since I got up. Had a shit to take my mind off it, but that didn't help. Had a cold bath—that made it worse. How about I borrow the teabags, go home, make the tea, have it off with the missus, then perhaps come back for that beer?'

As David speaks, he is fidgeting and drooling, with his right arm going inside his dressing gown. Wilf has never seen a man so desperate for sex before, even during his short stays at Her Majesty's pleasure.

'I think you better go, David, before I do something I regret,' warns Wilf.

David, with last night's alcohol still in his bloodstream, tears off his flea-bitten dressing gown, throws it down on Wilf's hallway floor and stands before Wilf, naked, with no shame in hiding his fat and lily-white body. David holds both arms to the heavens, yelling as if he was at the top of a mountain, 'Jesus Christ, man, I need a bunk up. Watch me have it off with my wife. Think about it, Wilf? Seeing my bum going up and down, up and down, up and down, up and...'

Wilf can't take it any more and delivers a powerful right upper cut, sending David Hughes into the open communal corridor of the 1930s-built Hudson Close flats, with all the red brick flats looking onto each other. As David's bare backside hits the cold concrete, Mrs Day is coming down the stairs on her way to visit her sister in Acton. The shock is too much for Mrs Day, who screams out, 'Sex maniac! Sex maniac! Help!'

All the neighbours know her voice only too well, and do not come to her aid, apart from Wilf's next-door neighbour, Bill Todd, who is on his way out to have a walk around White City to clear his head. Bill Todd looks at the fat naked man, shrugs his shoulders, leans against his front door and lights up a 555 State Express.

David slowly gets up and walks with caution towards the communal stairs, passing Bill Todd without making eye contact. Mrs Day screams out again, 'Sex maniac! Sex maniac! Help! He's bloody Welsh!' Whether Bill Todd hates the Welsh as much as Mrs Day no one knows, but Mrs Day's closing declaration answers her original plea.

Bill Todd lamps David with all his might, yelling, 'You bloody dirty Taff!' Again, David is knocked to the floor.

Hearing a spot of bother with his father, loyal son Wayne, a 15-year old aggro lad, comes flying out with his trusty DM boots on and starts to kick the naked David hard, with Bill Todd looking on with pride.

'That's it lad—kick the Welsh bastard,' eggs on Mrs Day to Wayne, while Bill Todd's wife Moira and daughter Samantha carry on watching TV in the front room. Wilf, watching this from his front door in total disbelief, steps forward, barging the Welsh-hating Mrs Day out of the way, and jabs Wayne enough to knock him off balance, while delivering a straight cross to Bill Todd, knocking him out in one punch.

A shell-shocked and bruised David gets up and heads towards the stairs. Wilf runs back into his flat and returns as David is slowly climbing the stairs. Wilf taps David on the shoulder, who turns around expecting to be punched again. Instead, Wilf passes him his dressing gown, five teabags and four small cans of Double Diamond, saying, 'Here, go and get your leg over.'

'Thank you. Sure, you don't want to watch?'

'Yes, quite sure. Now, piss off before I change my mind.'

■ ■ ■

A month later, a rugged and handsome Larry is drinking in The Cromwellian

Club, South Kensington, dressed in an all-denim safari suit, 'me-pulling out-fit' as Larry calls it. Larry believes he married too early, seeing his wedlock as a prison sentence with casual sex his freedom. Larry envies Ian, who seems to enjoy married life, and is fiercely jealous of Wilf and Tommy with their devil-may-care attitude. So, to find what he believes is happiness, Larry likes to rub shoulders with pop stars, the London aristocracy, local villains and models, while trying to bed some young naïve girl at The Cromwellian Club.

At the bar, Larry notices a stunning blonde in a pink floppy hat wearing a pink floral dress, dancing provocatively like a member of Pan's People to Sweet's 'The Ballroom Blitz'. The blonde looks gullible, just the way Larry likes them. Larry, the hunter, watches the blonde like she is prey, waiting to pounce with his inviting smile. The blonde and Larry briefly make eye contact, then he goes in for the kill. Larry smiles, holds up a glass of champagne, and playfully beck-ons the dancing blonde towards him with his finger. The blonde points at her-self, mouthing the words, 'Who? Me?' Larry smiles his cheeky smile and nods.

'Cor, Larry, you don't 'arf know all the crooks,' says the slightly drunk blonde. Larry thinks: one more yarn about the Krays, one more drink, then a taxi back to hers—a drill he knows and practises all so well.

Suddenly, Larry hears a tough voice whisper in his ear, 'I wouldn't say too much about The Firm. The twins still have men on the outside.'

Larry turns round to see a well-built man, dark hair with a round face, late thirties. Larry thinks: maybe a former boxer or army.

Larry doesn't reply with words, just gives his well-rehearsed menacing stare. Yet the man is not fazed. 'Lose the girl, my friend. Reckon you're a face, a rogue. If you want work, I've got work. But that's if you're a pro, not a bullshitter.'

Larry, sizing the man up, quietly replies, 'Who are you mate? Can't you see I am entertaining my lady?'

The blonde giggles. The blonde, Eve Berry, a 21-year-old, beautiful woman, has been turning men's heads for many years now. A travel agent at Thomas Cook, Baker Street, she's been yearning to be whisked away to some exotic location by an international playboy. In the meantime, Eve with her 'girlfriends' patrol the happening night clubs of London for generous and stupid men. On entering the venue, Eve picks her man—from instinct, she can sense the men that are vulnerable and anxious to impress with their cash. Once Eve has chosen her prey, she makes her move by dancing erotically near them, allowing eye contact. Once contact is made, the man, believing he is in control, beckons Eve over.

It's a manoeuvre that to date has never failed pretty Eve Berry from Pinner, now flat-sharing in Bayswater. The moment Larry entered The Cromwellian Club, Eve noticed him and whispered to herself, 'He's the one.'

Eve, now bored with the situation and the conversation, as every wannabe villain who chats her up professes to be connected to the Krays, the Richardsons or the Great Train Robbery firm, decides to gather her friends and head to another night club.

'Larry, I better go. Do you know what time the number 19 leaves here, please?' asks Eve with her well-practised puppy-dog eyes.

Larry, relieved that Eve's decision to depart means he can avoid any confrontation, replies, 'Here, take a fiver, get a taxi home,' trying one last attempt to act the generous and caring gentlemen.

'Gosh, Larry, I'll pay ya back. Promise. I better go.' With that, Eve pecks Larry on his left cheek, to find her friends, Caroline and Ingrid.

Caroline and Ingrid, like Eve, are head-turners, and are being bored to tears by two musicians in their twenties, Joe and Mick, telling these girls that they have jammed with The Kinks, David Bowie and The Who. Joe escalates the lies further by saying Mick Jagger begged him to join The Stones. Like Eve with gangsters, Caroline and Ingrid always end up being chatted up by out-of-work musicians or actors with delusions of grandeur.

Eve briskly walks over to Caroline and Ingrid, exercising their well-used getaway plan. 'Girls, I've just called home to tell them not to wait up. Sob, me mother, she's been, oh my God, she's been hit by a car. Got to go–she's in A&E.' As they say their dramatic goodbyes to Joe and Mick, who give them a pound to share for their taxi home, Eve, Ingrid and Caroline head for the exit.

Just as the girls are about to go up the stairs towards the exit, Eve hears Larry yell out, 'Love, I don't have your number.'

Eve turns around with a mischievous smile, ready to shout back, 'I know,' then run off like Cinderella, is overcome with a sudden magnetism for Larry. She reaches into her fringed handbag, pulling out her mascara, along with a paper handkerchief, as she quickly scrawls her telephone number down on it. Eve runs towards Larry like Cathy to Heathcliff from Wuthering Heights. Placing the handkerchief along with the five-pound note in the palm of Larry's right hand, Eve kisses Larry full on the mouth, pulls back and whispers, 'Call me soon, Larry, please?' then Eve, along with her friends, disappears into the night.

Larry's heart is pounding, yet his feeling of ecstasy is broken when the man coldly says, 'Let's talk business, Larry.'

■ ■ ■

'It ain't a scam. It's a proper job, a tasty number,' snaps a dishevelled Larry.

'You call a meet round 'ere, smelling like a brewery, looking like a dog's dinner, telling us you've got a job, a big one? Mate, no one has seen hide nor hair of ya for yonks,' says Wilf, annoyed that Larry thinks it is OK for him to disappear, then resurface like a hero.

'I've been away planning this.'

'And with a bird—I can smell stale perfume. Larry, you've still got lipstick on your collar, unless the fella you met down The Cromwellian Club is an iron? Is this what this meeting is all about? You are coming out of the closet? Look, we don't mind if you are,' says Wilf turning to Ian and Tommy with a smile, as all four of them stand in Larry's front room, 72 Bloemfontein Road, White City.

'Shut up, Wilf. Course there's a girl on the go. Eve—good-looking girl, great body, a real dead-ringer for that Linda Hayden. You know, the one from Taste the Blood of Dracula,' says Larry, a keen fan of Hammer Horror films, as well as women.

'Ain't seen it, Larry. You know I don't like 'orror films,' says Wilf.

'Yeah, cos you leave the pictures with brown stains round your arse,' jokes Larry. Tommy and Ian both laugh, as they are used to Wilf and Larry's bickering.

'You are funny, Larry, a real bloody wag. OK, so you've been knocking off some dolly, planning the next Great Train Robbery. Where's Rita and the girls?'

'Gone to her sister's. When I came back this morning, found a Dear John under the bread bin,' says a nonchalant Larry.

'You OK about it, Larry?' asks a concerned Tommy.

'OK about it? I am bloody over the moon about it. Makes it easier for me and Eve,' says Larry, as he visualises him and Eve holding hands, walking along a secluded beach, somewhere in the Mediterranean, as the sun is setting. Wilf, Tommy and Ian all look at each other with half smiles, while shaking their heads.

Wilf, deciding to take order, breaks Larry's romantic train of thought. 'OK, you've got a nice girl, I am happy for you, I really am. But what's with this job? Who's the fella, what's the crack?'

Larry clears his throat, ready to tell his friends about a life-changing opportunity. 'As you know, met this fella, Warren Spiers, ex-army, Sergeant Major—well, to quote him, "Warrant Officer Class 1, Regimental Sergeant Major". Spiers tells me he was badly injured in Northern Ireland—a bombing by the IRA, County Tyrone, May last year, killed five of his mates. It was on the news.'

'Yeah, I remember that,' confirms Ian. 'Anyway, he was a good soldier, loyal, hard-working, all that. So, the army set him up as a clerk or somefink for The Security Group down Leather Lane, city way.' Larry pauses, waiting for the usual cutting remark from Wilf. Yet Larry is pleasantly surprised to see that Wilf's eyes are fixed upon him. 'Spiers tells me the pay is peanuts, just beer vouchers. One of his jobs is the timetables, so he knows well in advance when money comes in, goes out. Cos he's ex-army and all that, he's trusted. Spiers knows in three months' time there's a pick-up from Heathrow, dollars and sterling from the States.'

'How much?' asks Wilf, now engrossed with Larry's plan.

'I'll get to that in a sec, Wilf. Two vans in the morning pick up the dosh from Heathrow, get back to the depot for midday for a second count. Then, in the afternoon, off to The Bank of America, Mayfair. Between noon to one is their lunch break. There's a café on site, but no one eats there as Spiers tells me the food is shit, so they all piss off to the bakers, supermarket, chippy, whatever, for their grub. Leaving the main gate open for an hour, their guard is down, cos they're more bothered about their bellies. I've seen it, walked past on me jacks. It's a bloody stroll in the park.'

'But we ain't blaggers, Larry. We're tea leaves, kiters. This ain't us,' says Wilf, trying to conceal his nerves.

'Wilf, what do you want to do? Sell stolen candles all your life, break into the odd meter for small change, have sex-mad Welsh neighbours banging on your front door? A quick pint plus a hand shandy from Sue down the Queen Adelaide?'

Wilf, contemplating Larry's words of wisdom, retorts, 'Why us? Why not Mick King? Heard every blag has to go through him. I don't want to step on his toes—heard he's a loon.'

'Don't worry about King. Listen, Spiers ain't stupid—we ain't got form for this, so the Sweeney will be banging down King's door, not ours. We've been tearing it up all our lives, tools or fists. I can't see it being a problem for us, rushing in with shooters in balaclavas screaming give us the money. Bang— over and done with in five minutes.'

'How much? You said you'd get to that in a second,' says an excited Ian.

'The best part of quarter of a million in ten minutes before the Old Bill show up. In other words, grab all we can in that time. Still a lot after expenses, split five ways.'

Ian makes a loud whistling sound.

'Expenses. What expenses?' Wilf, asks trying to be rational.

'The guns—that's about a grand. He's going to give us a two grand to live off, so we can sack the candles and all that shit. As for the cars, well we agreed to nick them before the job, so only two to three gees, Wilf. I fink we could afford it.'

'Where does an office clerk get the odd grand or two ?' questions Tommy.

'As I told ya, he's trusted. No one finks he's been picking up the odd loose bundle of notes for the last six months. 'Ere who wants a bull's eye up front?' says Larry, as he pulls out a roll of five-pound notes, impressing Wilf, Ian and Tommy at the same time.

'I'm in,' says a now-converted Wilf.

'Me, too,' yaps Ian.

'Oh yes, I'll have some of that,' adds Tommy.

As the excitement is dying down, Wilf turns to Larry, inquiring, 'When do we meet Spiers?'

'You don't. I am running this.'

8

The Adventures of Rockin' Wilf—Part Two

'I am not dressing up as a woman,' Ian screams irately.

'Look, Ian—you are the smallest with the prettiest face. Me, Wilf or Tommy would look like bleeding Danny La Rue. Listen, all you've got to do is walk past the entrance pushing the pram, with a shooter under the covers. Get the pram stuck in a crack in the pavement. A bleeding-heart security guard will come to your aid. Pull out the shooter, screaming at the same time. It's on. Then bang—me and Tommy come running round the corner, armed, followed by Wilf in the motor, it's that simple,' says Larry, with an air of authority, as he, Wilf, Tommy and Ian sit in his front room.

'Yeah, that simple, cos it's what we do every day,' snaps Ian.

'I've been studying bank robberies. Gone to the British Library, looked at old newspapers. It's all about the element of surprise, disguise and, of course, planning. A mother pulling out a double-barrel shot gun from a pram—what's going to happen? The guards will shit themselves, as they won't be expecting it,' explains a rather irate Larry.

Ian, still unconvinced, retorts, 'Whose idea was this anyway?'

'Well, it was Spiers', mate. I must admit I was sceptical at first, but after we talked, it makes sense—the element of surprise. Remember to scream or shout in different accents—Irish, Scottish, whatever. As long as it ain't London, we don't have to be bloody Mike Yarwood's.' As Larry finishes his sentence, he returns his focus to Ian, gazing at him like a school teacher waiting for an answer from an unruly pupil.

Ian lets out a loud sigh, looks at his friends and with a great deal of reluctance replies, 'OK, I'll do it—for us, for the money. But I swear this goes no further.'

'Of course, it ain't going to go no further. Bloody Hell, Ian, we ain't going to talk mate,' reassures Larry.

■ ■ ■

'OK, next Thursday. You boys ready?' orders Spiers, as he downs his Johnnie Walker Red Label scotch at their weekly meeting at The Star Tavern, Belgravia, SW1, a public house where many underworld scams are hatched.

'Yes. Ready, Mr Spiers,' says Larry, savouring the role of leader.

'Good, there will be three vans.'

'Three? Thought it was just two coming back from Heathrow?'

'Yes, the other is a weekly wage pick-up from the banks to go out to the factories in the afternoon, but that's peanuts. They get back for midday, always do. You strike at 12.27 on the dot. That's when the gate is open, the guards will be having a snout, waiting for their grub. You've got to be out by 12.37. I'm calling the Old Bill at 12.31, as my office looks right into the courtyard, so I will be the first one, apart from the guards, to see the robbery. The Old Bill won't be there within six minutes. Larry, just grab as many bags as you can, don't be foolish.' Larry takes a big gulp from his half pint of Worthington 'E, as it dawns on him that this is the real deal. 'Don't worry Larry, I know you can do it. That bird you're knocking off, does she know?'

'No, she just thinks I am a normal tea leaf, not a blagger,' says Larry, making direct eye contact with Spiers, hoping his poker face will cover his lies. Larry has told Eve pretty much everything since their first date.

■ ■ ■

12.25: Wilf's heart is pounding harder than it ever has done before as he sits in a stolen light blue Ford Escort Mark 1 Estate, gently revving the engine up in Worship Street, while keeping a watchful eye on the entrance of Curtain Road. Wilf's heartbeat intensifies when he sees Larry and Tommy walking towards the entrance, both donning sheepskin coats, dark glasses and indiscreet blonde wigs.

'Bloody Hell. If the Old Bill goes past now, they are bound to get a collar,' Wilf mutters to himself.

Then, right on cue, Ian dressed as a pretty young mother pushing a pram gets within ten feet of the entrance. Wilf looks to the heavens and says with pride, 'This one is for you, Granddad Bernard.'

12.27: Ian's finest hour. Apprehensive at first, yet now relishing the opportunity to dress up like a woman. Ian sees the crack in the pavement, the crack he has walked past so many times in the past two weeks, ready to execute a manoeuvre that will make him and the lads wealthy. Ian observes the guards gathered in the courtyard, smoking cigarettes while swapping jokes and anecdotes.

With perfect precision, Ian pushes the front left wheel into the crack, tilting the pram abruptly. 'Oh darling,' screams Ian in an attempted female Yorkshire accent. 'Don't worry, love,' says an overweight security guard, as he notices what he perceives as a damsel in distress but failing to understand what Ian is saying.

As the chubby security guard gets within two feet of Ian, Ian lets go of the pram, pulling out the double-barrel shotgun and yelling out in his abysmal female Yorkshire accent, 'It's on.' The chubby guard looks at Ian with some confusion as he can't comprehend what Ian is saying. Ian is offended, as he has been practising his accent all week. He shouts out in his normal voice, 'It's a robbery, you fat bastard.'

Then the guard is forcefully pulled by Tommy and Larry, as they come up behind him, heading towards the entrance. Tommy, Larry and Ian, along with the frightened security guard, run into the courtyard, wielding their guns as they do. Then Tommy, Larry and Ian shout out in a mixture of Yorkshire, Irish and Welsh accents, 'Give us the money.'

The guards fail to understand their pronunciations, yet seeing the fear on their colleague's face, accompanied by two armed men and an armed man dressed up as a woman, they understand it is a robbery. The guards fall to their knees, with their hands in the air. The chubby guard is thrown face down to the ground. As he lands, Ian kicks him with all his might, as Ian is still annoyed the guard didn't understand his accent.

12.28: Wilf pulls down his balaclava and hits the accelerator, as he doughnuts the Ford Escort Mark 1 Estate outside the gate, with the rear reversing into the courtyard. Wilf slams the brakes hard; the stolen car comes to an abrupt standstill. Larry, Tommy, Ian and the surrendered guards are taken aback by his stuntman-like driving skills.

Wilf leaps out, runs around the back, opens the boot, then gives Ian and Larry a hand with the bags, while Tommy hovers over the security guards with two pistols. It is clear from their faces none of them want to be heroes today.

Larry pulls out the stopwatch from his sheepskin coat and yells out in an attempted Welsh accent, 'One minute to go.' Tommy and Wilf look at him perplexed, as they don't understand what he is saying. Reverting to his London accent, while looking at the stopwatch, Larry yells out, '45 seconds to go.'

12.37: Wilf pulls out of the courtyard into Curtain Road and heads towards the A501 then King's Cross, for the lads to dump the getaway car, a quick change of clothes, divide the bags then drive off in two stolen cars, both Ford Escort Mark 2s, with Ian and Wilf going in one, Larry and Tommy in the other, before heading to a rented workshop in Streatham to drop off the loot.

12.59: Eve Berry, at Thomas Cook, Baker Street, hands a young jetsetter couple their return plane tickets plus accommodation for Barbados. As the couple politely take their tickets, the new radio station for London, LBC, (London Broadcasting Company) announces a newsflash. 'Armed robbery at the Security Express depot today at Curtain Road. More details to follow.' Eve's face breaks into a smile, aroused, as she is now sleeping with a wanted man.

13.59: Wilf, Larry, Tommy and Ian sit apart on Platform One, Streatham train station, each holding different non-descript sports bags containing the guns, maps, disguises and a further £100 in cash each—enough to tide them over until the money from the robbery is divided. The money was in envelopes in the lockup, as Spiers told Larry counting the money then and there would be time consuming, therefore he was prepared to front the 'tide them over' money himself. Spiers also told Larry he would arrange in two weeks' time to pick up the bags, along with the articles, apart from the cash, to be discarded.

Wilf wanted to dump all the incriminating evidence straight away, but Larry insisted they follow Spiers' instructions.

■ ■ ■

'World in Action? But we only did the job last week. How do you know it's on the telly tonight?' asks an anxious Wilf, who is starting to feel the pressure of their latest criminal endeavour.

'Cos it's in me current bun, that's how I know. Don't ya gander at the papers?' replies Larry, who unlike Wilf is savouring their recent caper.

'Clearly not this morning. 'Ere, has the press given us a name? You know, like the Curtain Road Gang or somefink?'

'No, they ain't given us a name yet, Wilf. Don't worry about that. Just enjoy it, cos me and Eve will,' says a gratified Larry.

Wilf pushes his half-eaten plate of eggs and chips to one side at Alf's Café, Loftus Road—the lads' sporadic rendezvous, packed with local builders and lorry drivers on the fiddle, who know better than to eavesdrop. 'Then she knows?' snaps Wilf.

'Wilf, she won't say a word,' says Larry in Eve's defence. Infuriated, Wilf gets up, looks at Larry, and says with menace, 'You'll shout this brekkie, won't ya?'

■ ■ ■

Even though he, along with Tommy and Ian, find Eve to be funny, warm and highly attractive from the handful of times they have met her via Larry, Wilf can't believe that his friend could be so careless over something that could jeopardise their freedom. Wilf is equally annoyed that only last night Larry told him in the Queen Adelaide that Spiers had moved the stolen money to a secret location to be divided equally in about a month's time.

■ ■ ■

As Wilf's clock strikes eight, the dramatic theme tune of World in Action fills his front room in Hudson Close. The music starts to fade, and a well-spoken voice announces with urgency, 'Tonight on World in Action, we look at The Drag Queen Robbers. A ruthless gang of men who like to dress up as women, who recently pulled off a heist as big as The Great Train Robbery.'

Wilf looks with total disbelief at the opening shot of uniformed policemen walking around the courtyard of the Security Group in Curtain Road, as if they were going for a stroll in the park, then Wilf mutters to himself, 'The Drag Queen Robbers, that's the bloody name.'

Wilf returns his attention to his Philips colour TV, as the well-spoken narrator continues, 'On 3rd May this year, four men, all dressed as women, held up The Security Group Depot, Curtain Road, East London. A depot that has been compared to Fort Knox.'

'Fort Knox? Leave it out!' shouts Wilf at the TV, then focuses again on the narrator.

'With armed robberies on the rise in London, many gangs are wearing the standard stockings or balaclavas as a disguise. Yet what makes this robbery more sinister than others is that a leading psychologist in Great Britain believes that that the men are living out a sexual fantasy. Dr Gerald Brummel, Professor of Psychology, Oxford University explains.'

World in Action fades out the camera shot of the policemen doing nothing in Curtain Road, then fades in with a camera shot of a middle-aged bearded man, smoking a pipe in a tweed jacket and a black polo neck jumper, against a backdrop of leather-bound books in an expensive-looking bookcase.

'These men are possibly still living with their mothers, probably virgins, perhaps homosexuals unable to come to terms with their own sexuality and more than likely victims of bullying. So, unable to have long-lasting relationships with a woman, coupled with a deep-down hatred for their mother, they take what they believe to be revenge on society, by dressing up in their mother's Sunday-best and arming themselves with guns to carry out a brutal and aggressive robbery. Money is not the real issue—they want the world to see their suffering, their pain. I believe this armed robbery is just the start.'

Wilf sits in his front room, with his mouth wide open, as the narrator announces, 'Eyewitness accounts confirm Dr Gerald Brummel's theory.'

A camera shot cuts in of a man lying in a hospital bed, with the caption, 'William Taylor, Security Guard at Curtain Road on 3rd May'. A weak and feeble-looking man pulls his head up from the pillows, looks directly at the camera and says, 'They all looked like the wicked stepmother from Cinderella. I went to Hell that day, sob. I haven't come back, aaagh.'

The shot of William Taylor is abruptly cut, then Dr Gerald Brummel reappears, this time walking towards the camera in a huge stately garden. 'I would go on to say they have small penises and they probably masturbate each other for minor sexual satisfaction. The robbery was maximum sexual satisfaction and they probably ejaculated the moment the guns were pulled out. This is the closest they will ever get to having sex.'

Wilf, unable to take any more, gets up and puts his boot through his TV. Looking upwards at the ceiling, Wilf says to himself, 'Bloody Hell, I've got to see Sue.'

■ ■ ■

Wilf wakes up in Sue's flat, around the corner in MacKenzie Close, just after ten. Wilf needed a stiff drink and female companionship yesterday evening before closing time, after being denounced on British television as a cross-dressing man obsessed with his mother. Sue had to go to work early at the Queen Adelaide to help with the bottling up, as she had left the pub early last night to entertain a very confused and annoyed Wilf. As Wilf reaches for his Embassy Number One cigarettes, he hears a loud knock on Sue's front door. 'Bloody Hell, not another pervert needing some tea bags?' he says to himself.

A familiar voice shouts through the letterbox, 'Wilf, open up. It's Larry. Just seen Sue outside the pub, she told us you were here.'

A stressed yet elegant and upbeat female voice cuts in. 'Please open. It's important.'

Wilf recognises Eve's voice straight away, to the point it excites him.

'We are buggered, Wilf,' are the first words Larry says as Wilf opens the front door in his white vest and Y-front underpants.

'You're telling me. That crap on World in Action—all bullshit,' snaps Wilf.

'It's worse than that, baby,' says a worried Eve.

'How can it get much worse?' says an exasperated Wilf.

'You tell him, sweetheart,' sighs Larry.

'On the way to work this morning, there was some commotion outside Bayswater Tube Station. I think some fellas had tried to turn the newsstand over. Saw a few bobbies, then I see him, Spiers in a suit. I remember him well from the club. All the bobbies were calling him, "Sir". So, I peg it back to my flat to wake up Larry, phone in sick, get a taxi to the Bush, and here we are. Spiers is Old Bill, you've been fitted up.'

'It all makes sense now. It was way too easy. The gates left open, the way the guards didn't put up a fight, we weren't chased. It has been bugging me from the start. Bloody Hell, Larry, you fool.' Wilf pushes his friend hard on the chest, Larry steps forward, they both take their stances as if ready to fight.

Eve steps into the middle of them, screeching, 'No fighting, that's not the answer. You need to get rid of anything that ties you to the robbery, anything.'

Eve's wise words puts a much-needed calm to the situation. Wilf winks at her, she smiles back with affection.

'OK, you two, get to Tommy's, I will run to Ian's. Have you called them?'
'No, you're the first one we've spoken to,' says Larry.
'OK, meet at mine, about four. Now go, get all the gear, guns, cash, everything and dump it,' says Wilf as he closes the front door, returning to Sue's bedroom to get dressed, stressed yet pleased to be the leader again.

■ ■ ■

Wilf makes it to Ian's home at 14 Maurice Street in record time, only to be confused by Ian's attitude, as Ian thought last night's World in Action was excellent. Ian was happy to part with the sawn-off shotgun, plans and money, but wanted to keep the dress and wig as a reminder.

Wilf returns to his flat in Hudson Close after prising Ian's cherished dress and wig out of his hand, questioning the sanity of his friend, and pleased that Ian's wife Dawn was at work. Wilf gathers his armed robbery paraphernalia, along with Ian's, and throws them into his large black Dunlop bag. Knowing that time isn't on his side, Wilf catches a taxi from the Uxbridge Road to Scrubs Lane Bridge. After finding a few broken bricks and placing them in his Dunlop bag, Wilf throws the bag into the Thames, hoping that the elements will erode the evidence.

Wilf, thanks to Eve's beady eyes and love for the lads, now knew that the Flying Squad would be knocking on his front door soon. Yet Wilf didn't have the foresight to think that his front door would come flying off its hinges at four in the morning, followed by the war cry of 'Armed police—don't move.' Wilf braces himself for the attack, as he hears heavy footsteps marching towards his bedroom door.

'Wakey, wakey, ducky,' a voice, where the years of drinking straight scotch and chain-smoking has taken its toll, bawls out.

Wilf's bedroom door is brusquely pushed open. In the door frame stands a 6'1" man, with a beer gut pushing through his light-blue, open-neck, wide-collared shirt and light-blue crumpled trousers, wearing a dirty old beige Burberry mac, which has certainly seen better days. With an ageing weather-beaten face, dark sunken eyes, a thick black moustache with matted down greasy hair that would take a tornado to move a thread of it. The man steps forward towards Wilf as he lies in his bed. Standing behind the overweight man is a younger, thinner and better-looking 5'9" man with mousy brown hair in an off-the-peg suit, clean-shaven with a smug expression on his face.

'Get up you, poof,' orders the older man. Wilf leaps out of his bed, naked and stands before them, placing both hands on his hips for both men to see that he is well-endowed. 'My God, man, put some clothes on. I haven't had my Ready Brek,' demands the older man, while the younger man is transfixed with jealousy. Wilf slowly puts on his denim shirt and jeans with a beaming smile.

'I am Detective Sergeant Rodgers and this is Detective Constable Wright. Wilfred Percy Savage, you are arrested on suspicion that on the date 3rd May 1974, with persons known and unknown to you, took property unlawfully from The Security Group, Curtain Road, London, by force or threat of force. You have the right to remain silent, but anything you do say may be used in evidence against you in court. Do you understand these charges?'

Wilf calmly nods his head and replies, 'Rodgers and Wright? You sound like a poor man's Morecambe and Wise.'

'Oh, a fucking comedian. Well, laugh on this, sweetheart,' Rodgers says, as he tries to punch Wilf with a left jab. Wilf, a skilled boxer, sees the punch coming, ducks, as Rodgers is too out of shape to catch an experienced fighter off guard. As Rogers' left arm passes over Wilf's hair, Wilf comes up with a strong and well-placed upper right cut, which lifts Rodgers off his feet and backwards into Wright, sending them both out of his bedroom and landing on his hallway floor.

Rodgers and Wright get up, dust themselves off and run towards Wilf, followed by six wooden tops, some wielding pistols, others truncheons. It takes the police ten minutes to restrain Wilf. 'Never go down without a fight,' his grandfather always told him.

Wilf is bundled into a waiting police van, parked in the communal car park of Hudson Close. The uniformed police handcuff and seat Wilf, with Rodgers shouting out, 'Oh shut that door,' as he slams the van door shut, with all the police, and even Wilf laughing. The police van screeches out of Hudson Close with screaming sirens, followed by Rodgers and Wright in an unmarked police car, as they head towards the Westway en route to New Scotland Yard, St James' Park.

■ ■ ■

The police van drives into New Scotland Yard's underground car park. Wilf is dragged out of the van by two uniformed policemen and made to stand to attention to Wright. Wright steps forward and gives Wilf a strong stomach punch, making Wilf keel over. Wilf looks up to see Rodgers nodding with approval at his protégé. 'You bastards,' roars Wilf. His words are met by a karate chop to the neck by Wright, which is so forceful that Wilf is knocked out.

■ ■ ■

When Wilf regains consciousness, he finds himself sitting on a cold wooden upright chair, reminding him of his schooldays. Wilf's eyes start to gain focus, with Rodgers coming into his vision, as he sits opposite Wilf, with his elbows resting on a wooden table with a green well-worn plastic cover, and a silver ashtray, blackened from fiercely stamped out cigarettes. Wilf looks to his left and notices a small frosted window blocking out all daylight, while feeling the presence of Wright standing behind him.

'Wilfred, Wilf or should I call you Rockin' Wilf? Aren't you a little too old to be into all this rock 'n' roll shit?' ribs Rodgers, with Wright sniggering behind Wilf.

'So, that's what you've nicked me for? My taste in music? Bloody Hell, I must be looking at least five years.'

'Don't get smart with me.'

'Well, don't be a silly sod then.'

Rodgers stands up, walks towards Wilf as if he is going to hit him. Wilf doesn't flinch. Rodgers, swayed by Wilf's fearlessness, returns to his chair, sits down, pulls out his Benson & Hedges Gold from his left breast pocket, opens the packet, pulls two cigarettes out and passes one onto Wilf.

'Ta,' says Wilf, as he puts the cigarette in his mouth, waiting for a light. Rodgers takes out his gold Zippo lighter from his right trouser pocket, lights his cigarette, then puts the lighter back into his pocket.

'Oh no, you don't get a light,' says Rodgers, blowing out smoke.

Wilf takes the cigarette out of his mouth and throws it to the ground. 'Well, I wanted to give up anyway, so you are doing me a favour.' Wilf receives a rabbit punch from Wright, knocking him off his chair, making both detectives laugh out loud as Wilf lands on the left side of his body.

'You stashed the loot, the shooters, the dresses, the lot. Tell us what you know. Your friends, Detective Sergeant Legg, Sergeant McDonald, told us this ain't your usual game. Who's been turning the thumbscrews on you to make you go from being a thief to a blagger? Wilf, I can help you, be your friend,' says an infuriated Rodgers, as he believed arresting and questioning Wilfred Savage would be an effortless operation and Wilf would break under pressure, therefore leading to the arrests of Ian Potter, Tommy James and Larry Jenkins. Wilf was the prime suspect, chiefly due to his family's involvement in criminal enterprises for many decades. Moreover, the Yard didn't have the time and resources to arrest the others. Detective Sergeant Legg, annoyed that he wasn't involved in the dawn raid on Wilf, did suggest to New Scotland Yard that they arrest all four suspects, not just one. Detective Sergeant Legg's suggestion was met by Rodgers saying he would skin Legg alive if he ever questioned his methods again. Detective Sergeant Legg made a mental note to take Rodgers to a brothel with his trusty camera one evening.

'Oh, bless them. Bet old Half is gutted he ain't here. Am I going to be here much longer? Because I am starving,' says a self-assured Wilf, knowing that Rodgers will be just as hungry as he is.

'Hmm, the first thing you've said that makes sense. Wright, pop down the Wimpy, get three cheeseburgers, three fries and three cans of cokes. Tell Stavros it's on the Yard account.'

'But, guv,' whines Wright.

'But guv what? Bugger off, before I piss all over you, put you on desk duty covered in urine.'

Whether it was a threat or a previous punishment, Wright obediently leaves the interview room to get their food.

'Bet the Wimpy bill never gets paid?' says Wilf.

'Of course not. Who's going to chase the Yard for money? One chap did. George Burroughs—had a greasy spoon just round the corner. Kept turning up asking for his money. Then, funnily enough, we found enough cannabis to get all of London's layabouts and hippies high for years. Burroughs got five years for possession with intent to supply. He's got about two years left to do. Thing is, everyone says he's clean-living and honest. Would have been easy for me to have found a gun, marked notes, map, easy, say the dresses were dumped yonks back,' says Rodgers in a quite sinister tone.

'How come you didn't, you know, find anything?' asks Wilf, in a relaxed manner.

'Because contrary to what you villains think, a lot of coppers like Wright and the wooden tops are family men, looking to keep the law and order of the land. Yeah, Wright is learning to be heavy-handed, but I wanted him to find the evidence. You know, give him more confidence, more belief he is doing the right thing. I was hoping you would buckle under questioning, give the lad a boost, but you didn't,' says Rodgers to an intrigued Wilf.

'Let's not beat about the bush. You know and I know this is a fit-up, so I suggest you let me go and mum's the word,' replies a confident Wilf.

'Wilf, my dear Wilf, not one court, not one paper, will support you. I mean they might believe you, but to give the boys in blue a bad name over a Shepherd's Bush scoundrel? No, we need to win the public back. You see we've had enough of the public loving the rogues. Can't go into one pub in East

London without some old dear going on about the bloody Krays. Had enough of all this 'honour amongst thieves', a code of silence, like those bloody wops from The Godfather—shit film. That Pacino? Shit actor. Can't see him lasting. He's a wanker.'

'Well, I liked the film and Pacino. Thought Brando was a bit dull though.'

'Shut up. You ain't Barry Norman. Anyway, we thought we'd have some fun, create a new gang, one the public will hate and be scared of. Make the public love, trust and respect the long arm of the law again.'

Wilf is astonished, yet not surprised that the Drag Queen Robbers is a publicity stunt by the Home Office and the Metropolitan Police, along with Granada Television, to gain popularity with society and to overcome the police's jealousy of the underworld.

'My family know some good coppers, local lads like you said, keeping law and order. There's a sort of mutual respect. But you, you are a nutter. Now, as I said, let me go and mum's the word,' demands Wilf.

'No, no. I've got you now. But I'll do a deal, off the record like. You confess to the robbery, taking full responsibility, saying you planned and funded the whole thing. You don't know the names of your accomplices, as they were muscle for hire, and you've got a thing about dressing up in your mother's clothes. If you agree to that, I will see you are incarcerated in Broadmoor Hospital for cooperating. You'll get a nice cosy cell with a TV, warm blankets.'

'And if I don't?' asks Wilf, not believing what he is hearing.

'I will nick King and other blaggers within two hours of your release, along with your mates. Word will be out that you are singing like a canary.'

Wilf shakes his head, then replies, 'What a waste of the taxpayers' money. No doubt you kept the money that was nicked, maybe the odd bag was returned, a bit like the Train Robbery, if you know what I mean. Do you, the rest of the Yard, the government and bloody TV think some Monty Python sketch about fellas dressing up as women, robbing security vans, is going to make the public flock to the Old Bill? I am going, you ain't got nothing on me and I'll be fucked in giving you a confession.'

The interview room door swings open. In marches Wright clutching three brown paper Wimpy bags with the grease oozing through the paper and onto his suit. 'You can have mine DC Wright, I'm going home,' orders Wilf. Wright gives Rodgers a surprised look.

'Savage, you know what will happen—by tea time, your name will be dirt. You'll have to leave town,' warns Rodgers.

Wilf shrugs his shoulders, gets up slowly. 'You going to escort me out?' asks Wilf.

'Oh yes,' replies Rodgers with an evil smirk.

■ ■ ■

Wilf, with Rodgers and Wright by his side, marches in silence into the foyer of New Scotland Yard. As the door opens, Wilf is blinded by the flash of cameras.

'You one of the Drag Queen robbers?' shouts out an irritating voice.

'Perfect,' says Wilf to Rodgers.

'Perfect for what, Savage?' asks a muddled Rodgers.

'For this.' Wilf pulls Rodgers by his shirt collar towards him. When Rodgers' nose presses onto Wilf's lips, Wilf opens his mouth, then with all his might, bites hard into Rodger's nose. Wilf hears the bones snap in Rodgers' nose as the warm blood trickles into his mouth. Rodgers screams out in pain.

Wright punches Wilf in the kidney. The impact is enough to make Wilf release his bite. Wilf spins round and, with a right cross, knocks Wright to the floor, with the national and regional press snapping photos of Wilf's attack.

Seven uniformed officers, bearing truncheons, steam into Wilf, who meets the assault by singing, 'He rocks in the treetops all day long, hoppin' and a-boppin' and singing his song. All the little birdies on Jaybird Street, love to hear the robin go tweet, tweet, tweet.'

As the batons rain down hard on Rockin' Wilf, he knows will go to prison as a legend, not a grass or a cross-dresser—something his grandfather would be very proud of.

9

The Rise and Fall of The Magnificent Seven

'Let's pop down Stuart's in a bit, grab some nice gear for tonight's party. Jamie's picking up some decent puff from Rooster. Osc, you've done some good tapes, ain't ya son?' says a vibrant Eddie to his long-time friend Oscar and new friend, Desmond, in his bedroom. Both feeling Eddie's fervour, they smile eagerly as they nod in unison, amusing Eddie as they do. 'Jesus, both of ya like a pair of nodding dogs.'

'Piss off, Ed, you sound like Captain Flack from bleeding Trumpton,' quips Oscar.

'Pugh, Pugh, Barney McGrew,' adds a nervous Desmond. Yet his anxiety is brief, as both Eddie and Oscar mildly chuckle at his quip.

'I thought Rooster was inside? 'Eard he got busted,' says Oscar, who has never seen eye to eye with Rooster.

'What planet have you been on? Charges got dropped, since Mac bloody Mac walked out. Uxbridge Road nick is in turmoil. Happy days for a bit. Sure, the Met will bring in a real bastard,' contemplates Eddie.

'It was a nut house with Mac bloody Mac running the show. Where's Mac bloody Mac gone anyway?' enquires Oscar.

'Don't know, anyway fuck him. You've got those tapes, yes or no? Cos I'll be fucked if I am going to dance to Stars on 45 records all night long,' says Eddie, going back to the party tonight at 23 Sinclair Road, W1, just behind the Olympia. The other week, Eddie chatted up Gemma Robertson, a Saturday girl at Kensington Market. Eddie charmed her so much that Gemma foolishly invited him and the rest of The Magnificent Six—now the Seven, due to Desmond joining late in the summer—to her seventeenth-birthday party at her parents' house on 24th September.

'Yes, Captain Flack. All done. Got them back at mine,' Oscar replies with an air of authority.

Desmond, feeling slightly left out, feebly asks, 'What records did you tape?'

Oscar, sensing his insecurity, replies with no eye contact, 'Not mine, new kid. Moved in about a month before you, from Streatham, Leroy, his brother Max. He's got two turntables, tape deck. He done me the tapes, just for a few Benetton shirts, like.' Then Oscar turns to Eddie and says, ''Ere, Max was telling me about his posse, Shake 'n' Fingerpop. They take over some old disused warehouse, set up their sound system, 'ave a real good dance until the sun rises. Max tells me all the chaps are well togged up and the girls, he reckons, the best looking in London.'

'Like the sound of that—Wickers has been empty for yonks. We should throw a party,' says Eddie in an entrepreneurial spirit.

'Good idea. Tell ya, these tapes—I ain't heard nothing like it. It is one step ahead, not one step beyond.'

Oscar's closing words trigger a memory in Desmond of when he was Des the Skinhead, the most feared teenager in Brighton until one fateful day a skeleton that his father Archie and he believed they had firmly locked in the closet was accidently unlocked by his mother Yvonne.

Heartbroken and shamed, Desmond and his father left Brighton under a black cloud and relocated to Shepherd's Bush, White City, whilst his mother and younger sister, Debbie, stayed by the sea. Archie simply turned up at Hammersmith and Fulham Council, and told the housing officer, Horace Rawlings, that he and his son were homeless. Archie slipped Mr Rawlings fifty pounds and a promise of his lifelong collection of Knave Magazines in return for a home. Within a day, on 11th August 1983, Archie and Desmond Wilson were the newest residents at Havelock Close, White City. Archie, Acton-born, originally tried the same bribe at Ealing Council the day before. Housing officer Penelope Pryce fainted at the suggestion of the dirty magazines but was quite receptive to pocketing a 'bull's eye'.

Archie landed a job on a nearby building site as a brickie six days a week, leaving Desmond alone in the flat. It wasn't until the second week of being alone that Desmond decided to venture out one Saturday lunchtime, dressing up in—in Desmond's eyes—his smartest look: a dark blue Fred Perry tennis top, as Archie forbade him to wear anything red ('Red means you are a queer and a commie. You ain't a poof socialist, are you son?' 'No, dad'), and bleached Levi's jeans rolled up ankle-high to show his trade mark ox-blood DM 18-hole boots with his grade one, all over crop.

As Desmond approached Kents' Newsagent, Bloemfontein Road, to buy ten Benson and Hedges Gold, he noticed two teenagers, one with mousey brown hair and the other with chestnut brown hair, drinking Slush Puppies on a hot summer's day. Both are wearing Lacoste tennis tops, one in white, the other in red, and Ellesse tennis shorts, while sporting bright white Stan Smith Adidas trainers. Straight away, they exchange menacing stares.

'Fucking Casuals,' Desmond mutters to himself. He hates them, with their carefree attitude, charm and boyish good looks.

Desmond gazes at them with sheer hatred, a stare that has frightened many youths on a Tuesday night at the Top Rank Suite, Brighton. However, Desmond's usual method of intimidation doesn't go to plan, as the smartly dressed teenagers exchange glances, which are followed by loud laughter. 'What are you laughing at?' yells Desmond, mimicking the borstal daddy, Ray Winstone, as Carlin from Scum.

'Mate, I am laughing at a clown,' mocks one of the teenagers. Desmond now knows he has no choice but to fight them, which he doesn't mind, as long as the adversaries are smaller than him as these two are. Desmond takes his boxing stance, believing his posture and size will frighten the lads. Yet his intention to scare has the reverse effect, as the mousey brown-haired teenager aggressively throws down his Slush Puppie, steps forward and side-kicks with his right leg into Desmond's stomach.

Winded, Desmond falls straight to the ground with a thud on his back-side. The mousey brown-haired teenager follows up with a kick to Desmond's face, knocking him backwards. The chestnut brown-haired teenager runs over, pours his Slush Puppie over Desmond, then proceeds to kick him hard on the right side of his ribs, while the other follows suit by kicking Desmond on the left side of his ribs.

The speed and the power of the kicks prevents Desmond from getting up as these boys are experienced in giving someone a beating. Desmond screams out in pain, begging them to stop, knowing this would break his father's heart.

'Never ask for mercy son. Never. Take your hiding.'

'Yes, dad.'

Then, amidst the kicking, a commanding voice booms out, 'Jamie, Q—leave it. He's had enough. Let him up.'

The teenagers stop upon this order. Desmond, winded, with bruised ribs, face caked in blood, and soaked in Slush Puppie, gets up. Standing before him is a teenager with short blond hair, well built, fresh-faced, with a bright blue jumper over his shoulders, wearing a light-blue Pierre Cardin short-sleeved button-down shirt, cut down Levi's' 501 jeans and a beaten pair of black suede Adidas Gazelle trainers. Standing next to him is a dark-haired, slightly smaller teenager, in a Sergio Tacchini white polo shirt with a bright red chest line, Adidas shorts and Puma Roma leather trainers.

For the first time, Desmond is taken aback by how smart Casuals look, as he feels a connection straight away to the blond-haired teenager. They both smile at each other, whilst the dark-haired teenager points at him and mouths to the mousey brown-haired and chestnut brown-haired teenagers, 'Who's he?'. They both shrug their shoulders.

'Here—clean yourself up,' says the blond teenager as he passes Desmond a clean white handkerchief. 'Seen ya. You moved in a few weeks back with your old man. Lads, this is a White City boy, not a stranger. We look after our own, don't we?'

'Yeah, Eddie, but he was being cheeky,' snaps the mousey brown teenager.

'So, what? He's one of us now. What's your name, mate? Where you from?'

'Desmond, from Br... Reading.'

'Well, Desmond from Reading, do yourself a favour. It's 1983 not 1979—get the European look,' butts in the dark-haired teenager with an air of arrogance.

'Leave it out, Oscar,' demands the blond teenager.

'Desmond, I'm Eddie, that Paul Weller-wannabe is Oscar, and you've already met Jamie and Quicksilver.' Desmond starts to laugh. 'That's good—a laugh a day and all that.'

'It's a smile a day, Eddie,' says a smug Oscar.

'Hark at the bloody Encyclopaedia Britannica. Come on, let's get some chips. Oscar is buying at Pilcher's.'

'Me? Why?' a confused Oscar asks.

'Cos you owe me from yesterday, I done all the work, told Raj, you helped me out no end, so he wouldn't give you the tic tac. So, you get the chips and we're evens,' states Eddie.

Oscar, snarling at Eddie, replies, 'OK, but not him,' pointing aggressively at Desmond.

Eddie puts his arm around Desmond. 'Yes, him, cos I think underneath this skinhead is a Casual just waiting to get out.'

Within one week of the melee with Jamie Joe and Quicksilver, Desmond changes his appearance, thanks to hand-me-downs from Eddie and catching Archie drunk after he got an overtime bonus from work. Gone are the ox-blood Doctor Martens boots, replaced by a pair of black leather Adidas Sambas. Gone are the trusted bleached tight Levi jeans; now Desmond sports Lois jeans and such like. Gone are the Fred Perrys as Desmond wears with pleasure Lacostes, as he impatiently waits for his crop to grow out. With a new meaning to his life, Desmond is happy—not for the first time but for a long time. Most nights, before he crosses over from being awake to asleep, he recalls with fondness his caring mother, Yvonne.

■ ■ ■

Yvonne Mitchell met Archie, when she was a Bunny Girl at the Playboy Club Mayfair, on 6th May 1963. A light brown-haired girl with light brown eyes, naïve and pretty from Hartlepool, like a sweet Rita Hayworth, Yvonne came to the old smoke to pursue her childhood dream of becoming a dancer.

Yvonne often says that at first, the dark-haired, handsome and strong Archie Wilson was charming, kind and funny, with a sort of Robert Mitchum-look about him. Then Yvonne sighs and cries. 'Then I got to know the real man,', as her childhood dream of becoming a dancer faded away.

Then, after many failed business ventures and sackings, Archie persuaded Yvonne to move to Brighton at the start of 1966, as Archie was growing tired of London. 'Too many coons are moving in.'

'Yes, dear.'

Desmond Albert Wilson was born 3rd December 1966, whilst three years later, Deborah Alice Wilson was born 28th March 1969. Even at an early age, Deborah was a dead ringer for her mother. Archie showed no affection to either child when they were born, so both at an early age bonded with Yvonne.

Yet, when Desmond turned 12, Archie broke the bond. He took his son to the local pubs and football to see his old man have a good tear up. 'A boy that hangs out with his mother ends up becoming a poof. You ain't an iron, are you son?'

'No, dad.'

By the age of 14, Desmond Wilson was 11 stone and 5'11" with the physique to be an athlete and the brains to be a grade A student. Yet Desmond didn't focus on his positive physical and mental character traits. Instead, he felt a desire to inflict pain and misery, brought about by change in the family dynamics. So, Desmond bloomed into a brutal bully, replacing love with hate, pleasure with pain.

One thing Desmond hadn't conquered was girls and he was still to pop his cherry. Girls scared him, so he would avoid any contact with them when he could. Yet the local girls, from all different walks of life, were attracted to Desmond the bully, with his above average looks, light-brown hair and brown eyes, with no zits and not an ounce of fat. After leaving Falmer High School, Brighton, in June 1983, Desmond was determined not so much to lose his virginity, but to at least have a kiss and cuddle with a girl. So, in a rare moment of vulnerability, Desmond asked Archie for advice.

'Son, girls love a bad boy. Listen, just give them one, a real good seeing to, just like I did with your mother. Look at her, she couldn't be happier.'

'Yes, dad.'

Wanting to help his son overcome his fear of girls, Archie arranged for Yvonne and Deborah, now called Debbie, to spend the day at Black Rock,

Brighton. He knew there wasn't much for them to do there, but at least it would get them out of the house. Archie was to pop down to the County Oak Pub, about an hour's walk away, allowing Desmond a few hours alone with the Brighton belle and fellow Falmer High School leaver, Amanda Young, who has had the hots for Desmond the bad boy for about a year. It didn't take much persuasion for Amanda to come over one lazy Sunday afternoon to see Desmond—just one telephone call from a very nervous Desmond.

Alone in the living room, a worried Desmond makes his move. He closes his eyes and moves forward to kiss Amanda. To his sheer excitement, he feels Amanda move closer towards him. But his exhilaration is shattered when he hears, 'My God, your breath stinks. You certainly didn't do the Swish this morning.' Whether through nerves or sheer laziness, Desmond had forgotten to clean his teeth and use mouthwash to erase the odour from last evening's homemade curry.

A shocked Desmond takes a swing at Amanda. A girl used to seeing boys turn when challenged, she sees the oncoming punch, sways her head slightly to the left and comes back with a left upper cut that knocks Desmond off the sofa. 'You dare try and hit me, Desmond Wilson?'

'I'm sorry, I really am. I'll go and clean my teeth,' begs Desmond.

Amanda, now in a bad mood, not just because Desmond tried to hit her but because she has nowhere else to go as her parents have friends round—the Parkinsons—and her best friend Tracey is at her gran's.

'I'm hungry,' says Amanda, thinking she might as well get something to eat before she heads home, as the attraction she once had for Desmond is well and truly out of the window.

'I've got one of them Brevilles. Fancy one? Cheese and onion?'

Amanda, enjoying seeing him grovel, says, 'Well, OK. Got any Tizer?'

'Yeah, got Tizer. So, will you stay?'

'Well, OK. Where's my Breville and my Tizer?'

'Coming right up,' replies a relieved Desmond, who quickly heads to the kitchen at the back of the living room.

Then his happiness is cut short when the front door swings open. 'Hello, we're back,' announces Yvonne, merry after a few sherries.

Desmond darts back to the living room, hoping to cut his mother off and take Amanda out for some chips. Yet his hopes are dashed as his mother and Debbie are standing over Amanda. Debbie sees her red-faced brother and says, 'Didn't know you had such a beautiful friend, she is gorgeous.'

Amanda blushes like it was the first time anyone has admired her looks and replies, 'Didn't know you had such a beautiful sister and mother—they are stunning,' making Yvonne and Debbie blush, too. Desmond just nods, knowing they are both right. 'Your son is just about to make me a cheese and onion Breville.'

'Yum, Dessie,' jokes Yvonne.

'Don't call me Dessie—it's Des or Desmond,' says an angry Desmond.

'Well, you will always be my Dessie. Now go and make me, your sister and this beautiful young girl a Breville. I'll have cheese and onion, too,' orders his mother.

'I'll have tuna and mayo, please, Dessie,' says a giggling Debbie.

As Desmond waits for the Breville to heat up, he pops outside for a crafty cigarette, knowing full well that his mother and sister will be engrossed in a conversation with Amanda. It is a choice that Desmond will regret for the rest of his life. As he puffs away Yvonne is showing Amanda a family photo album from the 70s that has not seen the light of day for many years.

After Desmond finishes his cigarette, he throws the butt over the garden fence. Desmond walks back into the kitchen. As he does, the words that come out of the living room make his heart stop.

'No way that's Desmond in a tutu. Was it fancy dress?'

'No, Dessie wanted to be a ballet dancer or an ice skater. He loved it—had posters of Wayne Sleep and John Curry all over his bedroom wall. Well, until my husband tore them down and burnt the tutu.'

Desmond storms back into the living room, shouting, 'That was a long time ago. Now give the album back.' Yet Desmond's anger is heightened further as Amanda pulls up the photo album level with her face, showing a photograph of a young, baby-faced Desmond posing in a pink tutu. Desmond sees red and goes to strike Amanda one more time.

As Desmond steps forward, pulling his right arm back, Amanda screams, 'Your son is going to hit me again.' She knows full well she could take him, but Amanda knows that playing the victim will cause a major argument between him, his sister and his mother.

'What do you mean 'again'?' asks a concerned Yvonne.

'He hit me earlier when I refused to kiss him, then forced me to stay for a Breville, I want to go home,' cries Amanda. She puts her head in her hands, hiding her face as she breaks into a wry smile.

'You're just like your father,' Yvonne yells as she starts to lay into Desmond, Debbie joining in by kicking her brother hard on the shins.

Amanda looks at the madness unfolding before her eyes and decides to leave, as an afternoon with her parents and the Parkinsons now seems a better option. Then Amanda has a eureka moment. In her hands, she possesses a photo album that will bring down Desmond the skinhead—payback for Desmond trying to hit her.

Amanda clutches the incriminating photo album and makes a mad dash for the front door. As Desmond is trying to fend off the onslaught from his mother and sister, he sees Amanda escaping. 'The cow is getting away with the photos,' Desmond yells out, making Yvonne and Debbie stop, hurt that someone could steal from them.

They slowly pull back allowing Desmond to give chase. But Desmond is unable to prevent Amanda getting to the front door of 28 Lucraft Road and to the outside world, as he fails to see the lowdown coffee table by the fireplace, which makes Desmond trip over as he starts to run, landing on his head on the marble top, knocking him straight out.

■ ■ ■

'You need to get the photo album back. No one can know me son is a mincer,' are the first words Desmond hears when he gains consciousness.

'You are pathetic, Archie Wilson,' snaps Yvonne.

'Shut it. I should have bleeding burnt them yonks ago. I didn't bloody think you would show them to anyone, especially some bird,' yells Archie.

'Well, I am proud of him. He's more of a man then you. Shame you thought street fighting was a better option,' Yvonne says in Desmond's defence.

Outraged, Archie replies, 'Ain't nothing wrong with that. Me old man took me brawling when I was 11.'

'Yes and look how you turned out,' barks Yvonne.

'Get in the kitchen woman—it's belting time.'

'No, it's not, dad,' screams Debbie. Yvonne, Archie and Desmond gasp at the young girl's bravery. 'I think it's best you and Desmond go, leave me and mother alone. You are horrid and mean.'

'Debbie, this is my house. You and your mother leave. Let me and the boy go scrapping and a shagging. You would like that, son, wouldn't ya?'

'Not sure, dad,' replies a confused Desmond.

'What? You don't like scrapping? You don't want to go shagging with your old man? Your granddad would turn in his grave,' says a rather hurt Archie.

'Archibald Wilson, you are ill in the head. What father takes his son out on the pull?'

'My old man used to. Me mother never minded,' says a rather proud Archie.

'I remember you telling me, but if you remember about my parents, they gave us the deposit on this place when Maggie gave us the right to buy. So, as long as the mortgage is in my name and my name alone, this house is mine.'

Archie is shocked yet knows the woman that he once loved but now bullies is correct. 'Yvonne, I'm sorry,' Archie pleads. Not that he feels bad about his anger, but he doesn't want him and Desmond to be homeless.

'Pack a suitcase. Please just leave us. Please, dad, just go,' pleads a tearful Debbie, as she runs to Yvonne, who opens her arms and hugs her daughter with every ounce of love she has in her body.

Desmond, seeing the love between his mother and his sister, starts to weep, then looks at his father, who is picking his nose. Desmond starts to wail. As he does, he cries out, 'Dad, let's go. Please.'

Archie and Desmond move to Martha Spear's bed and breakfast that very evening

The following morning, Amanda rushes to her local newsagent and pays for fifty photocopies of the best photo of Desmond in a tutu, which makes the owner, Mr Patel, chuckle as for years he has had to endure racist remarks from Desmond. The photocopies quickly exchange hands amongst the younger generation of Brighton, with more copies being photocopied that are either handed out as flyers or simply fly-posted.

After a long sleep in, Desmond decides to go for a walk to take out his frustration on some innocent kid. However, Desmond quickly retreats to the B&B as the kids he once bullied—and even his old friends—point at him and laugh. Some adopt a ballet pose, whilst others hum Swan Lake.

Desmond storms back into the room he shares with Archie, who is engrossed with a well-used copy of Knave, and says, 'Dad, we've got to go.'

■ ■ ■

While Desmond is out with The Magnificent Six, he phones his father from one of the telephone boxes in the Uxbridge Road. Desmond is relieved to hear that Archie is back from work, as his father usually finishes early on a Saturday. Desmond asks Archie if he can switch the immersion heater on, so Desmond can jump straight into the bath when he gets back. Archie grunts, states he is busy. It takes Desmond about ten minutes and a handful of tuppence pieces to persuade his father to honour his request.

Desmond walks into the flat with a purpose and pride, but this is shattered when he sees a familiar sight: Archie slumped on the sofa, clutching a can of Tennent's Lager Lovelies—the nearest he has been to a woman since Yvonne made him leave.

'Dad, did you switch the bath on?' asks Desmond, hoping that the answer will give him a little bit of reassurance.

'I ain't your slave, son. Been busy, can't you see?' Archie replies in a sleepy manner.

'I ask just one thing, one bloody thing, dad,' barks a furious Desmond.

Archie, sobering up from his late Saturday afternoon booze up, leaps up and performs the vicious ritual of removing his thick black leather belt with a huge stainless-steel buckle. 'Hic. Back-chatting your old man? Get in the kitchen—it's belting time and I want you to sing the song, too. "It's belting time, na nananana, it's belting time."' It's a song that Desmond has sung on numerous occasions before feeling the brute force of Archie and his belt.

A few months ago, Desmond would have been the obedient son and accepted his undeserved punishment. Yet, late in the summer, Desmond has started to see the world as a beautiful place, a fun place, not a place of chastisement and agony. Desmond is no naïve fool—he knows there are dangers, plenty of them, rival gangs, be it Scooter Boys, Mods, Punks, other London Casuals, policemen. Yet, for the first time, he has friends, equals, not the weak people that used to surround him.

'Nay, dad, I ain't singing the song, I ain't going in the kitchen.'

Archie is shocked by his son's confidence. 'So, you think you are above a belting? Me old man used to belt me, made me sing the song, so, son, I'm passing it down, father to son, if you like,' Archie says with an evil smirk.

Desmond feeling stronger by the second, replies, 'No wonder you've turned out like you have. Granddad was a loon—best place for him is six feet under.'

Archie swings his belt, smashing into the three flying ducks on the wall. 'Now look what you made me do, boy. It's going to be a belting to end all beltings for disrespecting me and my old man.' Then Archie starts to sob, as he reflects with a pervert sense of fondness of his father belting him in the kitchen in front of his mother, as the young Archie wholeheartedly sings the traditional Wilson's belting song, which has been adapted over the years to suit current musical trends.

Desmond, seeing his father's defence down, steps forward and punches Archie with a straight jab in the throat. Archie holds his neck, falls to his knees facing Desmond and starts to choke. Shocked by his actions, Desmond heads to the front door to escape from the scene of the crime.

As Desmond runs out of White City and on to India Way, he tries to reassure himself. 'I'm just a boy. I'll tell the Old Bill it was self-defence.' Desmond looks to the skies and cries out, 'I want my mummy.' Then his recent life as a skinhead bully starts to flash back, recalling with agony his poor innocent victims. Desmond falls to his knees, puts his face in his hands and cries out again, 'I am so sorry, please believe me, I am.'

'I am sure they know you are truly sorry.'

Desmond raises his head from his cupped hands, and sees two men in their early twenties, medium build, both with blond hair, in checked, short-sleeved button-down shirts and sporting black bow ties standing over him. As Desmond catches their eyes, the men smile a caring smile the likes of which Desmond has not seen for ages. The smile reminds Desmond of happier times, before he became a skinhead, when he would play with his sister, hug his mother and go to ballet lessons or the ice rink with pride.

Yet Desmond is wary of these men, they are too nice—far too nice for him to trust. 'Piss off you poofs,' he snaps.

The men, resilient to belligerence, smile their loving smile and one of then simply replies, 'The aggression and anger of youth. The sign of a lost soul, a troubled soul. Tell us your problems, we are the ears for God, and via us we can pass on God's love.'

The word love starts to melt Desmond's heart. One of the men moves forward and puts his hand on Desmond's shoulder. Desmond puts his hand on top of it. The warmth of the man's hand gives Desmond hope.

'Tell me your name, child of our beloved lord.'

Desmond closes his eyes as he holds the man's hand tighter. The man gently pulls Desmond up from his knees and they embrace. This unexpected and much needed moment of tenderness moves Desmond like he has never been moved before.

'My name is Desmond... and... I... miss... my... mother... my... sister... I have... harmed... my father... kids... other kids... I am so sorry... please forgive me...'

The other man joins in. Soon, they are group-hugging on India Way.

'Desmond, God forgives you. You have learnt from your mistakes. God sees that, God sees all.'

All three gently break away from their hug and face each other. Desmond is overcome with emotion. 'Does God really forgive me?'

'Yes, son. Where are you going tonight? To help a little old lady with some housework? Feed the poor?' asks one of the men.

Desmond shakes his head in shame. 'A party.'

'A party is where the Devil will steal your soul with sex and drugs.'

'I don't want the Devil to steal my soul. Help me, please,' pleads a confused Desmond.

One of the men replies, 'We will save you. God has found you. Come with us to the church. We can all pray together.'

Sniffling, Desmond replies, 'Is it far?'

'A short journey by car. We can stop for burgers if you like. Would you like that?' says one of the men in a caring voice.

Desmond nods then starts to cry. 'I have nowhere to sleep.'

'We have beds. We can even find you a job. We can save your soul from the Devil and get God's forgiveness,' replies one of the men, offering reassurance to Desmond.

Desmond falls to his knees again, looks up to the heavens and says, 'I am saved, I've seen the light.'

Both men exchange glances and smile. 'Come, Desmond. Come with us.'

'Yes, I will come with you.'

With this, Desmond gets up and starts to walk alongside the two strangers down India Way.

tales of aggro: book two
matteo sedazzari

baby let's smash this place
become a social disgrace
a lie tells more than the truth
honey, I'm living proof

10

The Theatre of Temptation
by Oscar De Paul

Curtain rises at 5.30pm
At The Theatre of Temptation
The play—Broken Dreams
A rip-roaring alcoholic drama

With the continuing characters
Performing to a familiar crowd
The usual scenario of mishaps and misadventures
Amid the laughter and tears of three men

Men who have lost the optimism of youth
Replaced with the cynicism of old age
Nursing an historical hangover
As they contemplate the world

They try to foil the government conspiracy
Of their underachievement
Their lack of funds and job prospects
Anyone and anything to blame for their lonely nights

As they plead their bitter-laced case
The landlord lends a sympathetic deaf ear
And with each nod of empathy
He pours the men another drink

As the clock hands move slowly
With smoke-stained windows blocking out the sun
One of the men takes centre stage
As he transcends into a drunken clown

His monologue begins with his sad childhood
Deprivation a dispassionate teacher
Then his emotions move to sudden joy
As he is passed another pint

His peers cheer him on with passion
Here, here, they chant
Get high with me
Stay low with me, their motto

The supporting cast arrive, fresh from shit
They are united in tales of sexual conquest
Chat about how the Pakis are taking over
And it's England's right to win the World Cup

Fucking wops, one of them says
Cheating pasta-eating cunts, says another
Their hatred is broken by beauty
As a young girl enters the scene

They smile like leering maniacs at the girl
As she asks the landlord for directions
A chance to shine, they think
Get your tits out for the lads, they bellow

Classical!

The girl hastily exits at the rear
The men chuckle with pride
She fucking loved it, they say
Then, in a brief sober moment, they remember past loves

The sound of a fruit machine
Breaks their train of thought
Fucking Jacko won the jackpot
Lend us a fiver, you cunt, they yell

Jacko smiles and leaves the scene
For tonight he is a cameo, a mere spear-carrier
The main cast applaud his exit
As they down another drink

Charlie enters through the main doors bearing gifts
The three men jump up with joy
Charlie passes each of the men a small parcel
The men slink into the piss-stinking toilet.

Ladies and Gentlemen: there will be a snort interval.

Act Two
The men take centre stage once more
This time full of life, zeal and joy
With smiles that show their rotting teeth
Chattering as the snot runs down their nose

Ambition is for nancy boys, one says
I feel part of the community, says another
Childhood dreams start to fade away
As a nightmare of self-loathing begins

With each visit to the toilet
The men feel more invincible and ready for action
Their voices louder and their words ruder
Folk nearby move away

What is their problem? they scream
Don't they like the working man?
A feeling of violence overcomes them
As one of them throws an ashtray

A woman screams, a table is kicked over
Followed by the sound of smashing glass
A family man tries to calm them down
Fuck off, cunt, is shouted, as punches are thrown

The landlord shouts, as his pit bull barks
The men stop and bow their heads in shame
Peace is restored with tears of apologies
And a round of drinks

The landlord collects the glasses. Time please, gents
Tonight the men have entered the twilight zone
They have stayed in limbo, treading dirty water
As the world has moved inexorably forward

Bravo!
Curtain fall

Tomorrow night at 5.30pm
Repeat performance
Of Broken Dreams
In The Theatre of Temptation

11

Let's 'Ave It with Eddie the Casual

The stench of verbal bullshit is overwhelming, making my lager taste sour, as all I can hear is the foghorn voice of Honest Ron. He's doing his usual anecdotes, with a few backhanded compliments thrown in for good measure to the cute and curvy brunette barmaid. But I am not listening, as I've heard them all before. Yet this unsuspecting babe is being reeled in hook, line and sinker, like they all do, which amazes me and the rest of The Magnificent Six no end. Pretty silly that after all these years, I still call the lads, every now and then, by our school playground nickname. Yet here we all are at the Elephant and Castle boozer to meet Roy Harper. I didn't call this meet on—oh no, Rooster did—and Ron and Jamie Joe are here on his behalf.

Roy Harper is one of the infamous Harper clan, Elephant and Castle underworld royalty, I suppose a bit like me—my family's the Savages, well known around the Bush and beyond. I think you all know my uncle, Rockin' Wilf. I think the whole of England do after his little, shall we say, encounter with the Flying Squad. I ended up buying Hudson Close off the council in 1989. Homeowner by the age of 22 and bought my second flat last year, Granville Mansions, right opposite Bush Green. You should pop over some time for a cup of tea and a smoke. Wilf still lives at Hudson Close, not rent-free but near enough. Let's just say it's beer vouchers, because I am doing all right now. I am going to make an offer for Braybrook Street soon, the original Savages family home.

I make my dollars from the building game. Got into it when I was 16, a few months after I left school with one of Wilf's mates, Raj. I thought I was going to follow into the family's trade—you know, a bit of this and a bit of that. Just thought it was my destiny. Then, after a few months with Raj, I was making good money, honest money. I was getting bored with the shoplifting and all that. To me, even at 16, I saw it as kids' stuff, unlike Oscar. Oh yeah, Raj had Oscar on the tools for a bit, but he had to sack him. Bet Oscar has never told you that. Raj's sons weren't that interested in his business. Just wanted the money at the end of the week, spunk it over the weekend, skint on Monday, asking for a sub.

Unlike them, I could see something big going on with Raj. Soon, I was pricing jobs with him, meeting potential clients, closing the business, doing the graph and making a profit. We're business partners now, Walia and Savage Property Developers, and business is booming. But once a rogue, always a rogue, I suppose, because I still dabble. Declare this, don't declare that. Got a nice cash nest egg stashed away for a rainy day. But I ain't telling you where—you'll either nick it or tell the taxman. But, you see, as long as the taxman gets his cut, he leaves you alone. Just make sure you hand in your returns, show a small profit and pay your bill once a year, easy-peasy.

Even the DS (drug squad) will give you no grief to a degree if you're working or own a business. Ron is flying it as a financial advisor to firms in the City, no shit, but it's a cover-up, as all his punters are on the bugle, so it's an excuse for him and the City boys to go on a bender. Jamie has got into the restaurant game—bought a French diner in Chiswick last year. Even Rooster has got his own scaffolding business now, Rooster's Scaffolding. His workers double up as his debt collectors. Walia and Savage use them all the time for building work and to collect any outstanding's. But it's all a huge smoke screen for them to launder their money, pay the taxman and keep the Old Bill off their backs. Everyone is sweet.

I know fellas who have been banged up because they were signing on yet drinking champagne and tucking into seafood platters for lunch at a riverside pub in Richmond on a Monday, while showing off rolls of pink ladies (that's fifty-pound notes, in case you didn't know). The downfall of so many wannabe dealers and villains is vanity and fucking stupidity. Trust me, the Old Bill always prefers an easy collar, because real detective work means just that—they must work for a living. Cos just like villains, coppers like the easy life, too.

As for the rest, Quicksilver works with me, oversees the jobs. I haven't touched the tools for a while. Dino is getting into computers, buying and selling them. Reckons there's a fortune to be made. I am seriously thinking about investing in him. Oscar is still doing telesales—reckons it's a stopgap while he writes his novel about us being Casuals and getting into Acid House. I hope he does, I really do.

Acid House was so nice. No. It was beautiful, as it was wonderful to go out and not get into a melee, just dance, flirt, smile and shake hands with a stranger. Of course, Es had a lot to do with it, creating a sense of euphoria. But, also, I think everyone had had enough of aggro. It was getting out of hand. You couldn't even leave the front door without getting into trouble. I remember our last scrap me and the lads had, before we got on one matey at Shoom Fitness Centre. It was November 1987, with seven drunk Irish navvies in Pilcher's. We turned them over, but fuck we were battered and bruised the following morning. Then, a month later, there's me and the boys, with all these football lads, gays and beautiful girls, as one, no trouble, just a sweaty room full of love, peace and unity. Oscar believed Acid House would bring down Thatcher and her Conservative government. I love his passion, but he can be a romantic fool at times.

Now, it seems to have gone full circle, as people are getting territorial and aggressive again, me included. I nearly slapped a fella the other day at my local Pizza Express when I was out with my fiancée, Louise. Why? I made out he was giving me the dirty. I don't think he was. Well, he wasn't. I had been on the nosebag the day before with Jamie Joe, old time's sake, so I was rather snappy, but I know that's no excuse. Lou walked out, paged me, telling me to get help or I can forget the big day. I must, but this evening, I want aggro. I need it, because it's been about six years since we had a real good tear-up.

If I know I'm up for aggro and need to see a shrink, you are probably wondering why me and the lads are in a moody local's boozer. Well, like I said, Rooster called this meet with Harper to sort out some business. I don't know the whats and wheres, as villain chat bores me, especially when it comes from Honest Ron.

Anyway, Ron calls me, saying that he and Jamie are meeting a fella for Rooster in the Elephant and Castle pub. Ron asks me if I fancy coming along

as a bit of backup to him and Jamie. I ask Ron abruptly why Rooster isn't going. Ron tells me that Rooster is away seeing some Doris in Ireland that he
met the other week when he was out and about in London night life. The fella
might be a loon, but in the last few years, Rooster has certainly become attractive to women of a hedonist nature. Ron goes on to tell me that Rooster gets a
call from Harper. Old Rooster has got one of them mobile phones—I am getting one next year. It's urgent, according to Rooster, so he calls his messenger
boy Ron to sort it out. Bloody gangster bullshit. I still find it hilarious that
Rooster started to trust Honest Ron after he found his 'nicked' bike and we all
know who nicked it. Do you know, still, to this day, Rooster is none the wiser?

I suppose, out of friendship and boredom, I said okay, fine, but as long as
we are not carrying anything back, not one pill, not one rock, not one gram
of coke, because I haven't got the energy or the time to have a 'no comment'
interview in some nick in South-East London. Ron tells me it's just to size
things up. No exchange, just a meet, that's all. I said no problem. Word soon
gets back to Oscar, as it always does around White City, that me, Honest Ron
and Jamie Joe are off to the Elephant and Castle pub, so he calls Dino and
Quicksilver, thinking it's a jolly boy outing for The Magnificent Six, prick. So
here we all are.

I haven't been to the Elephant and Castle pub for yonks—two years probably—when me and the rest of the lads, and the girls sometimes, Louise,
Stephanie and their lovely friends, would come here on a Sunday morning,
off our nuts, to dance to some garage. A lad, Matt Jam Lamont, used to run
it. He's gone onto bigger and better things. Nice fella, always sweet with us.
It was a bit moody, but that was to put off the 'club tourists', as Oscar calls
them. You know, the ones that just live for the weekend. Like Oscar, I can't
abide weekenders, as the Flowered Up record goes from last year. Good band,
Flowered Up—Oscar reckons they are the Small Faces of Acid House.

Oscar and me, out of the lot, have always been elitist, be it the playground, when we were Mods or Casuals, or Acid House. I could be distant to
outsiders, then sometimes welcome them with open arms, like I did with a lost
skinhead ten years ago—Desmond. Desmond is now the vicar of The Church
of St Stephen and St Thomas. He thought he had killed his old man. He
didn't, just knocked him out. He ran away, bumped into some Bible-bashers

and found God. Now him and his old man are as sweet as a nut. His old man moved back to Brighton for a second chance with his wife, a nice happy ending. Desmond is going to marry Lou and me—that's if she takes me back.

Did you know the area, Elephant and Castle, is named after this pub, not the other way around? Me neither, until Oscar went to the library and told me and the lads. I do love him for his endless source of useless information.

All this nattering with you lot has made me lose track of time. My word, it's 8.45pm. 'Ron, it's quarter to nine. I'll give him until 9pm then I'm off.'

'Relax, Eddie. If Roy said he will be here then he will be. Fancy a game of pool?' Ron replies.

Ron points through the smoke-filled pub to a well-worn and torn red felt pool table, which has certainly seen better days. As the smoke subsides, I see two chaps, about my age, playing pool. Casually looking on are three more blokes. I must give credit where credit is due—these boys are well turned out: an array of smart, button-down and polo shirts, chino trousers, Levi's jeans, all sporting smart shoes, not a trainer in sight. Three of them have short and smart haircuts, one still has a bob hairstyle from 1988, and the other, long blond hair tied back in a ponytail. I bet they are former ravers now smartening themselves up again, probably ex-Mods or Casuals, or both, like we were. I hope they like a scrap, I really do.

As Ron points in an aggressive manner, the lad with the out-of-date bob is about to take a shot, but he stops, rests the cue on the table and looks in our direction, making the rest of this local firm take notice of us. Ron sees their gaze and says, 'Winner stays on lads,' attempting to break the ice and size them up. A game of pool usually eases the tension—we find out that we've got mutual friends, been to the same clubs, exchange jokes and anecdotes, and by the end of the night we are the best of friends. Or sometimes it can just kick off. I really hope it's the latter, I really do. I need a good tear-up for old time's sake.

'How about a game of doubles?' asks the lad with the bob in a slightly confrontational manner as he points to Honest Ron and me. 'Doubles, singles, triples, even invite your old Auntie Irene down. Makes no odds to me—I'll still whip ya,' says Ron in an upbeat manner and a smile, as I am sure he just wants to do his business with Harper without any bother. But I don't. I want a good old-fashioned pub fight. Ron and I both move closer to the lads and the table. None of them are smiling. Poker faces.

'I'll play ya,' quirks the fattest one of the lot. Didn't really see how fat he is until I was this close up. We're lucky—we haven't got a fat kid in our gang.

'Alright, mate, it's your funeral,' harps Honest Ron.

'Where you from mate?' asks Fatty.

''Ere and there. You know, from around,' says Ron in a cheeky manner.

Again, they fail to laugh, even smile. I can sense the trouble brewing, I can feel it. I love it. I look at Oscar, Dino, Jamie and Quicksilver, and nod my head towards the pool table and Ron, a sign we need backup. My boys don't need to be asked twice—they know the cue. We've been watching each other's back since Christopher Wren. We know our roles and mine is to knock out the opponent's top boy—always has been, always will be. I am a bloody Savage, for Christ's sake. It runs in the family.

The rest of The Magnificent Six—oh shit, there I go again, calling us by our old nickname—step into the arena with puffed out chests and frosty stares. Our rivals sense the hostile advance, mirrors our aggression and stand shoulder to shoulder. I go behind the lads, with Jamie Joe stepping forward, to give the pretence that he is the top boy. It's a bit unfair to say that it's a pretence because we all know Jamie can have a row. But it's just a ploy so I can go incognito and work out who's who and what's what.

Then I see him, and he sees me. A good-looking boy in a short-sleeved green Ralph Lauren shirt, Stone Island jeans, black Patrick Cox loafers, with short black hair, well built, but with a little bit of a beer gut. He's mine. It will be a battle, but I can take him.

I use a bit of reverse psychology. I turn away to avoid eye contact to give the impression that I am bottling it. Out of the corner of my eye, I see him smirk, as if to say 'chicken'. 'Pretend to be weak that he may grow arrogant,' as Sun Tzu says in The Art of War. I live and breathe that book.

The sound of Ron racking up the pool balls breaks the South-East London boy's concentration. Nice move, Ronnie. 'The whole secret lies in confusing the enemy, so that he cannot fathom our real intent.' Sound advice from Sun Tzu, but I don't think that is Ron's intention. I think he really does want a game of pool. Not for me, though. I want blood—their blood.

I glance around the pub. No other real contenders: a couple on a night out, a few old geezers who probably used to knock it down the Old Kent Road. They would love to join in, but their tickers would probably play up.

I look at Quicksilver, who returns with a knowing stare. Oscar is looking on edge. I give him a wink, just to reassure Oscar that we are one. He smiles back nervously. His hands are shaking as he sips his pint. Then Bobbi notices as he waits for Ron to break. 'A bit nervous, mate? It's only a game.'

'Na, mate. Just a bit chilly in here. Ain't your landlord heard of central heating?' Oscar replies.

'Says 'e in a Paddington coat,' pipes up the lad with a ponytail in a strong Newcastle accent. So, they've got the token northerner in their posse. Geordie turns around to his friends, they all start laughing. Of course, it's not endearment, just a tried and tested form of intimidation. We've all done it.

'My word, that is original. Suppose you'll be singing, "'Cause the fog on the Tyne is all mine, all mine. The fog on the Tyne is all mine, all mine" later,' says Oscar, who seems to be growing in confidence.

'Aye. Ain't ever heard 'hat afore ever, 'ave I, lads?' says Geordie to his boys.

'Never, Andy. First time for everything, I suppose,' says a dark-haired lad with a real Soul Patrol wedge haircut. This lad has got a familiar face, probably from a few years back when we were all loved up. He's well turned out. Probably, out of this lot, he's the real ladies' man; ours is Honest Ron and he's the ugliest out of the lot of us.

Quicksilver, who's always had his fair share of snogs over the years, looks at Ladies' Man and says, 'You look like you're a contestant for Blind Date. "Pick me, number one, cos I am the bubbles in your champagne, babes."'

'Hark at the lad with the silver flick. You look like you have just been buggered by Dracula,' he replies, which is met by a long roar of hostile laughter by these 'Sarf' London boys.

'Says the bastard son of Cilla Black. I bet deep down you're really into fellas, cos you're the one that brought up buggery, not me,' replies Quicksilver in an aggressive tone.

'He's got a point. What made you say that? Must be on your mind nonstop. I mean you are all brushed up. Is that for the ladies or you trying to impress your mates? Hoping tonight is the night you can come out of the closet?' says a forceful Jamie Joe.

'Piss off, mate, I ain't no poof. I like me birds, don't I… lads?' snaps Ladies' Man. Yet this time, he doesn't get the support from his boys, as they look at each other, thinking maybe he is, maybe he isn't.

Excellent move, Quicksilver and Jamie breaking their unity. 'If his forces are united, separate them.' Yes, you guessed it, good old Sun Tzu again.

Talk time is over. Now for a much-needed ruck. Sometimes, it is better than sex, it really is.

I creep towards Ralph Lauren. He's mine, he's dead, it's on. But suddenly, he turns to face me. As he does, Ralph Lauren throws his beer glass directly at me. I duck. It flies past, smashing onto a pillar. The sound of breaking glass is the catalyst for the much-needed and long-awaited kick off. It's on. It's fucking on. Oh yes.

Oscar grabs a pool cue from the rack on the wall, breaks it over his knee and leaps onto the table, just like Johnny Boy from Mean Streets, a film he has watched countless times. He is swinging the cue and kicking out with his practised evil glare. He hasn't actually made any contact yet, but he sure looks mean.

Dino grabs Bobbi and pushes him against the wall. Quicksilver and Ladies' Man start doing windmill impressions. Quicksilver, this ain't a school-yard bundle. Ron now knows the game of pool is a distant memory, has no choice but to join in, so he screams out, 'Let's 'ave it', and with this, he tries to kick Fatty in the gut but misses. Fuck it, Ron. Trust you.

Jamie Joe runs straight into Geordie and head butts him square in the face. Strike one, Jamie, 10 out of 10. You are the master of the Glaswegian kiss. Blood spills out. Geordie is dazed, but still standing.

Then Jamie Joe uses his favourite trick. Ladies and Gentlemen, may I introduce you to 'The Bar Stool'. He grabs the nearest stool and, with all his might, smashes it into the right side of Geordie's head. Geordie hits the floor upon impact. I hear screams and yells in the background. The couple are running for the door. 'Better than EastEnders, mate.'

My troops are in warfare. I must focus. It's on.

Here I am, facing Ralph Lauren. We utter no words, just sizing each other up, waiting to strike, top boy versus top boy, these are the rules. Ralph Lauren goes into a southpaw stance. Good, he's a boxer. So am I. It's going to be a good fight, the best. Fuck, do I need it, do I want it.

As I go into the orthodox stance from boxing, ready for battle, a clenched fist whisks past my nose. I turn my head to my left and see a red-faced Fatty willing to die for their leader. Then I see Honest Ron approaching Fatty's right side, who's oblivious to my oncoming friend, which is perfect for Ron, as there is no guard, so Ron launches a powerful right hook, making Fatty wobble like a Weeble.

The commotion between Honest Ron and Fatty gets the attention of Ralph Lauren, who is looking annoyed and concerned that the gut-buster of their gang is getting a hiding. Excellent, he is distracted. Good boy, Ron, good boy.

Time is now of the essence. I clench my fists tighter, swing my hips from my right side. My right hook flies straight into Ralph Lauren's jaw, a full-on connector, as The Magnificent Six used to call it. Ralph Lauren begins to sway, leaving his face and stomach exposed. So, I follow through with a front-house kick to his gut. His reflexes are slow. Too much ale, Ralph. He falls to the floor. He's down. Fuck Queensberry Rules—I want to take him out, hurt him. It's on.

I boot him straight in the face, the power of my kick sends him backwards, leaving his crotch exposed. I stamp down on his cock like a pneumatic drill, constantly using my heel. He's squealing like a pig, just like Ned Beatty in Deliverance. My adrenaline is reaching a climax. This is an amazing sensation, inflicting pain on a stranger. I will forever be in his memory. I don't need love, I don't need Louise, I need violence. Pain is beauty, yes, it is.

My bliss of vehemence is suddenly broken when I feel a thud on the side of my head. I spin round and there's Fatty standing with a broken bottle. Over Fatty's shoulder, I see the dwarf of The Magnificent Six sparked out on the floor. Fuck you, Ron—Fatty was yours. Again, I'm fighting for two.

Remember The Magnificent Six's Art of War rules, Ronnie?

Rule 1: never hesitate

Rule 2: follow straight through

Rule 3: by any means necessary

I touch the side of my head and feel a dampness. It's nothing. Fatty will have to do better than that to put Eddie The Casual down. Fatty steps back to admire his handy work. Fatal mistake, Fatty, giving your opponent time. Huge mistake, Fatty. You see, tonight I'm Mike Tyson, Chuck Norris, Batman, The Tasmanian Devil. The blood on my head is my baptism. I feel 18 again. I feel my strength. I feel my anger. Eddie the Casual is back.

He stares in my face and utters the immortal words, 'You want it or what?' Typical thug, he's expecting backup. No dice, Fatty. He swings from the left and the right, missing each time.

I scream my famous battle cry: 'I'll rip your lungs out.' With this, I give Fatty a well-placed and powerful right upper cut. I feel the flab from his double chin wobble on my knuckles. My punch pushes Fatty into a pillar, which prevents him from going down. Shit, I was looking forward to kicking the shit out of this gross beast. Our eyes meet, then Fatty breaks away from my gaze, as he scours the floor looking for a tool. Old Fatty spots a pool cue. He stoops down to pick it up. Bad move, fat boy—I'm going to hurt you, really hurt you.

With Fatty bending over, his back is the only part of the body I can attack, so I leap on it and with all my weight, I force Fatty onto the ground, face down. I press hard on him and put his left earlobe into my mouth. I bite hard. He screams out like a girl. I can smell his BO and bad breath with my nose buried in his face. His salty sweat oozes into my mouth.

I let go of his earlobe. I put both my hands flat on the floor and push myself up with my knees on his back, just to give this idiot some more pain. I hear Fatty moan as my left kneecap cracks into his back. From my knees, I quickly manage to stand up. Fatty stays face down, crying like a baby, holding onto his left ear as the blood pours out. What a beautiful sight. I wish I had a camera to keep this moment.

Now to slaughter the pig, so I start to kick him fast and furious on the right-side of his rib cage. Then Fatty starts to cry out, 'Leave it out, mate.' What? Fatty doesn't want to play any more? It's on, he's mine.

I need to catch my breath. So pleased that I have, because Ralph Lauren is standing in front of me. Fuck, I thought he was out for the count. He's holding a blade—it's a bloody flick knife. Fuck, this isn't West Side Story.

I step back two paces and put my hands out to say, 'No trouble'. But I don't think Ralph Lauren is going to listen to me. I mean, I did kick him and Fatty while they were down. Then, like Spider-man, Jamie comes flying in with a bit of four-by-two. Ralph Lauren feels the full force and goes down. Where Jamie got this bit of wood from who knows, who cares? All I know and care about is that Jamie Joe stopped me from getting sliced up. I turn around and I give Fatty a goodnight kick.

Then this glorious nightmare is broken by the sound of a dog barking. It's over…

I look over my shoulder and see the landlord with his black Staffordshire bull terrier. 'Fuck off. You've done Harper's boy and his mates. I would walk while you still can. You've got five minutes then I'm calling the Old Bill. Give ya a head start.' I nod at the landlord, as it is slowly sinking in that we've just turned over the son of Roy Harper and his boys.

I look around the pub, and see that Jamie, Dino and Quicksilver are all standing. Honest Ron is now getting up off the floor, while Oscar is still standing on the pool table, clutching a broken pool cue with that insane look upon his face, fucking looney toon. As for our adversaries, Fatty and Geordie are still on the floor while Bobbi and Ladies' Man are on their feet, war-torn though. Ralph Lauren is picking himself up. Fuck, he was battered by me and Jamie Joe, but he still won't go down.

Ladies' Man goes over to help Ralph Lauren, who pushes Ladies' Man back and says, 'Get off me, you fucking poof.'

'I ain't a p…' Ladies' Man doesn't complete his sentence, as Ralph Lauren gives Ladies' Man a right hook, knocking him out.

Ralph Lauren then looks at the landlord and says, 'Frank, don't be stupid, no one is calling the Old Bill. We'll have them sniffing round 'ere. The old man won't want that.' Ralph Lauren returns his attention to us, with a degree of respect, looks directly at me and asks, 'You ain't Honest Ron?' I shake my head and point to Ron. Ron steps forward like he's some superstar. 'Got a message from me old man. I am George Harper, his lad. He's running late. Asked me and the lads to come down 'ere an' look after ya like. Soz about the confusion. Ya fellas can certainly 'ave it. Let's 'ave a return match, your manor soon?'

Ron and George Harper both start to laugh, as do the others—well, apart from Fatty, Geordie and Ladies' Man, who are still seeing stars.

I rush to the toilet to be physically sick. I have created a world of madness, violence and mayhem. Dear God, I am sorry. All I had to do was to let Ron play a game a pool. Why the fuck did I kick it off? Is this my life now, is it? I need help, I need love, I need Louise…

12

Stephanie's Song—Part One

I never thought that Oscar and I would stay together. Do I still love him? Not sure. Maybe. Who knows? But I can't dwell on the past, it's all about moving forward, living in the present, and Oscar wouldn't.

I am Stephanie, you know the cheeky girl that shouted out, 'It's The Magnificent Six!' to Oscar and his mates one day at Christopher Wren School. I used to see them, we all did, strutting around like peacocks. The words just came out of my mouth. I went bright red with embarrassment when they turned around and smiled, but at least I wasn't invisible any more to them. I was hoping to be chatted up by one of them—I wasn't bad looking back then, I've certainly blossomed out now. I know that is vain, but if you've got it then flaunt it, baby.

About a year later, one of them did ask me out, Oscar, when I was on my way to Hammersmith Park to play tennis with Lucy. Oscar looked so angelic with his arrogant swagger, in his dapper Casual clobber. I was attracted straight away, as I was getting into the whole Casual thing. I loved the look and the music, jazz funk, electro, hip hop.

After tennis, I rushed back to my bedroom to whack on Wham's Fantastic album. That was mine and Lucy's album for that summer, and boy did I dance to Wham's 'A Ray of Sunshine'—you know, the one that goes, 'Sometimes, you wake up in the morning with the bassline, A Ray of Sunshine. Sometimes, you know today you're gonna have a good time and you're ready to go.'

That was exactly how I felt until the following evening, when Lu and me popped down Pilcher's to buy some chips, as you do, and everyone was talking about The Magnificent Six going to some all-night drug-fuelled orgy. I ran home in tears. I was inconsolable. Even a hug from mum couldn't mend my broken heart, even though Oscar wasn't my boyfriend then. But silly me, I just thought he was different.

I think it was the next evening I saw Oscar with the rest of The Magnificent Six outside Wormholt Park. He smiled and waved in a cocky manner. I can't remember what I said, but I more or less told him to piss off as I didn't want a sex maniac near me. Soon after, I heard that the orgy was all bullshit, made up by that prat Toby Brown. Lucy's been with him—yuck. He makes my skin crawl: he tried it on with me once, once only. I told him where to go. Please believe me, I felt bad, as I had told Oscar to go away. I was a stupid cow. I saw Oscar a few weeks later walking along on his own towards me, strutting it like he did back then. It made my heart flutter. I gave him a big beaming smile as he approached me, but the arrogant sod just walked straight past, without even making eye contact.

I know Oscar wanted to make me feel guiltier than I did, but baby, I wasn't going to beg—never have, never will do. So, I left it. Oscar wasn't worth chasing, oh no, so I started going out with Ashley Hughes—nice looking lad, but way too controlling. But by the time Ash and I had broken up, Oscar and I weren't talking, as we were both leading separate lives. I went to Hammersmith and West London College to do my A-Levels—oh yeah, clever girl me. Met and started seeing Paul Hudson from my English Literature class. Like Oscar, Paul was a bit of a lad, cheeky chappie and all that. I thought he was the one, then I found out he liked to play away from home, silly boy. But Paul did break my heart. He asked for another chance: 'It was a mistake'—all the usual bullshit men say. But there was no way I was going to be his downtrodden girlfriend, so I told him to fuck off and he did, thanks to Lucy's brother, Aaron, having a word. That was just before my A-levels. I didn't find solace in the bottle, no. Studying and junk food—I was one burger away from being obese.

It was Oscar's cheek that made me get my figure back. I had just finished my final A-level, History, so I popped down Pilcher's for a celebration portion of battered sausages and chips.

''Ere, you've porked out a bit, Steph,' were the first words Oscar said to me in nearly four years, as he and his sister Olivia stood behind me in the queue. I turned around with a look of shock on my face, as did Olivia. Me and her were never friends: civil, yes; friends, no.

Then I started to laugh, as it was a humorous wake-up call. I needed to lose weight. So I went on a crash diet. Within a month, Oscar and me, at long last, were going out together. Me and Oscar went out for five years: clubs, parties, holidays, eating out, all the things lovers do. We were even saving up to get a place together.

But something inside me started to doubt it, not just him, but everything. I had an excellent job: campaign manager for Sapphire Advertising in Soho. Got the gig through some girl I knew, Tara Fuller, from around town. But I was bored with that, too: full of superficial and shallow people. I left college in 1987, full of ideas, but got into the whole hedonistic way of life. We all did. Still gutted that I didn't go to University. Then I started to think, 'Is this it? Marry Oscar, become a darling of the advertising world?' It wasn't me. I was living my life for other people to make them feel fulfilled.

Oscar started drinking a lot—every night—and most of the time he was merry. No, he was never abusive or aggressive, just a cock, a real cock, and like me a few years back, Oscar porked out around the face and gut. Then, one night down The Queen Adelaide, when me and him were having a quiet drink, I kissed him on the cheek and said, 'Sorry Oscar, I can't do this any more.' Oscar didn't say a word, just looked at me with his sad and sunken eyes, like he was expecting it. My beautiful one-time Soul Boy was now just a fucking beer boy. I walked out in tears, but I didn't look back.

Then a month or so later after leaving Oscar, March 1992, I moved here, 15a Norfolk Place, Paddington, above Micky's Fish and Chip Shop—not a patch on Pilcher's,. We're still here now, Lucy and me. Both single but we both like to mingle, if you know what I mean. My parents moved out of White City two years ago to Peel Road, South Woodford, so I have nothing to do with the area now. Lucy does, as her parents still live there.

A lot has happened to both of us since we set up home here—all good. Lucy has taken up photography after buying a camera and doing a few courses. Now it's her career, freelance work. My girl is so happy, a joy to be around.

Me, during a drunken night with Lucy—I think it was about two years ago, January 1994, I can't really remember—anyway, me and her were singing along to all our favourite songs, from Grandmaster Flash to Diana Ross, with hairbrush in one hand and a glass of wine in the other.

Lucy looked me in the eye, and said so sincerely, 'You've got to be a singer.'

'Shut up, Lu, you're drunk. I ain't a singer.'

'Look at ya. You are beautiful, sexy, you can dance, you can sing. Steph, seriously, you know you can do it.'

Lu was right. I could sing—been told that since I was a kid, when I would sing along to The Beatles, Slade and all stuff like that, at the family knees-up on Christmas day. I just never got around to doing anything about it. Not that I lacked confidence, just more being lazy than anything else. However, Lucy's slurred words were a sign to me that the time was right to chase a dream for me.

The following weekend, I popped down North Kensington Library to look up any amateur musical theatre groups near me and found Showcase in Ealing. I didn't have the experience to go pro, not yet anyway. But I passed the audition with ease—well, actually I blew them away with my rendition of 'Knock on Wood' and 'Don't Cry for Me Argentina'. After joining, I appeared in Oliver!, The Pajama Game and then got the lead of Reno Sweeney, the nightclub singer, in Cole Porter's Anything Goes. I quickly learnt how to be ruthless and tough to get the part. To be honest, I became a hard-nosed bitch—I had no choice, otherwise it would have been the chorus line forever.

I loved singing 'I Get a Kick Out of You' from the show, especially the lyrics 'some get a kick from cocaine', which reminded me so much of Sapphire Advertising—coke-sniffing really got in the way of productivity. They laid me off not because I wasn't any good, but because I refused to partake in snorting that shit up my nose. Been there, seen it, done it. They gave me three months' money. Nice. So now I am a PA for a recruitment company in Bayswater: less money, but more free time for me.

I loved Showcase, and it made my family and my Lucy so proud of me. I hate to say this, but out of all of my serious boyfriends—there's only been three by the way—I really wished Oscar had been there to see me perform. Hmm, oh well, it was me that walked out on him.

After Showcase, I got myself an agent, Yvonne Laurie, Soho, a bit of an Okay Yah. She tried to get me some auditions for West End musicals, but no luck, so she put me forward to do some backing singing for two French DJs based in London, Louis and Timothée, for a dance track called 'Dance Like Marcel Marceau'. Yes, it was as bad as it sounded, but I was getting paid cash. Double nice. So, I went to a recording studio in Hackney Road, Bethnal Green. Both Louis and Timothée were fucking undressing me with their eyes. I told the perverts to stop or I was walking with no refunds. I wasn't being over-sensitive—I know creeps when I see them.

Then the producer, he owned the studio, a jolly black guy in his early forties, overweight but it suited him, Isaac, asked me to do the vocals, without Louis and Timothée. I said okay, but I wanted another £100 now and for them to only come back when I had left. They both agreed, thanks to some let's just say 'gentle persuasion' by Isaac. I knew Isaac had an alternative motive, but I could sense it wasn't sexual.

'Could you hold fire for ten minutes? I want my partner to hear you sing,' Isaac asked with a kind smile.

I knew straight away it was an audition of some kind. 'No worries. I'll come out of the live room and wait in the control room, if you don't mind, Isaac?'

'Yeah, of course. Make yourself at home, Steph. Won't be long.' About five minutes later, Isaac walks into the control room with a well-built white guy, early thirties, in a bright white shirt, rolled-up sleeves and the first top buttons undone to show off his Curb gold chain, with matching bright white Nike trainers, as he sports a pair of perfectly ironed khaki chinos. But what really struck me was his over-the-top glowing tan, a real lobster look. I had to put my left arm over my eyes, he was that bright.

'Steph, this is Doc Savage,' Isaac says, as both of them sit down to face me.

'Hello, Doc Savage.'

'Hey, Steph. Please call me "Doc".'

'I take it you aren't a real quack then?'

'No, no, no. Doc Savage. Never heard of him? He's the first superhero. The Man of Bronze?'

'No, not really into the whole superhero thing. Had a boyfriend who was bonkers about all that.' Great, I thought, I am going to be auditioned by a 30-something fella, naming himself after a superhero.

'I'll lend ya some of me Doc Savage books and comics if you like?'

'As I said, not really my thing.' I wasn't going to say, 'Yes, please.'

'Direct—like it. Okay let's hear you sing then,' requested Doc with a smile.

'Direct demand—like it.' Both Isaac and Doc chuckled. Good, because I learnt from an early age to make sure any relationship, business or social, is on an even keel from the onset, otherwise the fuckers will have control over you all the time. 'Happy to sing guys, but not this song: "Oh dance, like the clown, oh dance, never frown, oh dance, yeah dance... like Marcel Marceau."'

Again, Isaac and Doc giggle. Then Isaac leans back, grabs an acoustic guitar, leans forwards and says, 'Okay, name a song and I'll see if I can play it.'

'Light My Fire.' Fuck, that was one of Oscar's favourites.

'Nice. Love it. Okay, S, on the count of four.' The opening lyrics, 'You know that it would be untrue, you know that I would be a liar if I was to say to you, boy...' (I changed the lyrics slightly) '...we couldn't get much higher' flew out of my mouth like a nightingale. I had them in the palm of my hand.

As Isaac strummed the final chord of 'Light My Fire', Doc looked at me with real respect and said, 'Okay, we are creating an all-girl group to rival The Spice Girls. Isaac is the music man—he knows how to pen a song or two, there ain't no instrument worth playing that he can't play. Top producer, he's got this studio, which we can use any time. Me, I am the manager, business man. I'll get the PAs, the DJ and radio plugs, the interviews, the money, the record deal, we ain't fucking about. We've got three girls already, just need a fourth. You interested, Steph?'

'I'll think about it,' I casually replied, but deep down this little White City girl was really doing somersaults in her heart.

■ ■ ■

'You must be Steph,' are the first words I hear, as I walk into Isaac's studio to meet the rest of the girls for the first time on a Sunday morning. I turn around to see a beautiful young black girl, who could easily pass as the kid sister of Naomi Campbell. She looks confident and bubbly with her jet-black hair tied back, in a tight white T-shirt, three-quarter-length light jeans and cute Adidas trainers with a gold stripe.

'That's right. You're Chelsea?' I reply, as Doc and Isaac have given me a lowdown on all the girls, and no doubt they've given the girls the lowdown on me.

'So, my reputation precedes me,' says Chelsea, grinning ear to ear.

'Hey, Steph. I'm Lacy Blanc,' butts in a cute, petite freckle-faced girl with skin so white, like a china doll, in a red polka-dot dress matching her red corkscrew shoulder-length hair.

Doc tells me that Lacy is French, but she sounds as much French as I sound German. 'Hi, Lacy, love your dress.'

'Oh this? Got it from Portobello,' Lacy replies with a sense of pride.

'I've spent a small fortune down Portobello,' I say, as I start to feel a good vibe from Chelsea and Lacy.

But my positivity is short-lived when an icy voice cuts in: 'We 'ere to talk about glad rags or fucking music?' I look round and see an olive-skinned girl with long wavy black hair, dressed in a black laced sheath dress with flat closed-back thong sandals, sitting by the mixing desk in an attempt to give the air of authority. Zeta Zahaf, from Westbourne Park, Greek father, Libyan mother, went to Italia Conti but got expelled for knocking out a teacher, which I do find amusing.

'Hello, Zeta.' I emphasise her name as I say it.

'Hello, Stephanie,' replies Zeta in an equally cutting tone. Zeta and I start to eye each other up.

Then the studio door swings open, Isaac and Doc strut in, making Zeta jump out of the chair and stand next to me—chicken. 'Okay, girls. Now we've got the pleasantries out of the way, let's get down to business,' announces Doc as he steps into the middle of the control room, with the girls and me huddling around him ready for a team talk, while Isaac walks over to the mixing desk and obviously his chair.

'Girls, you've all been hand-picked by me and Isaac, all of you have done a bit of studio, live work and all that, so we know we can hit the ground running. Time is of the essence—we'll record a track today, see how we work together, get it in the can. But listen, girls. I am telling you, if we stick to the plan, we will be signed within six months, number one within nine months.' As Doc is speaking, I can't help but notice how much brighter his skin is than when I first met him.

'Nice words, Doc. Okay, girls, ready to make some music?' chirps Isaac and, like obedient school children, we all turn to face him. I wonder if The Supremes went through the same introduction.

'Okay, we are going to do one track today. No lead vocals. You'll get a line of the verse each, then all together on the chorus. It's a funky little number called 'Raspberry Ripple'. And, girls. Ta-dah! That's the name of the band—Raspberry Ripple. You like it?'

'No, I fucking don't,' I snap. There's no way I'm recording or going on stage with that name. From my outburst, I sense a slight silent hostility.

Then Zeta states, 'Isaac, that's a kids' name. Look at us—do we look like kids?' Zeta and I exchange glances: she is strong, just like me.

'Okay, I hear ya, Steph, Zet. Let's do the song please. Raspberry Ripple—you like the name, Chelsea, Lacy?' says Doc, quickly bringing order.

'Not really, Doc,' says Chelsea rather sheepishly, with Lacy nodding beside her. Brilliant, we've shown to Doc and Isaac we ain't no pushover.

'Okay, girls, you don't like the name, huh? But you're going to love the song,' says Isaac. As he hits the large green playback button, the sound of a wah-wah guitar, a thumping bassline and funky drums pumps out of the speakers. I like this, oh boy, do I like this.

Isaac gets up, starts to dance like some drunken uncle at a wedding, then breaks into a kind of sweet Marvin Gaye-type soul voice. 'Hey, I am your raspberry ripple, please don't tickle, I am your raspberry ripple, my love is worth triple, I am a naughty raspberry ripple, a sexy raspberry ripple, squeeze your raspberry…'

'Fuck no. This is worse than "Dance Like Marcel Marceau". Sorry, Isaac, you can make a tune, but you ain't Bob Dylan.' I told you, I always speak my mind.

'Steph, we've got to record this, get a tune out there. Now, come on, girls, get in the live room and sing,' orders Doc.

'I ain't singing that shit either,' pipes up Zeta.

'Thanks, Zeta,' I say, as I am genuinely taken aback by her support again. I look at Chelsea and Lacy.

'I'm with Steph and Zeta,' says Lacy.

'Yeah, Isaac, the music is fucking cool bruv, but the words, nay,' says a rather rattled Chelsea.

'Then you write the fucking words,' screams Isaac. I do love a bit of aggro—hanging around White City and The Magnificent Six, you sort of get a love for it.

'Okay, we will,' I retort.

'Fine, Doc and me will piss off down the pub, be back in two hours. So you'd better crack on.'

With that, he and Doc storm out of the studio. I don't think they expected a mutiny so quickly, but the uprising has brought me, Zeta, Chelsea and Lacy closer, like a real band, not puppets.

'That's the title and chorus, girls,' I announce to my new song writing partners.

'What is, Steph?' enquires Lacy.

'"Crack On". Goes nice over that guitar,' I reply with relish.

'Hmm, that girl has got soul. Love it,' says an enthusiastic Chelsea, as she puts her arm around me. I look at Zeta—she is smiling, but behind that smile, I can see her plotting. Nevertheless, I smile back.

The writing of 'Crack On' is going well. Nearly finished it. We haven't decided on a band name yet, but we are really getting to know each other. Chelsea is a chirpy Brixton girl. Doc discovered her at his cousin's wedding, singing backing vocals with some Motown cover band. Her voice is okay, but she is stunning—I think that is what got her the part. Chelsea loves her soul, funk, R 'n' B, hip hop music—she's a bit of an anorak, to be honest. So am I, too, when it comes to music.

Lacy, a Hampstead girl, still lives with her folks, as does Chelsea, but they are only 21, bless. Lacy is a bit more of an indie, Britpop girl. Loves Oasis, Blur, Pulp and all that. Got a real soft singing voice. Isaac discovered her the same as me, as Lacy was doing backing vocals for her then boyfriend's band, Great Expectations. He got jealous after Isaac approached her, so she called it a day. Good girl.

Zeta doesn't give too much away. She's 25—Jesus, I am the oldest in the band. Anyway, Zeta got the gig for the band, because Isaac knew her from here and there. Works for some bank. Just bought a place in Wapping. That's all she is telling us. But, I hate to say it, her voice is good. Is she better than me? I don't know, but we are both sopranos, we can span five octaves, whilst Chelsea and Lacy are mezzo-sopranos, span three—I learnt all about different vocal ranges when I was doing musicals.

The studio door opens slightly, then Doc's head pokes out, 'All right girls? You struggling? Look, Isaac is a bit pissed off. You turned down "Raspberry Ripple"—it's got number one written all over it.'

'It's got shit written all over it. Listen to this—"Crack On" ' I announce, as all of us stand up and go side by side like the England team before singing the national anthem. I count, 'One… two… three… four,' then me, Zeta, Chelsea and Lacy go a cappella: 'This is your finest hour, knock out all doubters, this is your finest hour, they will all admire. Crack on, don't crack up, crack on, don't crack up. This is your finest hour, bloom like a flower, this is your finest hour, feel the power, crack on, don't crack up, crack on, don't crack up. I said: sisters, crack on, don't crack up, you hear me, sisters, it's your finest hour, knock out. I say knock out all doubters, KO KO KO, crack on, don't crack up, don't crack up.' We all fade out on: 'Don't crack up.'

'My word, girls, that is a hit. Let's go to work—I'll go and get Isaac before he gets too pissed,' says a highly impressed Doc.

■ ■ ■

I am home now, feet up, cold Bud in hand, listening with pride to the final mix of 'Crack On' on a cassette. It's a belter. So proud, happy and slightly drunk. Only problem we had was Zeta. She went full Mariah Carey, trying to hit a seventh octave, bloody show-off. Zeta doesn't want to be in a band. She wants a solo career. I can feel it. She's using us to help herself. Fuck her. Anyway, I've got to think of a name: something powerful, strong, sexy, catchy.

Lucy will be back in a bit—I'll send her out to the offie for some more booze. I am a lazy cow, but I really fancy getting pissed.

Lucy told me when she got in that she's got the chance to travel to New York to pursue her career. So, we spent the evening, dancing, drinking, reminiscing, chatting and crying. We are both at the start of a new adventure. Going to miss her. She's my girl.

Called Micky the landlord this morning from work to hand our notice in and the day just got better, as I've been fired with immediate effect. Nice. All my own doing—been late too many times, too many sick days, all the usual shit. Cried when they told me, jumped for joy when I left the office. I love it when a plan comes together, as Hannibal from The A-Team says.

I'll move in with my folks, South Woodford, sign on. Double nice. Going to turn down any auditions or studio work from my agent, as I am going to put everything I have into this band. Also, I ain't short of a few quid. Still got my deposit in a savings account for the place Oscar and I never bought, but I won't bother telling the Job Centre. Why should I? It's my money.

Having a band meeting tonight at The Churchill Arms, Notting Hill way. It's Doc's local. Been there a few times: nice pub. The meeting is mainly to chat about a name for the band–no need, though, as I've got one—song writing, as Isaac is going to give us loads of tracks on a cassette for us to pen some more words, and a cover version, make it ours. I like that concept a lot.

Doc and Isaac have just walked in as me and the girls are chatting. Well, Zeta isn't really joining in—fuck her, arrogant bitch. Jesus, Doc looks like a bleeding Oompa Loompa from Charlie and The Chocolate Factory, he is glowing so much. I've put my Ray Bans on—not to give it the Liam, but Doc is literally burning my eyes.

'You been on the sunbed?' I must ask, even though I know the answer.

'Yeah, treble session today. They had a few cancellations, so I slipped them a few quid, you know for a drink, then had a quick top-up, just 20 mins like, on my sunbed at home' says Doc.

'Looking good, Doc, a real Ibiza hunk,' says Zeta, in her creepy way.

'Thanks, Zeta, I've got to look the part for those A & R record executives.'

'What, looking like a bronze statue? Doc, you are going gold, just like Shirley Eaton in Goldfinger,' I say with jest.

'Who?' asks Chelsea.

'You must know it. The girl that is suffocated by gold paint from that James

Bond film, Goldfinger. Fuck, that's the cover we should do: "Goldfinger", by Shirley Bassey. What a song.'

'I know that song. Shit it's good. "Goldfinger, he's the man, the man with the Midas touch, a spider's touch, such a cold finger,"' sings Lacy. I smile at my beautiful friend.

'I know that tune. It's wicked, yes,' adds Chelsea. Three out of four band members: we all look at Zeta.

'If we're going to do James Bond, I'd rather do "Live and Let Die".'

I don't bother replying, just look at Doc and Isaac, who look at me, then Zeta, then the rest of the girls, and Isaac replies to all of us, 'Guns and Roses done that a few years back. I reckon "Goldfinger", loop those horns, beef it up, yes that will work. A real mutha fucka choon.'

Good, a step in the right direction, as Zeta doesn't get her way. I know the next battle will be the lead vocals, but I'll wait until we are in the studio, save my energy, as I've got a bigger fight now: the band's name. 'Look, I've got an idea for a name. It came to me last night after reading a book of mine from my middle school, round at my parents.'

'What's that then? Jack and Jill?' cuts in a bitchy Zeta.

'I meant to say history book. Found it in the loft. Anyway, that ain't important. We should call ourselves Boadicea,' I announce with gratification.

'What the fuck, girl?' asks the ever-educated Zeta.

'Da Boadicea. You know the woman from AD 60. Rode a chariot with blades on the wheel. Led her people to stand up to the Roman Empire. A real rebel. A bit of a looker as well. Zeta, surely you know of her: a famous historical figure, an inspiration to all women? Now that's real fucking girl power.'

Doc Savage jumps up and says, 'Fucking yes! Steph, you are a genius.' Everyone seems delighted, apart from Zeta, as she puts her head down in annoyance and jealousy.

■ ■ ■

This afternoon, we record "Goldfinger". The lead vocal is mine—going to fight Zeta for this. We haven't been in the studio for ages, as Doc wanted us to hang out, work on our vocals, be creative, pen some more lyrics, and choose the best two tracks for the demo, along with "Crack On" and "Goldfinger". We have, two class songs, "Midnight Folk" and "I Wanna Be Free, I Wanna Be Me", lyrics written by me and the girls. Oh yes, Boadicea is taking shape. Watch out, Geri, Mel C, Mel B, Victoria and Emma—Stephanie, Zeta, Chelsea and Lacy are coming… Yay.

I am a little late getting to the studio, as the tubes were a bit fucked and I needed to pick something up from Boots. As I enter, I feel a sombre mood. Chelsea and Lacy are huddled together on the couch, crying. Isaac is sitting down, looking so sad. Zeta sees me then starts to cry, like my entrance acted as her prompt to become a victim. Then she looks at me and says abruptly, 'Doc's dead.'

'What?' I can't believe what I have just heard.

13

Stephanie's Song—Part Two

I gaze at Chelsea, Lacy and Zeta: Chels and Lac are clearly grief-stricken, whilst Zet seems to be shedding crocodile tears—nothing about her seems genuine.

'How?' I am sure this question has been asked numerous times this afternoon, but I need to know. All possibilities are entering my head: drug overdose, heart attack, stabbing, road accident.

'Baked himself alive, that's all we know,' sobs Lacy through tears and snot.

'I found him this morning under his sunbed. Got 'ere an hour ago—had to wait for the Old Bill,' says Isaac, as he tries to regain his composure.

'No way, Is. You're taking the piss. He's going to bowl through that door any second now,' I reply in desperate hope.

'Steph, I wish it was a wind-up, but Doc is dead,' says Isaac in a matter of fact manner.

I take a deep breath and with an air of authority ask, 'How? I mean, people don't just burn themselves alive under a sunbed. We need to know, Isaac.'

Isaac grabs his grubby and torn packet of 20 Benson & Hedges Gold from the mixing desk, pulls out his silver Zippo lighter from his light grey jogging bottoms, sparks up his cigarette, takes a long drag, blows out four perfect smoke rings, and then says, 'We all saw Doc was getting addicted to the sunbed. I mean, he bloody glowed in the dark. Yesterday, we had a meet to discuss your photo shoot this Tuesday and a cheeky trip for Doc to Ibiza to get you girls a PA at Amnesia & Pacha.'

'We are still doing the photo shoot and the Ibiza gigs aren't we?' asks the self-centred Zeta.

'Z, shut it,' I snap.

Zeta is about to reply but is cut short by Isaac. 'Not now, baby. Let me tell ya what happened.'

'Okay, hon.' Baby... hon... oh my God, Isaac is sleeping with Zeta. Doc and I predicted that.

'Yeah, hon, please go on,' I reply with raised eyebrows. Isaac snarls his right top lip slightly at my sarcastic tone.

'Hmm, so I go to meet Doc. He calls me on the mobile just as I'm getting to Notting Hill. "Is, got a bit of agg at Marco's Lettino. Need backup." I put the pedal on the metal, thinking Doc is about to get a hiding. I lose the motor...'

'Did you find it again?'

My God, can you believe this? Either Zeta is dense or she can't stand not being the centre of attention.

'It means parking the car, baby. So, I run to Marco's. That's his favourite sunbed and tanning shop. Been there before, but as you can see, don't really need a sunbed. Ha!' Zeta is the only one that chuckles. 'As I get there, he's squaring up to Marco, saying shit like, "You fucking wop. We won the war. You fucking cheated in the World Cup. Fuck Paolo Rossi, fuck Dino Zoff, fuck all you eyeties. Shit food, shit country." Marco ain't a geezer to mess with. I can see he's about to lamp Doc, so I step in the middle, pushing Doc back. Marco looks at me and says, "Isaac, tell your friend no more sunbeds. He's crazy, he'll get cancer." I look at Doc, he doesn't look right—he's bright orange.'

'Doc never struck me as a racist, Isaac. Always seemed to respect all races and religions,' I state in Doc's defence.

'Before he got into Acid House, popping pills, he was known as Nick the Nazi round Barnet in the early 80s,' says Isaac.

'Why Barnet?' asks Chelsea. My word, she's joined the dense crowd, too.

'That's where he's from. Nick Shaw, Barnet lad, told me. Him and his mates started going to Acid House to smash up the black kids, but he started taking Es. Loved the vibe, started serving up, loved the money. That's how I met him—not the summer of love, but the following year, 89, some do in Clink Street, Shine or something. Good crowd. I was doing the sound system, just on the water, Nick was there, selling pills, we got talking, gave him my number, just thought it was E chat. But he called me a week later about a sound system for a do in Mill Hill. He liked me, I liked him, he started investing money in the sound system, then we called it Isaac's Bangers.'

'Then it started to grow, Nick was out and about getting us gigs, warehouse parties, clubs, house parties, garden parties, weddings, even the odd bar mitzvah. We were coining it in. I was putting my money aside. Nick must have been saving his money too, cos in 92, he pissed off to Asia. That was it. I bought him out and sold Isaac's Bangers' sound system and client list. Sold my motor, downsized my house. My wife went spare, divorced me the following year, took my kids, but I wanted a recording studio, wanted to be the Hit Factory of East London. Never made it as a musician, thought I was getting the breaks, supported Aswad, Misty in Roots, all the big names.'

My God, Isaac is telling us his bloody life story. Shall I put the kettle on, pull up a pew? 'That's interesting, but what about Doc?'

'Okay, Steph. Hold your horses. Nick comes back from India three years later, all tanned up, now calling himself Doc Savage, a name he got from DJ-ing in Goa. Doc tracks me down. He's got a bit of money. I didn't ask questions, you don't with Doc, but he can always pull in a few quid. He invests in the studio Happy days. But we didn't get the hit acts or the up-and-coming bands, so that's when we decided to form our own group.'

'Yes, we've worked that one out. Please, Isaac. Doc, your best friend?' I am now getting highly irate.

'Sorry, you are right, Steph. So, I get Doc to the motor, no dramas, but he's weeping like. I know he's got a sunbed in his bedroom. Fink, I'll get in there, cut a wire or take him to my place. But he insists he wants to go home for a sleep. He seems calm now. So, we get to his flat, he's all subdued. I find a parking space, we both get out.'

'Then Doc kicks off again: "I need a tan for Ibiza, I need that tan for the clubs. I need it. Fuck." "Doc, your tan ain't going to make or break the deal, you look like the Tango Man." Then he gets all shirty again, "Come again? Do I fuck look like the Tango Man." "No, the Tango Man looks like you," I

144

snap. Doc goes berserk: "You know what? Fuck you, fuck Boadicea. You are all sacked. I'll get meself another producer, songwriter. There's loads of girls that can sing, better looking ones."

'That was it. I shout out: "Fine, Doc." I get into the motor and come here, throw meself into the music, get the track ready for today, work on some new ideas for you girls.

'Fuck, the barnies Doc and I have had over the years, I know from experience, it always blows over. Always. So, I call his landline, mobile, no answer. Fall asleep 'ere, wake up, no messages on the studio answer machine, no missed calls on my mobile. So, I go over to his place—got the spare keys as he's got the spares for my pad. As I get there, I smell smoke: you know, like when you've burnt a pizza in the oven after the boozer. I open the front door, all this smoke bellows out. Lazy fucker couldn't be bothered to put new batteries in his smoke alarm. So, I head to his bedroom, see the smoke coming out of the sunbed, and by the side is an empty bottle of Jack Daniels and a few roach ends. Must have had a drink and smoke beforehand.'

'I dive over to the sunbed, open it up. There he is, burnt up like a jacket potato. All I needed was some tuna and sweetcorn mayo and a side dish of coleslaw and I would have been in Spudulike.'

I just say, 'I'm out of here,' turn around, open the studio door and head out into the street, laughing and crying. I need a drink or two. Went to the Marksman pub, only a five-minute walk. They know me there as that's where we would go after recording or a quick meet.

■ ■ ■

'What a surprise, Lacy. And you didn't think to call my mobile or find me in the Marksman pub?'

She's just called me at home, two days after I went AWOL from the studio. Been too cut up to see anyone, as I do feel like I am surrounded by imbeciles, cowards and traitors. It seems that intelligence, bravery and loyalty are dying traits.

'Soz, Steph. I called your mobile, it went straight to your answer machine.'

'You didn't think about leaving a message?'

'I don't know how. I haven't got one of them telephones—too complicated for me.'

'It's the same as leaving a message on a landline. Bloody Hell, Lacy.' What did I say about imbeciles?

'Sorry, Steph.'

'Why didn't you come and look for me then?' I need a drink. I know it's only ten, but boy, do I need a drink.

'Didn't think about that. Thought you had gone home.'

'Why didn't you call my house then? You could have left a message. We've got an answer machine. You know how to use one of them?'

'Yes, I do. My parents have got one.'

I put the phone down and head to the kitchen. Cornflakes or a beer? The telephone rings again. I know it's Lacy, but I can't be fucked.

Well, Boadicea went ahead and recorded 'Goldfinger' without me. Yes, you've guessed it, Zeta done the lead and my so-called friends, Lacy and Chelsea, done the backing vocals, with Isaac in the chair. I thought they would be mourning. Yes, I know life goes on, you have no choice, but to do it the day after he died and when one member of the band (me) is clearly upset is well and truly out of order. They could have waited to at least after the funeral. I mean, we ain't going anywhere.

I am having cornflakes. Have a beer later: folks are away, Hayling Island, they've got a holiday home there. Gave me the keys once. Once only, as I went down there with Oscar and the rest of The Magnificent Six, and a few girls. It was madness, especially when Rooster turned up with loads of goodies. Let's just say we had a Rolling Stones weekend.

I suppose I might as well tell you the truth. Doc and I were speaking and meeting a lot. No, I didn't fancy him and he never tried it on with me. I never felt uncomfortable with Doc. He had a vision, to get to the top, and saw in me his captain in Boadicea who shared his vision. He had even talked about sacking Zeta, either replacing her or going out as a three-piece girl group. He said I argued about the band cos I cared; he knew that Zeta argued cos she loves chaos. She made a few advances on Doc but he backed her. He was a pro, a real pro, a ducker and diver, yes, but he had an energy that is sometimes hard to find. With him gone, I have lost a good friend and a powerful ally. I

146

wish Lucy was here: I need my girl. Even Oscar, he always got me, cheered me up, when I was down.

Doc's funeral was a sombre affair. Sorry, I am stating the bleeding obvious, as they usually are. It was at Bells Hill Burial Ground, Barnet. I went on my own. It had been the first time I had seen Lacy, Chelsea, Zeta and Isaac since the day I walked out. Went to the wake after at his parents' home, a mixture of grieving relatives and 30-something clubbers.

I was sitting in the corner, drinking perhaps my third drink of the day, when Isaac came over. 'Steph, we want you back. It's been a difficult time for all of us. I know you are annoyed that we went ahead with the recording but that was our way of dealing with it. Look, come to the studio next Thursday and we'll do "I Wanna Be Me, I Wanna Be Free."' I didn't say a word, I just nodded.

■ ■ ■

'I wanna be me, hic, I'm going to be me, you can't stop me, from being free, hic, free, free, free, you can't stop me from being me. Ain't no job, ain't no law, ain't no lover, you know, that can't stop me from being free, free, free, free. I wanna be me, oh yeah, hic… Take five, Isaac. Give me a second, I can nail it,' I plead as I look through the live room window into the control room. Yet my request isn't met with open arms, as Isaac is clearly annoyed. Lacy looks certainly concerned, Chelsea is reading a magazine, whilst Zeta looks pleased that I am falling apart before her eyes. My fault, though, as I thought a few drinks before going in the studio would calm my nerves. Big mistake.

'Steph, look, this is your fifth take and the worst one. I can't waste any more time. You're going to have to let Zeta give it a go. Sorry, but that's the way it is,' shouts Isaac through the control room microphone.

Like a spoilt child who can't get her own way, I storm out of the live room and head straight to the pub. I need that drink and to get away from them. As I walk to the pub, I am starting to believe this was a set-up for me to fail. I know it, I can feel it. Call it intuition.

'Been yonks, Steph. How you been?' I put my fifth—or is it my sixth?— Bud down and see Edward Savage, aka Eddie the Casual, looking as dapper as ever, in a nice two-button brown blazer, white shirt, dark jeans and dark black Gucci loafers.

'Bloody Hell, Eddie. How's Oscar?'

'I'm good, Steph. Thanks for asking.'

Shit, the first thing I ask is about the welfare of my ex-boyfriend from years ago. 'Sorry, Eddie, how's you and Lou?' I always liked Louise: a real good laugh, but after I walked from Oscar, I cut myself off from all of The Magnificent Six and their entourage.

'Married. Just had our first-born. Little girl—Isabella.'

'Congratulations, Eddie. Seriously, so happy for you and Lou. Is Oscar well? You know, has he tied the knot?'

Eddie chuckles, pulls out his Marlboro Red cigarettes and gold lighter, offers me one. I turn him down. He should remember I don't smoke. Well, the odd spliff.

'No, he's lodging with Wilf.'

'No way! Hudson Close? Him and Wilf? Fuck, that must be insane.'

'It is.'

'You still live in the Bush?'

'Moved out six months ago Surrey way: a place called Esher, straight down the A3. Lou and me wanted to bring up Isabella "and hopefully more kids" away from White City.'

'Oscar always said you were the snob of The Magnificent Six.'

'Cheeky cow. 'Ere, why are you sitting 'ere on your Jack Jones getting slaughtered? That ain't the Steph I used to know.'

'In a band, but it ain't working out. Came 'ere to, well, you know. Anyway, what are you doing 'ere in East London now you're a Surrey boy?'

''Eard you were singing in a band. Bumped into Lucy's folks a while back, when I was seeing Wilf and Oscar.'

I am overcome with joy as I ask, 'Does Oscar know that I am, well, was in a band?'

Eddie smiles that knowing smile that I've always adored. 'Yeah, he does.'

'And?' My God, I feel like I am at school again.

'He was pleased for you, really he was.' I smile as I start to get butterflies in my stomach. 'To answer your question, I am here with Raj. He's gone to see his cousin up the road. We're looking at buying a few shitholes, doing them up.'

'I don't suppose you say: "This time next year", like Del Boy, as you probably are a millionaire already.'

'On paper, I am,' Eddie boasts. But who can blame him? He done it and I am so proud of him.

So, I reply, 'I always thought you would be. Well done, baby.'

Then Eddie's mood changes from one of pride to that of concern. 'Steph, get yourself a coffee, sober up and get back in there. Fight your ground. That's the Steph we all love. You're a White City girl—the best.'

I put my beer down, kiss Eddie on the cheek, then he pulls me in and we hug. Boy, does this feel good, just like the old days. I pull back, look into his eyes and say, 'See ya, Eddie. Well done on being a father. Give my love to Louise and Oscar.'

'Thanks, I will… Oscar… still misses you.' Eddie's final words fill me with belief and courage, as I turn around and head back to the studio. Come on, Zeta, if you want it.

Just as I am about to approach the entrance of the studio, I kick myself for not exchanging numbers with Eddie.

'That sounds like bloody Katrina and the Waves. Where's the soul, the passion? Jesus.' Clearly my emotions and the alcohol have got the better of me, but the playback I am hearing for 'I Wanna Be Me, I Wanna Be Free' is abysmal—a cheap Europop record. I visualised a real funky house track, loved by kids across the world. 'Listen, S. Since Doc's death, you've been all over the place, pissed most of the time. Go home,' snaps Isaac.

'Fuck you,' I scream, then I storm out, heading towards the Tube station.

■ ■ ■

Cold chicken korma is not the best thing to step on after a night of heavy drinking. Fell asleep in the front room, watching all my music compilation videos. The Tube, The Chart Show, Top of The Pops—still got them. First, I was inspired, loving it, dancing. Then I started to cry, as my dream—well, okay, it wasn't my dream two years ago, but it is now—is being pulled from under my feet by Zeta. The pressure got to me so much that I started drinking. Never been a heavy drinker before, just a social one.

The phone is ringing. 'Yeah,' I snap as I answer it.

'Steph, it's me, Isaac.'

'Yeah, I know.' The weak fat bastard really isn't my favourite person.

'Look, we need to talk.'

'What? Zeta given you the heave-ho?'

'I know you are kidding. Meet at the Marksman pub tonight, about seven. Stay on the orange juice, okay, Steph? Okay?'

'Yes, okay.' I slam the phone down and head to the kitchen to make a bacon sandwich.

I feel like an outsider. All the girls and Isaac are sitting opposite me. 'Steph, good to see you're not drinking,' says Isaac in a patronising manner.

'If I want a drink, I will have one,' I harshly reply.

'We want you in the band. You're a great singer, pen good lyrics—that's when you're sober. We are going to record "Midnight Folk" next week. I know a fella to act as our manager and we're going to…' Isaac pauses with embarrassment. Out of the corner of my eye, I see Zeta nudge her fat fella.

I snarl and ask, 'What are we going to do?'

'Change the band's name.'

'Come again?'

'Change the band's name,' Isaac meekly says.

'Yes, I did hear you. It was a rhetorical question,' I say with aggressive overtones. Don't fuck with a White City girl.

'Oh, I see. We are calling it Zeta, cos…' Isaac says rather sheepishly.

'Yes, because you are sleeping with Zeta and she…' I point directly at my adversary. '…has got you wrapped around her little finger, Isaac. Wake up and smell the coffee.'

'Listen, girl. Don't point your finger at me,' ripostes Zeta.

'Isaac, I am telling you now, she will drop you for a producer who's made it. You know that.'

Then my pent-up anger erupts as I leap over the table and start to lay into

Zeta. Should have done this on the first day. I am too fast and strong for the bitch. I hear the girls scream then I am pulled back. I look up and see Isaac and Henry the landlord.

'You're nuts, you're fucking nuts,' yells Isaac.

'And barred,' adds Henry.

'Fuck you, all of you,' I reply as I head for the entrance, knowing full well I have been sacked from the band.

■ ■ ■

I took the breakup of Boadicea so bad that I went on the piss non-stop for a month. Eventually, my parents sent me to stay with my older sister, Dawn, and her family in Poole, Dorset, to sober up. I went to a few Alcoholics Anonymous meetings in Poole but found myself having a drink after cos all I was hearing was despair, not hope, so I've cut down on the booze now, something called 'controlled drinking'.

I was only in Boadicea for six months, but it felt like a lifetime, as I gave the band my heart, soul and passion. I would go to bed not just dreaming but believing Boadicea would be bigger than The Spice Girls. Our music was more funky and soulful than theirs. Whilst Geri and the girls dressed glam and loud, Doc and I had this vision of Boadicea in hippie chic dresses, like we were dining out on the French Riviera in the early 70s. Think the elegance, beauty and sex appeal of a youthful Raquel Welch and Faye Dunaway and you'll get the picture.

From what I heard, a month after I was sacked from Boadicea—just before it became Zeta—Isaac, under the instructions of Zeta, sacked Lacy, kept Chelsea to do the backing vocals. But once Isaac and Zeta had recorded a whole new demo—I think it was six songs—Chelsea was given the elbow. But no record company, major or independent was interested, not one. Don't ask me why or how, just know it went tits up. Zeta left Isaac, surprise, surprise. Heard she pissed off to Ibiza. Sure she's got her claws into some other sucker by now. Of course she would, she loves using people—men and women.

I found all this out because I had to call Isaac. No, I wasn't calling him to ask for a second chance—fuck that—but to let him know that I had proof that I had co-written the lyrics for three songs and there was no way I was going to be shafted for my royalties. I waited for about three months when I was fighting fit again before I called the git. Isaac literally broke down on the telephone, telling me how he was used by Zeta, how he regretted sacking me, Lacy and Chelsea, that the pressure of the record companies' rejection drove Zeta to leave him. Then he had the cheek to ask if I wanted to reform Boadicea with Lacy and Chelsea. I politely told him to fuck off.

But I already knew that there was something wrong with the band, as my mother told me when I would have my weekly phone call to her from Poole, that Lacy and Chelsea had called a few times, asking for my new address or my new number, cos I ditched my mobile the day I got fired from the band. But the old girl, God bless her, wouldn't tell them because she knew I needed space and time to heal. But once I knew Boadicea was well and truly over, that's when I decided to leave Poole and return to London, my true home.

Here I am, back at White City, renting Lucy's old room at her parents' house. They are like family to me. I hate to say this, but I feel more open and relaxed with Lucy's old girl than my own. By the way, Lucy is rocking it in New York, living in Greenwich Village, taking the photos, making the money. Good girl, so proud of her, but I do miss my bestie. But she is coming back soon for a short holiday. Nice.

Why have I moved back to White City? One, South Woodford was a stopgap, before I thought I was going to hit the big time. How wrong I was. Two, never truly felt at home in South Woodford. Three, I can't afford to rent a flat yet and four, I have missed this place. It's been a few years, since I set foot here. The memories, good and bad, but it's my home, my true home, and it's what made me the girl I am today.

As for a job, start looking tomorrow. I did work when I was at Poole, in a bakers. Loved it. But I am going to find something to do with music. Yes, I know I am a late bloomer, but shit, I am only 28—I was 27 when I joined Boadicea. But I don't want to be a singer in a band, do backing vocals or be in a musical. Maybe A&R, management, songwriter, producer, something creative and behind the scenes. I'll probably start at the bottom somewhere, but I've got contacts from my clubbing days, my time in advertising, and Isaac owes me big time. I haven't forgiven him, fuck that, but I am going to use him just like he used me, prick.

At first, as you know, my sacking from Boadicea nearly broke me, but now it's given me strength, drive, belief and determination to be successful in music. Rejection and failure either makes or breaks you, it's that simple, it really is. Plus, I've got the money to buy a PC and that music software, Cubase. Heard that one of The Magnificent Six, Dino, dabbles in the computer game. How do I know? Because he flogged one to Lucy's old man, Dennis, the other month. Always liked Dino, liked all of them, and of course loved Oscar.

Here I am, walking past Hammersmith Park, down South Africa Road, heading to Pilcher's to get some chips, for old time's sake.

Oh my God. It's him. It's Oscar, looking lean and healthy, and he's gone all Mod again. I just knew he would love that Oasis look, and I bet he's over the moon that Paul Weller has made a comeback. The true love of my life, strutting towards me, just like in the summer of 1983, but this time dressed like a 90s Mod, not as a Casual.

Oscar has seen me. He is crossing the road. He's smiling, really smiling. I smile back. 'Good to see you, Steph. 'Eard you were moving back to the manor, bumped into Dennis the other day.'

'I am so sorry, I walked out on you, I really am.' The words just come flying out of my mouth. I can't play it cool, because I am still in love with him. The years apart made me see this, but I had to go on my own journey to discover who I am.

'Well, I ain't going to lie. I hated you for a few years, I really did. Then I gave up the gear, slowed down on the booze, started seeing things differently.'

I am touched. Maybe it was destiny, I don't know, but I do know I haven't been this happy for ages. 'Same here, Oscar.'

He just smiles and shrugs his shoulders, then says, 'Sorry your band never worked out. Lucy's old gal told me.'

'Shit happens. It wasn't meant to be.'

Oscar just chuckles, then asks, 'Where are you going?'

'Pilcher's. You barred?'

'No, Wilf put in a word. Mind if I join you? I am starving.'

Brilliant. He got my hint, when I asked about being barred. 'Oscar, it will be a pleasure. Please do.'

'Nice one, your shout—I think you owe me.'

'Cheeky sod.'

As we head to Pilcher's, walking side by side, a song starts to sing in my head, 'Sometimes, you wake up in the morning with the bassline, A Ray of Sunshine. Sometimes, you know today you're gonna have a good time.'

14

The Tale of Toby Brown

Toby Brown casually sips his pint as he puts on a front to all the punters in The White Horse down the Uxbridge Road that all is good with him and the world. But no one cares, as they are too busy watching England play Denmark in the World Cup, thinking maybe, just maybe, David Beckham will be lifting the FIFA World Cup Trophy on 30 June 2002 in Yokohama, Japan. However, there is no love lost between Toby and the pub's regulars, as they, like much of Shepherd's Bush, believe that Toby Brown is a slippery character. Yet Toby doesn't care about their low opinion of him, as being sneaky and devious are traits that give Toby much delight and pleasure.

Even when the then-young and dashing PC Graham Legg saved Toby Brown the teenager from a severe beating from The Magnificent Six, Toby failed to see Legg's kind act as a warning. For when the tears of relief had sub-sided, Toby carried on as before, manipulating people for pleasure and profit with his superficial charm.

Five years after nearly becoming persona non grata for an eternity with The Magnificent Six and the entire White City community, Toby did try his luck again with the lads as they were embracing Acid House, as many of their generation were. Yet, like previous encounters, his acquaintance with The Magnificent Six was short-lived and more or less went from 'Get on one, Matey' to 'Fuck off, Matey' overnight. After that Toby, swore he would never try to be friends with Eddie the Casual and his gang again, which was fine with them.

Soon after his brief encounter with the hedonistic lifestyle of clubland, Toby fell in love—well, pretended to fall in love—with rich kid Sophia Reece. The only child of a self-made millionaire and former barrow boy, Ronald Reece, who went from owning a fruit and vegetable stall in the original Covent Garden in the 60s to a chain of greengrocers across London in the 70s, Ronnie Reece's Costermongers.

One evening, a tearful Sophia told Toby that her father had been diagnosed with a severe case of bronchial cancer and Ronald had told Sophia he didn't have too long to live. With Sophia's mother passing away in 1986 from heart failure, it struck Toby, as Sophia was pouring her heart out to someone she believed loved her, that she was the sole heir to her father's estate. Whilst Sophia was becoming inconsolable after sharing her tragic news, Toby was planning how to get his hands on her inheritance, as he pretended to be the caring and dutiful boyfriend, with a performance that Al Pacino would have been proud of.

Yet, despite being terminally ill, Ronald Reece was still a street urchin and could smell a rat a mile off. He didn't trust Toby the moment he met him the first time but went along with the relationship to keep the apple of his eye happy. But now Ronald Reece was facing death within a year or so, and he knew that Toby Brown wanted to get his hands on his money. His hunch was confirmed when Sophia came waltzing in one evening, announcing that Toby had asked her to marry him. Sophia, overcome with joy and pain, informed her father that the marriage was to be in a month, so he could give her away before he died. Sophia was touched how Toby could be so thoughtful, but Ronald Reece thought differently and abruptly told his beautiful daughter so. Sophia stormed out of the family home in Hampstead and hailed a black cab down the High Street to drive her to White City, believing that her affectionate boyfriend would welcome her with open arms.

Toby hadn't told his now fiancée that his parents were away at Butlin's Bognor Regis. His brother Thomas had moved in with Betty Lace in Hackney, ten years older than him, so Toby had the place to himself. But after proposing to Sophia in Pilcher's, he went home, telephoned Debbie Franklin on the off chance as she lived just around the corner, to see if she fancied coming over to his parents. High as a kite on cocaine, she readily agreed. Debbie and Toby had a 'no strings attached' relationship, which suited both of them perfectly, just every now and then, when they got an urge or were high and, in most cases, both.

With impulse running high between Debbie and Toby when she arrived, Toby forgot to close the front door fully. So, when a tearful Sophia arrived to find the front door open, she walked in, thinking the worst, only to hear grunts and moans upstairs. Straight away, Sophia knew it was Toby—she didn't need nor want to see her supposed fiancé making love. Sophia just knew that she never wanted to see Toby again and that her father, Ronald Reece, was correct. As Sophia was leaving Toby's parent's house in tears, Louise Jones, Eddie's girlfriend was driving along in her MG Midget. Seeing a 'sister' in distress, Louise pulled over to offer a shoulder to cry on. Louise had seen Sophia around with Toby, often wondering, 'What does she see in that creep Toby Brown?' Sophia, touched by Louise's kind gesture bared her soul to her, and Louise gave what support she could. That evening they became friends forever.

Toby, after hearing the gossip of how he had tried to con the daughter of a dying man out of her inheritance and how Ronald Reece with his 'business connections' was looking for retribution for breaking his daughter's heart, knew it was best he left England as soon as possible. Being the lucky sod he can be, Toby managed to get onto Camp America at the last minute and he flew to New York at the start of the summer of 1989 to spend the summer at French Woods, Hancock, in the state of New York, working as a camp counsellor.

Toby didn't set foot on British soil again until the summer of 1999. Toby Brown had been away 10 years, yet no one had missed him, not even his family. But Toby couldn't care less. Toby hadn't returned to Old Blighty to make amends. No, he came back because he knew there was the potential to make a lot of money in the UK in the next few years. After seeing the film The Net starring Sandra Bullock in 1996 at a cinema in Philadelphia with his then-girlfriend, Tiffany Miller, an attractive and bubbly girl with a yearning to be an actress, making ends meet by being a bartender and her family trust, which Toby took it upon himself to manage. Toby had a visualisation that the internet was going to be huge in terms of usage and profit.

Being the blagger that he is, Toby left his job as a waiter at Henry's Diner

and found employment as a trainee web and graphic designer for Howlin'
Wolf Design in downtown Philadelphia, owned by blues enthusiast Marvin
Connor. For two and a half years, Toby learnt how to use Flash and HTML,
over the next three years, as well as developing an encyclopaedic knowledge of
the blues, so he could always sweet-talk Marvin over a pitcher of beer at the
bar down the road, Frosties.

Toby Brown had never been so focused in his life, yet it wasn't for the
common good. Toby knew these skills would soon be in high demand in the
UK, where he could charge an enormous fee as well as have control over his
clients, something that turned Toby on. So, without any warning, as Tiffany
was fast asleep, Toby crept out of the apartment for which her loving parents
paid the rent and caught a cab to Philadelphia International Airport. He then
purchased a one-way ticket to Gatwick Airport on Tiffany's credit card. In
Toby's perverse mind, he saw this as a nice leaving present.

Six months later, as the 20th century and the second millennium were
vanishing into the distance, and the third millennium and 21st century were
rising on the horizon, the World Wide Web was the newest craze in the UK,
with Toby Brown establishing himself as an oracle for businesses new to the
internet with Brown's Zen Web and Graphic Services.

Toby employed three school leavers, on a commission-only basis, to cold
call every small to medium-sized business across the Bush, Hammersmith and
West Kensington to get him meetings. Toby taught them every psychological
trick he knew so he could get his foot in the door. Once there, Toby charmed
and brainwashed the potential client, as he seldom left without a signed contract and a cheque for 50 per cent deposit.

Within 12 months of trading, Toby was able to buy his first flat outright
at The Grampians, Shepherds Bush Road, much to the relief of his parents and
the rest of White City. Yet Toby was annoyed, even hurt, that his growing business empire hadn't become the envy of his former community, especially with
the now 30-something The Magnificent Six. Toby hoped his success would
act as some form of revenge against these lads for the years of being ostracised.
But from Eddie to Jamie Joe, they couldn't care less, as Toby no longer existed
to them. However, in Toby's mind, he knew one day he would be a chapter in
the book of Shepherds Bush's folklore.

With no social life in The Bush, Toby Brown would venture out into the capital's nightlife, and frequent clubs like Tiger Tiger in the Haymarket or The Limelight in Shaftesbury Avenue, where he could be whoever he wanted to be, from a football agent to a music producer, as to him, being a web designer was a boring occupation. Toby's deceit gained him many male drinking companions, who also boasted they were living the dream. Yet his real desire was to sleep with as many women as possible.

Toby would tell women a variety of fabrications, including being friends with Michael Owen and such like, having VIP access to Stamford Bridge, the whole of the Juventus team being his clients, Noel was begging him to produce Oasis' next album and Paul Weller regretted not working with him. He even boasted that he had a cocktail named after him at the Groucho Club.

Some women believed him, some women didn't. Those that didn't, he left alone; those that did, became his prey. Once he had their interest and attention, Toby would create the illusion of romance so he could call them whenever he wanted sex. Once he was bored with them, which was usually after a month or so, Toby would discard them, just like a baby with an unwanted toy.

Toby didn't want to fall in love. However, one evening at The Limelight, Toby noticed a natural brunette with a curvaceous and buxom figure in her late twenties—a real dead ringer for Cindy Crawford, but without the beauty spot above her mouth—drinking alone at one of the upstairs bars. Toby was mesmerised. He wanted her and not just for sex. He wanted to get to know her, as there was something magical about her.

Toby kept his cool, made eye contact and when their eyes met, they exchanged pleasant and warm smiles. Then Toby calmly made his way to the bar, pulling out his black leather wallet, which was bulging with fifty-pound notes. Her eyes lit up when she saw the wad, then she returned her focus back to Toby, who said, 'Can I buy you a drink?' to which she replied, 'Yes, please. A JD and coke.'

Toby tells her who he really is, as he felt comfortable around her. The beautiful brunette is Catalina Garcia from Peckham. Her father is from Argentina whilst her mother is a proud South-East London girl. Catalina works as a PA at Funky Feet PR in Soho. Now on her own at The Limelight due to an argument with her soon to be ex-boyfriend, Toby and Catalina exchange telephone numbers. Eight months after their chance encounter, Toby and Catalina are still together.

Yet, of late, Toby has noticed a coldness from Catalina. There is no passion from her when they are intimate, laughter now seems like a distant memory and calling Catalina's new Sony mobile is a living nightmare for Toby, as she seldom answers her phone, responds to voicemails or replies to texts.

As the referee on the TV screen blows for full-time for England's three-nil victory over Denmark, all the staff and punters in The White Horse cheer and start to sing, 'It's coming home, it's coming home, football's coming home.' But not Toby. One, he doesn't know the song, as he was living in the USA when 'Three Lions' by Baddiel, Skinner and The Lightning Seeds was a hit record for the Euros in 1996. Two, he doesn't really like football. Just on occasions, he pretends he does, if he is drinking with his new friend, Stephen George, who sometimes pops into the pub when the England games are being shown live.

Toby bumped into Stephen George six months ago, one night down The Ministry of Sound, South-East London, when he and Catalina were out on a bender of alcohol and cocaine. Toby has developed his love for coke again since returning to the UK and was over the moon that Catalina was only too happy to partake. First of all, Toby froze with fear when he saw Stephen George leaning against a post on the dance floor, as he remembered him as the school bully at Christopher Wren School.

But Toby was so relieved when George noticed him dancing with Catalina and waved and beckoned them over to sample his batch of Colombian marching powder. Within ten minutes of a charged-up conversation, George suggested they exchanged numbers. However, Toby had left his Nokia phone at home. Lucky for him, Catalina was able to add George to her contacts, as she carried her phone with pride in her handbag. After dancing, drinking, snorting and talking with George and his cronies until dawn, George said it was sweet and for Toby to pop over for a pick-me-up, but made it clear to text first and wait for the all-clear, to which Toby heartily agreed.

When Toby and Catalina got back to his flat from their drug-fuelled shenanigans, Toby put Stephen George's number on his phone and ordered Catalina to delete it straight away from hers. She smiled and said, 'Of course, baby. I'll do it after this,' as she pulled out a gram of coke from her hand-bag. Toby, being so excited to do more drugs, forgot what he had just asked Catalina to do.

In Toby's eyes, a friendship was starting to bloom since their chance meeting at The Ministry of Sound, as he and George had gone back there a few times, which always ended with a little eye-opener back at George's and George ranting, as the coke was flowing through his bloodstream, his hatred for Eddie Savage, 'That cunt Eddie caught me off guard. I know it was yonks back, but I'm biding me time. Let that muppet think it's all in the past, then bang, good night cunt,' with Toby nodding vigorously in agreement. Yet Toby never took Catalina, as he was wary of George in that respect.

Toby finishes his pint in The White Horse and calls Catalina. This time, the phone doesn't even ring, just goes straight to voicemail. So, Toby sends her a text, demanding she get back in touch with him straight away. Then Toby decides to text George, as he is now entertaining the idea of an all-day drug and drink binge. He texts George, just to let him know that he is heading over to George's flat in Verulam House, Hammersmith, to collect some 'goodies'. As Toby hits the send button, he decides to put his mobile on silent so he can soak up the sunshine during the ten-minute walk from The White Horse to Hammersmith, believing that George will be more than happy to see his new best friend.

A rather merry Toby approaches Verulam House, presses number 5 on the main entrance intercom, and stands in front of the camera, as George insists all visitors do this. A harsh voice comes over on the speaker: 'Mate, didn't you get my text?' It's George and Toby can tell he isn't in the best of moods. Unknown to Toby Brown, one of George's foot-soldier dealers has gone AWOL with his money. George has been calling his dealer all day but to no avail, which is making George angrier with each passing minute. Coupled with missing the England game, George is ready to take his frustrations out on anyone that crosses him today and, unfortunately for Toby, that person is him.

Stephen George's ex-wife Vicki used to feel the brunt of his moods. It was George's unpredictable behaviour and the fact that he was a habitual adulterer that made Vicki leave George with their two sons 18 months ago. Since that fateful day, George has been trying to relive his club lifestyle from 1988 four-teen years before.

After hearing the irate George, Toby puts his left hand in his left jean pocket, pulls out his mobile phone, and sees he has received three text messages, one from his dentist reminding him about his check-up on Monday, one from Catalina at last ('Bubs... busy... x') and one from George, which reads: 'No mate, wait 4 me 2 call.'

Toby starts to shake, as this is the one man he never wants to cross. 'Sorry, so sorry, Stephen. Had my phone on silence. My bird has been chasing me all morning, you know what women are like.'

'I don't give a fuck if you are being chased by the Keystone Cops, you cunt. What the fuck do I always say to you?' Before Toby can answer like a told-off schoolboy, George says abruptly, 'Fuck it, you are here now. Might as well come up.'

Toby knows he is going to get a bollocking, but believes it will be worth it, as George is bound to give him a pick-me-up.

■ ■ ■

Stephen George, like his fierce opponent Eddie Savage, was born into a family of duckers and divers in White City. His father, Bill George, again nicknamed George, was a wheeler-dealer who tried to play with the big boys, only to get shot dead by a tough firm from South-East London when he tried to swindle them out of a grand in November 1970, when George Jr was just five years old. The murder of his father didn't change George—it just enhanced his brutal and spiteful manner, as he had shown at infant school just months before his father's death that he got pleasure out of inflicting pain on the other children. George, along with his older brother by two years, Herbert (known as Herbie), became local tearaways and bullies, as predicted by their teachers.

Stephen George was content being the local thug. He didn't even mind the odd short spell in prison, as being incarcerated helped his status and made him attractive to some girls, as they loved the local 'bad boy'.

Yet, his life turned the better for him when all 'the kids' were going to raves, dropping trips and popping pills in the summer of 1988. Prior to this, the only drugs George took were aspirin down his throat and Vicks Sinex up his nose. However, Herbie persuaded George to go with him and his mates to

Apocalypse Now at Wembley Studios in August of that year. George popped his first pill. Yet it wasn't the MDMA rush that he encountered that changed George's life. No, it was the twenty-pound notes George saw the dealer pocket each time he sold a pill. Stephen George saw his destiny—he wanted to be a drug dealer.

Within a month or so of setting up as a dealer at illegal raves, George's reputation grew and the money poured in. Yet George has never had his collar felt, let alone been pulled in for questioning for dealing. So, the rumour on the street, in the pubs, the clubs and even the playgrounds, is that George is a grass and donates generously to the Shepherd's Bush police's charity of their choice. The unsavoury gossip has never been proven, yet Rooster, Honest Ron and Jamie Joe are highly wary of him, so they refuse to do any business with George.

■ ■ ■

Toby presses the fifth-floor button in the lift, feeling slightly anxious, yet he believes his charm will calm George down. As the lift door opens, George is standing in front of Toby. He steps forward to shake George's hand, but instead of a firm handshake, he feels the impact of a powerful punch from George's right fist into his stomach, pushing Toby back into the lift. As Toby's back feels the cold metal through his T-shirt, he starts to slide down the lift wall. George steps forward, presses the ground floor button, steps back into the hallway and says as the lift doors are shutting, 'Now, fuck off and never come back, you cunt.'

As the lift starts to go down, Toby bursts into tears as he believed that Stephen George was his best friend. But George has had enough of Toby, from the non-stop texting to turning up at The White Horse unannounced. George was starting to feel uneasy, like Toby was becoming obsessed with him.

Toby heads to The Duchess of Cambridge pub on the Goldhawk Road, about a 15-minute walk from Verulam House. Toby had had the pleasure of being treated to Sunday lunch there on a comedown with his one-time friend George. Feeling rejected and shamed, Toby feels like getting wasted.

Drinking alone and slowly slipping into depression at the bar of The

Duchess of Cambridge, Toby decides to call his brother Thomas, to see whether he could pop over to Hackney for a few jars and maybe score some sniff. Yet his best-laid plan is short-lived as Thomas' phone rings twice before abruptly going to voicemail. Toby thinks to himself, 'What a wanker—rejected by my own brother in my hour of need.' Then he calls Catalina, believing this time she might pick up. But all hope is shattered when it goes straight to voicemail again.

'Fucking bitch,' Toby screams out, which brings attention to him from all the staff and punters in the pub.

'Mate, don't use language like that in here. You don't have to be Albert Einstein to work out you are having a bad day—I'll let it pass, just this once. 'Ere, have a beer on me and just chill out, fella.'

Slightly shamefaced, Toby looks up at the young blond-haired and handsome barman, who has just offered him a drink. 'Thanks. And sorry, mate: woman troubles.'

With each sip of beer, Toby is reliving the powerful stomach punch from George and wondering what is going to happen next. Toby is aware of the pain and torture that George likes to inflict on people, as he has heard it from the horse's mouth and from the word on the street. Toby knows that George likes to turn up in a balaclava with a hammer to a stranger's home, demanding their TV, stereos, kids' toys and the contents of the fridge. George has forced women and even men into prostitution to clear a drug debt. George has also kidnapped adversaries, stripped them naked, then forced them to take acid, making the poor soul have a trip that is sure to scar them for life. Stephen George is the devil of West London and Toby Brown has foolishly sold his soul to him.

Toby starts to cry, wondering why he befriended him. Was it all a ruse? A scam by George to fool Toby so he would trust George, then he would orchestrate a major fallout between them, so George could send Toby into the night to sell his body?

'I ain't selling my arse,' screams out a highly paranoid Toby.

'That's it, mate. Get out. You're barred,' yells the blond barman upon hearing Toby's banal drunken outburst.

Toby staggers out of The Duchess of Cambridge, believing that he will have to go back and knock George out; otherwise, he fears he will end up becoming a rent boy for George until his dying day.

Toby heads back to Verulam House, shadow-boxing as he walks, thinking he is Rocky, training for his showdown with Apollo Creed. In Toby's head, he can hear Bill Conti's 'Gonna Fly Now', the theme tune from Rocky—whilst the motorists and the pedestrians down the Goldhawk Road hear 'Dance of The Cuckoos', Laurel and Hardy's theme tune, in their heads as they lay eyes upon this drunken fool.

Toby buzzes on the tradesman's entrance to Verulam House to avoid detection as he enters the building and to have the element of surprise on his side. The doors of the lift open on the fifth floor and a courageous Toby steps out, a bravery heightened by the small bottle of vodka he purchased and downed at the off-licence around the corner five minutes ago.

Toby can hear the drum and bass music bellow out at full blast from George's flat. Toby knows no one in this block would dare tell George to turn his music down.

With all his might, Toby bangs on the door. Yet the music still blares out, so he bangs on the door again, this time more rapid and repetitive. The music slowly fades down, yet Toby keeps knocking. The front door slowly opens, with Stephen George standing in the entrance, looking shocked but not scared. 'You're either stupid or brave,' George chuckles.

Without warning, Toby goes for a right hook, but the alcohol has made him slower and weaker than usual. George weaves out of the way like a pro-boxer, punches Toby hard in the stomach again, which is followed by a brisk front roundhouse kick to Toby's face. Toby is knocked out cold. The triumphant victory that Toby had visualised over George was now nothing more than a pipe dream.

Toby opens his eyes to find himself sitting on a dining chair in the middle of George's living room. He tries to speak but he can't, as his mouth is bound with gaffer tape. Feeling like a mute, terror strikes Toby's heart, as he tries to stand up so he can get away but is unable to do so, as George has tied him to the chair with a towing rope in a series of tight knots.

George hears Toby's struggle from his kitchen as he is feeding his boa constrictor, Brutus, with live white mice bought in Shepherd's Bush market. As Brutus gobbles up the last trembling mouse, George steps back into his front room. Upon seeing the petrified Toby, he says with delight and pride, 'You silly boy, Toby. You should have walked, let it blow over, apologised and we would have been sweet, really sweet. But you had a skinful and tried to be a hero, fucking dick head. But fuck it, I've done ya. Fuck, it's been a while since I've bound and gagged a geezer. Fuckin' love it, Toby son. I could cut your cheeks with me old Stanley knife, nail gun your knee caps, cover you in tar and feathers, even shove me snake up your arsehole—that will make your eyes water, ha ha ha.'

Toby can feel the urine pouring down his leg as he has never faced terror or pure evil like this before.

George steps forward as if to hit Toby, yet stops in his stride when the front door intercom from the entrance on the ground floor buzzes. Toby fears the worst: a collection of George's cronies, a sheet of acid tabs and an afternoon and evening of torture.

George, easily sensing his victim's fear, says with malice, 'You're going to love this, Toby son.' George walks out of the living room to answer the flat's entry phone by the front door. 'Get up 'ere, girl. It's roly-poly time with Georgie Porgie.' Then George walks back into the living room and says to his hostage, 'Toby, listen and weep, my boy. I have been doing this for about six months. Best leg over I've had in a long time. She loves it, as her old man don't give it to her good enough.' George blows Toby a kiss, as he goes to open the front door.

'Get in the bedroom. I want me pudding and pie,' George says with delight, as he opens the front door. 'Oh, you naughty boy,' says a woman's voice, a voice that is so familiar to the bound and gagged Toby—the love of his life, Catalina.

Ten minutes later, Toby is listening with sheer horror to the pants and groans of a slightly more than satisfied Catalina, knowing that this incident will make a highly amusing chapter in the book of the folklore of Shepherd's Bush.

15

On the Road with Jamie Joe

'Oi! Roberto, I'm hungry. Where's me bacon sarnie?' yells Jamie Joe at the top of his voice. Roberto doesn't pay any attention. Nor do the other customers, as they have all grown accustomed to Jamie Joe's jovial loud and aggressive behaviour over the years at Café Paolo at The Vale, Acton.

Jamie Joe has been a regular at Café Paolo, along with the rest of The Magnificent Six, since their days at Christopher Wren School. Eddie the Casual is the only one of the lads to have never received a ban, whilst Jamie Joe received the most. However, Roberto Alesci, the proprietor since 1980 when he came to England from Naples to start a new life and open a café in memory of his father, Paolo, has always had a soft spot for the lads, especially Jamie Joe, as their boisterous behaviour reminds him of his fellow Neapolitans.

'J, we haven't been here for a while and you're kicking off like we are still at school,' rips Oscar.

'Save the fucking lecture. I've ordered a bacon sarnie and I fucking want a bacon sarnie. 'Ere, giz us a bite of your tuna roll. A man could die of hunger 'ere,' demands Jamie Joe.

'It's a tuna baguette, not a tuna roll, and no, you can't have a bite,' says Oscar in a matter of fact fashion.

'Hark at Little Lord Fauntleroy. You know something, Oscar? You've become a real bleeding mincer. The Oscar of old would have been devouring a sausage sandwich in white bread and ketchup by now,' says a rather narked Jamie Joe.

Oscar, now annoyed and unable to enjoy his tuna baguette, replies: 'You own a bloody French restaurant in Chiswick. "Mincer food", as you would call it, is your bread and butter.'

'Exactly. It's my bread and butter. I bet Colonel Sanders didn't live off Kentucky Fried Chicken. No, just made him a millionaire,' retorts Jamie Joe.

'It's KFC,' cuts in Oscar.

'What's KFC?'

'Kentucky Fried Chicken. It's now called KFC—has been for years. That's your trouble, Jamie, you still live in the past,' says Oscar in a condescending manner.

'Jesus, Oscar, you can be a real muppet sometimes, you know that?' snaps Jamie.

'You two ain't changed a bit. Here's your bacon sandwich. Now eat up and shut up, the pair of you,' says a rather amused Roberto, as he forcefully puts a plate in between Jamie and Oscar, bringing an abrupt end to their petty bickering, which was Roberto's intention.

'About bleeding time, Bobbie, and don't you dare mention Pirlo,' says a cocky Jamie Joe. 'Ha, he showed up that Joe Hart on Sunday night. What a penalty! Same old story: England going out on penalties.'

'Shut up, Bobbie. Jesus, this bacon sarnie ain't half ropey. Sure it's bacon?' quips Jamie Joe.

'Shut up, J. 'Ere, old Terence tells me you kicked it off the other night in Pilcher's and he had to chuck you out, you loon,' says Roberto, turning around and heading back to the grill behind the counter.

'I am innocent, Signor Alesci,' protests Jamie Joe in a light-hearted manner.

'Jamie, I was there with Steph and your missus, remember? An "old times' sake" meal? We had to pull you off two blokes, cos you said they were eating too loud,' confirms Oscar.

'Well, they were,' says a defensive Jamie Joe.

Oscar sighs deeply, looks at Jamie and says, 'Look, Jamie, there's no easy way to say it…'

'Then just say it, Oscar,' snarls Jamie Joe.

'Steph was out with Priscilla the other night, as you know…'

'What? You going to give me a bleeding lecture about relationships? I've lost count how many times you and Steph have broken up, got back together, then broken up,' says an annoyed Jamie.

'Mate, it's not about Steph and me. Anyway, things are good now.'

'Yeah, I bet, playing stepfather to someone else's kids,' states an irritated Jamie Joe.

'Fuck off, Jamie. I like them a lot and you know with those blockages I can't produce kids.'

'You're a Jaffa, mate. You fire blanks.'

Oscar, slightly hurt by Jamie Joe's remarks, then realises he can use Jamie Joe's cutting comments to his advantage. 'That's you all over, mate. You are getting aggressive over the slightest thing. Priscilla says it's near on impossible for you two to go out without you getting into some form of a ruckus. Slow down, Jamie. We ain't kids any more.'

Jamie Joe, who over the years has started to respect Oscar more and more, senses his genuine concern. 'I hear you, O. Nice to know the missus talks about me behind my back.'

'She's not slagging you off. She's worried. Look, Jamie Joe, you are married to an ex-Page Three girl that most of the fellas around here, me included, would have wanked over at some point in their life.' Jamie Joe's eyes light up with pride, as Oscar closes his sentence. 'Yeah, you know it,' says Oscar, seeing his friend smile. 'The restaurant is printing you money, as is your car lot. You've got two beautiful daughters, Brooke and Aubrey. You're out of, you know, the game.'

'I was never in the fucking game.'

'No, you mug. Not that game, the other game. You know what I mean. The one that Ron went down for and Rooster did a runner.'

'Yeah, I was held for 24 hours, my home, the restaurant and car lot searched. The Old Bill found fuck all. CPS had to drop it. Ron was caught red-handed and old Rooster was coming back from a night out on the tiles when he saw the Old Bill pull up, lucky bastard,' says a reflective Jamie Joe.

'I remember it well. It was two years ago. Dawn raid. I got a VO from Ron the other day, fancy it?' asks Oscar.

'Yeah, of course. Had the odd letter from Honest. The bastards ain't broken him. Fucking good,' says a proud Jamie Joe.

'Be good to see him. You heard, well, from Rooster?'

'Ha. Not a dicky bird. He knows the score. Probably fucked off to India on a moody passport, but I don't know. But one thing I do know: it was that mug, George. I don't give two fucks who hears. He is going to get it, the grassing cunt.' Oscar nods in agreement, as Stephen George, The Magnificent Six's arch enemy, seems to be growing in power.

'The grub and the coffees are on me. Look, Oscar, I will sort myself out. I've got to shoot in a second. Going down to Hersham, Surrey,' declares Jamie Joe.

'Hersham Boys, Hersham Boys, laced up boots and corduroys,' sings Oscar, but is cut short as Roberto shouts out in a jovial manner, 'Shut up', which makes both Jamie Joe and Oscar giggle. 'Just like the old days. Anyway, why are you going down to Surrey? See Eddie?'

'No, ain't spoken to Eddie for about a year. You?'

'Only on Facebook and the odd text. He's the lord of Esher, a real Surrey man, fucking sell-out,' jokes Oscar.

'You live in Holland Park now with Steph, with her songwriting cheques paying the mortgage.'

'Ha, she can sure pen a tune or two, but I pay my way, mate. Anyway, you live in Chiswick, a real family man,' retorts Oscar.

'I love Chiswick, but it's nice to come back to the old haunts every now and then. Reminds me of who we are. We had some cracks, really did. Look, Oscar, I'm sorry about what I said, you know…'

Oscar waves both his hands. 'Forget it. Heat of the moment. Me and Steph, we're trying to make a go of it for the umpteenth time. Ha, I do love her, I really do. Anyway, answer the question. Why Hersham? Bloody answer the question. Why Hersham?'

'Jesus, Sergeant McDonald… Mac bloody Mac. Fuck, forgot about him. What a loon he was. To answer your question, "Why Hersham?" Bloody to answer your question, "Why Hersham?" I'm off to pick up a mountain bike. I am going to give Bradley Wiggins a run for his money, before the Olympics hit London next month.'

'Bradley Wiggins? Plastic Mod from the top drawer,' says Oscar.

'My God, you talk about me needing to grow up—you're still an arrogant elitist. He's all right is Wiggo. You're just jealous that he's mates with Paul Weller.'

'No, not in the slightest,' says a chuckling Oscar.

'Yeah, right. Anyway, my old mate Vinnie from Hersham, he's got some BMC SpeedFox mountain bikes. You know, back-of-a-lorry job. They are usually a few grand, he's doing me one for 200 cash. Sent me a text the other evening, asking if I wanted a mountain bike,' says a more relaxed Jamie Joe.

Oscar smiles, then replies, 'Who the fuck is Vinnie?'

'A fella I buy a few cars from. He used to be a Mod back in the day.'

'Everyone used to be a Mod, a Punk, a Casual, a Skinhead, back in the day, if you believe what you read on Facebook. 'Ere, I never perceived you as someone wanting a mountain bike, and oh, by the way, Wiggins the plastic Mod rides racing bikes not mountain bikes.'

'Right, that's it. You're splitting hairs again. I am off. Text you when I get back. Pop down the restaurant this evening with Steph and the kids, have a bite to eat, on the house, of course.'

'Cheers, fella. How you getting to Hersham? In the motor?'

'No, catch the Tube from Stamford Brook to Wimbledon. A train every half an hour. One stop after Esher.'

'Easy journey. Are you bringing the bike back on the train then?'

'No, going to ride along the towpath by the Thames back to Chiswick. Going to pick up the path from a place near Hersham called Walton-on-Thames. Looked it up on Google Maps last night. You are going back to work now?' asks Jamie Joe.

'Jamie, I work for myself, you know that. Been doing freelance telemarketing for about ten years.'

'So, you never did write that book?'

'One day. See you later.'

'Adios, Oscar.'

■ ■ ■

Jamie Joe heads to Stamford Brook Tube station via Hartswood Road, as he loves to walk past the greenery of Wendell Park en route. As Jamie Joe approaches the park, he sees a chap, about 35, well built, 6'2", in smart jeans and a designer T-shirt, coming towards him.

Jamie Joe observes that the chap keeps touching his hair and checking his reflection in car windows. As they pass, Jamie nods to the chap, who nods back.

'Just got your hair cut, mate?' asks Jamie.

'Yeah, mate,' replies the chap in a proud manner.

'Well, if I were you, I would go back and get a refund, cos it makes you look like a real muppet.'

The chap gazes at the wiry 5'11", medium-build, 40-something man with mousey blond hair dressed in retro terrace gear from the 80s. 'Got a problem, pal?' threatens the chap.

To Jamie, a real geezer would have just said, 'Fuck off, mate,' and walked away laughing—an exchange of banter between two like-minded London fellas. Yet this chap clearly has an ego and fancies his chances: the worst mistake he could make today, if not all year.

'Pal, the problem is you. You've got the haircut of a muppet, but that doesn't surprise me, cos you are a muppet,' says an infuriated Jamie Joe, due to the chap lacking a sense of humour.

The chap steps forward with both fists clenched, thinking this will be a cinch, a real stroll in the park fight. When he gets within a foot of Jamie Joe, the chap pulls his right arm up level with his nose ready to strike, unaware that Jamie Joe is a seasoned fighter. Jamie Joe sees the gap and releases a left hook straight on the jaw of the chap.

The chap falls to the ground landing on his backside, which winds him upon impact, as he lands on the pavement. Jamie Joe follows up with a kick straight into the chap's mouth, splitting his upper lip, as Jamie Joe pulls his Adidas Samba trainer back. Jamie Joe puts his right hand in his right back jeans pocket, ready to pull out his trusty friend Slicey, a commando knife given to him by Rooster in the summer of 1983—a knife that has been used more for threatening than harming people, as Jamie Joe has seen a few of his associates go down for murder after stabbing someone in a moment of rage.

The chap puts his hand on his lip and can feel the blood; he looks at Jamie Joe, begging for mercy with his eyes. Jamie, sensing the chap's fear, decides against pulling out Slicey, as he has no need as the chap has already surrendered. But Jamie Joe believes he should be compensated for the inconvenience for the disruption to his journey to the Tube station. 'Give us fifty quid or I really will smash you up fella,' demands Jamie Joe. The chap is horrified.

The chap, believing he has no choice, reaches into his jeans' left pocket, and foolishly pulls out a roll of fifty-pound notes. The chap is a painter and decorator who's just finished a classy job in Kensington. Got paid in full last week and today drew out £500 in cash for his haircut, shopping at Harrods for a new shirt, then to wine and dine his latest girlfriend, Melissa.

Jamie Joe's eyes light up when he sees the wad of money. 'Thanks for your donation. That will do nicely.' He snatches all the cash out of the chap's hands. 'Now say, "Thank you, Sir."'

The chap is scared beyond belief, as he has never been knocked down so hard with one punch and is unable to talk. Then the chap thinks he might be saved when he hears a man from over the road shout out, 'Oi.'

'Oi yourself. Nothing to see here, mate. Just having a laugh, ain't we, mate?' quickly replies Jamie Joe.

The chap looks at a middle-aged balding man over the road and tensely nods in agreement. Then the balding man recognises Jamie Joe. 'Sorry, J. I'll mind me own business.'

'Yeah, as Del Boy says, you know it makes sense.'

Jamie Joe returns his attention to the chap. 'No one is going to save ya. There ain't no CCTV down here.'

The chap knows he has no choice, so in total fear, he says, 'Thank you, Sir,' as the tears start to flow.

The chap gets up quickly then starts to run. When he is far enough away, knowing Jamie Joe will not give chase, he turns around and shouts out, 'I'll find you, mate.'

Jamie Joe pretends to act scared. He knows the chap won't go to the Old Bill. He will ask around, find out who he is and shit himself for the rest of his life. Jamie Joe continues his journey towards Stamford Brook Tube station, £500 or so up, thinking to himself, 'Funny how one moment in one day can change your life forever, for the better or worse.'

■ ■ ■

Jamie Joe, real name James Joseph was born 21ˢᵗ January 1967 to Elsie Joseph, a working girl in the 60s from Acton, and as for his father, well, it could be a cast of thousands. When Elsie found out she was pregnant, she jumped straight into a hot bathtub with a bottle of gin. After that, she threw herself down the stairs. It was her mother, Dorothy, Jamie Joe's grandmother, who stopped her from having a back-street abortion. Yet, when Jamie Joe was born, Elsie passed her new baby boy to Dorothy, like an unwanted Christmas present. Elsie walked out, leaving Jamie Joe to be brought up by his grandmother alone, as her husband Bill, had passed away in 1962 from a heart attack.

For a few years, life was good on the South Acton estate for Jamie and his grandmother, as there was a strong bond between them. Elsie never showed her face, but Jamie Joe didn't miss her, as he loved his grandmother so much: they were each other's world. Then, one Sunday morning, 21ˢᵗ January 1973, the day Jamie Joe turned six, he woke up to total silence. Jamie Joe knew straight away something was wrong, so he ran into his grandmother's bedroom to see her laying on her bed, lifeless. Jamie Joe fell to his knees and broke into tears as he gazed at his grandmother, hoping and praying she would wake up. But, by late afternoon, Jamie Joe had accepted with pain and hurt that his beloved grandmother had passed away, so in tears, he called 999. Jamie Joe's entire world fell apart that day, as darkness entered his soul.

Jamie Joe's mother Elsie was in Holloway prison for petty theft and soliciting, and with no other close family, he went into a children's home, which was followed by a succession of foster homes, with only the Knights in Ealing offering Jamie Joe anything that resembled a family life. Just as Jamie Joe was starting to feel settled and doing well at school, in April 1981, Elsie was released from Holloway prison for the third time for petty theft, not soliciting. During her short incarceration, Elsie found God and became a born-again Christian. Elsie Joseph wanted to right all her wrongs, with being a good mother top of her list.

Social services welcomed Elsie's new-found faith with open arms and took Jamie Joe away from the loving care of the Knights and into the unstable clutch of Elsie Joseph overnight. Jamie Joe's protest fell on deaf ears, as Social Services believed it was only natural that a mother should bring up her only born son, regardless of her chequered past.

Within a month of being reunited, mother and son were given accommodation at 24 Champlain House, White City, on 23 June 1981. But their bond was short-lived. In a month, Elsie denounced God after a night on the booze and returned to thieving the following morning. Jamie Joe saw this as a revelation, believing that he would find the love he so desperately needed and deserved, by fighting his way into a local gang. From afar, Jamie Joe had watched the local junior Mod gang, Eddie Savage and his friends, as he planned his move.

Still to this day, Jamie Joe views his fight with Eddie at the Christopher Wren as a baptism of fire, as The Magnificent Six has given him more affection than his mother ever could or did. When Elsie passed away in 1994 from a heroin overdose in a bedsit in Hounslow, Jamie Joe didn't even shed a tear or attend the funeral, as they had stopped talking in 1986. Now, with Priscilla and his daughters, Jamie Joe is discovering a new feeling of love, as well as responsibilities. Yet there is no one in the world who could ever replace his grandmother Dorothy. Every day, Jamie Joe wishes that his grandmother had lived just one more day.

Jamie Joe's reminiscence of his grandmother is broken as the train bound for Hersham, Surrey, pulls into Wimbledon Station. Jamie Joe is pleased that the train is on time, as deep down he hates to dwell when he is alone and stationary, as healed psychological wounds become fresh cuts in his mind.

The exchange of cash and conversation between Vinnie and Jamie Joe is short and sweet, as Vinnie has to rush to 'attend to some unfinished business'.

Jamie just nods and says, 'Sure. See ya soon, Vinnie.' And with that, Vinnie jumps into his BMW 4 Series Convertible and spins off, leaving Jamie to ride home on his new bike, a bright red BMC SpeedFox mountain bike.

Before heading back to London via the River Thames' towpath, Jamie Joe decides to cycle around Hersham, so he can take in the scenery of the suburbs of Surrey.

Jamie Joe cycles down Molesey Road, a pleasant street with a mixture of 1930s semi-detached two-up, two-down, red-brick council houses and modern semi-detached houses that vary in size and style. Jamie Joe respects how these residents take pride in their homes, as they look pleasant and welcoming. Jamie Joe can't abide seeing houses or flats in disarray with boarded-up windows, cracked glass on front doors, overgrown grass or dirty patios, as this neglect reminds him of his mother.

Suddenly, Jamie Joe notices an overweight young teenage girl, all dressed in pink—pink sweatshirt, pink jogging bottoms, pink trainers—with her hair tied back, holding a family bag of Wotsits. She clearly wants to devour her crisps, but she can't as she is engrossed in a conversation on her bright pink mobile phone.

Jamie Joe slowly pulls up behind her, with a feeling of being mischievous. He thinks about stealing the phone, but he might get nicked, but he can't see tubby reporting him to the Old Bill for nicking a bag of Wotsits.

Jamie Joe rears to her left. She fails to hear him coming behind her, as she is chatting away to a mate. 'Mel, get some vino, nick it from the old girl's cabinet. Let's get fucking plastered in Coronation Rec, you fucking know it.' Just as she is finalising her plans for the evening, Jamie Joe whizzes past her and snatches her treasured Wotsits out of her hand.

'I'll have those fatty,' Jamie Joe yells out as he does so, but fails to see Slicey falling out of his pocket.

'You fucking wanker… No, not ya. Some fucking prick just nicked me Wotsits. Come on then, wanker.' Jamie Joe crushes the Wotsits in his right hand and throws them on the floor, as he didn't want to eat them—he just wanted to wind the teenager up.

Jamie Joe rides off, looking over his shoulder to see the girl run to her crumpled Wotsits on the floor like it was her baby that had fallen from a tree. She looks at the rumpled crisps in total horror, looks up and shouts to the fleeing Jamie Joe. 'Yes, you better run, prick. I'll get me brothers on you, fucking wanker.' Jamie Joe is crying with laughter, as he decides to keep cycling until he finds somewhere to eat, as Roberto's bacon sandwich hasn't filled him up and he has a long bike ride ahead of him.

Within five minutes, Jamie Joe stumbles upon Hersham Café further down the Molesey Road: a new and clean diner, yet trying to capture the feel of an old authentic greasy spoon café, something that Jamie Joe appreciates.

Jamie Joe polishes off their full English breakfast in 15 minutes. He compliments the owner as he pays the bill in cash, noticing three hoodies on their BMXs on their phones, as he collects his change. The youths are looking at his BMC SpeedFox mountain bike, which Jamie Joe left by the window while he ate.

Straight away, Jamie Joe gets it. His experience in fighting and being chased gives him the edge: that one step ahead that all good fighters need and have. He can feel one or maybe two of them are the fat girls' brothers. She's got on the phone and gave them the colour of his bike. Jamie Joe doubts that there are many bright red mountain bikes about in Hersham.

The hoodies clock Jamie Joe as he comes out of Hersham Café. One of them gives Jamie Joe an insane stare, by making their eyes large and moving their head from side to side. Jamie Joe knows he must strike first, so he punches with a fast and powerful left jab into the face of the hoody who was giving him the stare, roundhouse kicks another, leaving the final hoody frightened. But Jamie Joe shows no mercy. He rotates his hip, giving the petrified hoody a knock-out left hook. It's all over in less than a minute.

'Fuck off, you little cunts,' snaps Jamie Joe, which is greeted by loud cheers from the café. Jamie Joe looks over his shoulder and sees all the customers and staff clapping. Clearly, these kids aren't popular. Jamie Joe smiles and waves at his new fans as he gets on his bike.

The hoodies lay on the floor battered and bruised, leaving Jamie Joe at last to enjoy his day, which he could have done at the start if he hadn't stolen the fat girl's Wotsits. As he begins to pedal, he hears one of the hoodies shout out, 'You wait, geezer. Our cousins are going to get you. They will mash you up, blood, mash you up. You 'ear me?'

Not fazed, as he knows these kids and the people at the café have the same principles as The Magnificent Six (no police) and he doubts there are any cousins on the prowl, Jamie Joe carries on cycling, looking for a place to quickly stop so he can work out on the GMS on his Samsung Galaxy SIII how to pick up the Thames towpath back to Chiswick. Jamie Joe sees a large village green, old-school England picturesque, which he likes, as it reminds him of the photographs his grandmother would show him of yesteryear.

Jamie Joe parks his bike behind a well-preserved wooden bench. He sits on the bench, sparks up a cigarette and gets his bearings. Jamie Joe is pleased to see he is less than two miles away from Walton-on-Thames, where he can pick up the Thames towpath. After finishing his cigarette, Jamie Joe gets back on his new bike and puts on his headphones, so he can listen to his classic 70s and 80s American soul, disco and funk on his Samsung's MP3 player.

Riding off in time to Glenn Jones' 'I Am Somebody', Jamie Joe feels and hears a vehicle coming up his rear. He looks over to see three builder-type men with gritted teeth, huddled up in a beaten-up Renault Trafic white van. Jamie Joe pulls over to one side, allowing the van to pass, but it doesn't. Jamie Joe realises it must be the cousins. With Jamie Joe always ready for combat, whether it's picking up a pint of milk from the corner shop or going out for dinner with Priscilla, he knows it can kick off at any given moment, yet most of the time it is his own doing. So, Jamie Joe does not fear the current predicament. In fact, he relishes it.

Jamie Joe pushes the handlebars to the right and to his left leaps onto the pavement, putting the whole of his body into a forward roll position. The bike goes under the axle of the van, making it steer a sharp right to the other side of the road. The men in the van scream out.

An oncoming blue Ford Focus smashes into the side of the van, making the van steer further right as it ploughs through a small wooden garden fence and straight into the living room of a house on the road. The sound of crashing metal, snapping wood, smashing glass, shrieks of fear and the howl of a dog fill the skyline of Hersham. The noise of destruction and chaos warms Jamie Joe, as he lays on the ground with barely a scratch.

Then Jamie Joe picks himself up to appreciate his handiwork. The nearby residents come out of their homes and daytime drinkers from a pub a few feet away, The Bricklayers Arms, put their drinks down and go outside to see what all the commotion is.

The Ford Focus is stationary, Jamie Joe looks at the woman driver, a plump and round-faced woman who is alive but with a dumbfounded look on her face as she stares at her car's roof in total disbelief, but with some relief.

Men from the pub rush to her aid. 'You all right, love?' The woman just nods, still looking to the heavens. Jamie Joe looks at the van. The back half of the van is in a small front patio garden, whilst the other, which neither Jamie nor anyone else road-side can see, is in some poor sod's front room. The van smashed through the double glazing and brickwork.

A little bit of smoke starts to pour out of the van. 'Call the fire brigade,' shouts out a drunk builder from the pub. Then the front door of the smashed house opens, out steps a 30-something man dressed in just his boxer shorts, looking shocked. Then an even more shocked-looking Jack Russell dog pushes pass his left leg and bolts into the street. Then the drunk builder shouts out, 'He's been shagging his dog! How low can you go?'

'I think he already has. You can't get much lower than a Jack Russell,' shouts out another drunk builder. There are a few chuckles as the once-caring crowd now morphs into an angry mob, as they head towards the semi-naked man, all believing that he has had sex with a dog just because a local drunk said so.

Jamie Joe is delirious, as all the pandemonium works in his favour, as no one has given him any attention. Jamie thinks he can slip off and head back toward Hersham station, leaving his mark on this place. Suddenly, Jamie Joe feels a sharp pain in his side. He puts his hand where he can feel the pain. He feels a wet patch. He puts his hand to his face: it's blood. Then he feels another sharp pain, looks to his left and sees a familiar face: the fat girl. She steps back. He looks her up and down. There she is, all in pink and holding Slicey.

'That's for nicking me Wotsits, slapping me brothers and knocking me cousins off the road, you wanker,' she mutters in a sinister fashion. Jamie Joe falls to the floor, chuckling, as he wasn't expecting this.

16

The Rise and Fall and Rise
of Priscilla Pryce

If it wasn't for my beautiful girls, Brooke and Aubrey, I would stay in bed all day, as I am not in the mood to go and see Jamie lying in a hospital bed. But the girls insist—one last time, before he is brought home to rest.

When the police knocked on the door the other week to tell me that James Joseph had been stabbed, I fell to my knees and broke down. As I did, East 17's 'Stay Another Day' came on the radio. Spooky, as I once read that Tony Mortimer from the band said that he wrote this song about his brother's death.

Sorry, where are my manners? I haven't really introduced myself. Priscilla Pryce, ex-Page Three girl and proud of it. Remember me? Big in the 90s? No worries if not. I was never after fame, just freedom.

I hit the big time when I just turned 19, October 1989, after joining Yvonne Paul Management Agency. A nice middle-class girl from Farnham—well, Badshot Lea—former pupil of Weydon School, and then their sixth form, had a laugh there, made some good friends, boys and girls, the odd lover here and there. I was working at Farnham's Pizza Express, waitressing. Saving like crazy. Thought about travelling before I went to polytechnic or university after my A-levels. But my friend Zoe Turner at Pizza Express said I should go into hotel management and catering. Told me about courses at Brooklands Technical College in Weybridge, sort of up the road from me. Thought, 'Why not?' I had no dreams, no plans, other than people telling me

I should be a glamour model since the age of 16, but I just took them as cheesy compliments.

But it was some perv at Brooklands, one of the lecturers, who was a letch, who made me become a Page Three girl: Mr Batchelor, which was ironic as he was a bachelor, 40-something and still lived with his mother. Well, he kept saying at any given opportunity, 'What a lovely pear,' and shit like that. I was used to that, but this had a real sinister feel to it, as all the time he was undressing me with his eyes.

One day, Batchelor cracked a joke at my expense for the last time. The whole class roared with laughter. Usually, I would have gone red, put my head down. But this time, I got up, collected my things, stuck my chest and bum out, strutted out like a peacock, never to return. Caught the train home. Got in—mother, father and my brother Darren were all out.

I got out the Yellow Pages, let my fingers do the walking and called some model agencies. They all said the same thing: I needed photos. Then one girl, Susie—I can't remember from which agency—gave me the number of Yvonne Paul Management Agency in London. Susie said: 'Tell them you're the next Sam Fox,' as Susie said Sam was about to terminate her contract. So, on my last call, spoke to Angie Lewis, who warmed to my youthful arrogance. 'Okay, darling, I have 10 minutes free tomorrow at 4.30. Why don't you come in and show me your moneymaker?'

The next day, I turned up at their office in London at 4.20pm. Being a busty brunette, I went for the Victoria Principal Dallas look, but with more curves. Angie took one look at me and her jaw hit the floor. Well, when you've got it, flaunt it, baby. Angie couldn't get the contract signed quickly enough and arranged for me to have my first ever topless photoshoot, because she knew I had it. I thought I would get all nervous about having some stranger taking photos of my boobs in a blacked-out studio, but the photographer was a gent and a pro, not a sleazeball. I suppose, in his case, seen one pair of boobs, seen them all. After the session, Angie sent the best photos to her contact at The Sun. A week later, I graced Page Three and I was an overnight success, it was that easy. To be honest, it felt natural, it really did.

I suppose I have to thank Sam Fox and Linda Lusardi for making Page Three a national treasure, and for paving the way for the next generation of glamour models: girls like me, Maria Whittaker, Suzanne Mizzi and more gorgeous ladies. Maria and I got on OK, but I always had a soft spot for Suzie. Broke my heart when she died last year—so young, so beautiful.

The popularity I gained from Page Three not only boosted my confidence but my income, too, as well as my agent Angie's, as we signed a three-year contract with The Sun. Trust me, I was on Page Three more or less every other week. Soon, I was able to leave the clutches of my controlling parents in Farnham and move to London. A nice one-bedroom flat in Gloucester Road. Free at last, free at last.

It wasn't 24-hour party people. Well, sometimes it was, sometimes it wasn't. But I was just one happy bunny, as my life was on the up and I was making good money. Yet the fame side certainly had a downside because I couldn't even pop out for a pint of milk without some tradesman, builder or van driver shouting out my name or wolf whistling me. Then I had an epiphany moment—I could be the champion to these hard-working men of Great Britain.

So, I pitched an idea to Kelvin MacKenzie at The Sun (he was the editor back then). The plan was I would go out with a photographer, get a photo of me in casual yet chic clothing, with bricklayers, roofers, tilers, scaffolders, electricians, painters and decorators on the job. No, you dirty sod, not that 'on the job'. I meant working. You've got a one-track mind. Ha! I would get a few sound bites from these fellas—you know, favourite football team, favourite food, favourite this, favourite that—under the title of Priscilla's British Working Boys. MacKenzie lapped it up and gave me the green light.

As this concept came from me and not Angie, I was able to get more money without having to pay her a penny. Angie was livid, telling me how she had discovered me and all that shit. I politely told her to fuck off and terminated our contract via my new solicitor and sometimes lover, Ernie Harris. I was now well and truly a free agent.

I was so pleased that I axed Angie, as Priscilla's British Working Boys went mental on The Sun, with offers knocking on my door. Travis Perkins paid me a small fortune to use my intellectual property—me—for their billboards. Done a few TV ads with Dulux with their cute Old English Sheepdog—you must remember those. Me chasing the dog around a house after he's knocked over a can of paint? No? Oh well. Done loads of magazine and newspapers ads with Morphy Richards with me suggestively holding their kettles or putting bread in their toasters. Their sales went through the roof. Sex certainly does sell. The TV appearances followed—Wogan and all that. I was dancing with the stars, literally I was.

Even though I wasn't close to my parents or my brother, I paid my parents' mortgage off, bought them a Vauxhall Lotus Carlton (that was the car they wanted), paid for a trip to New York, a Mediterranean cruise and a bit more. Gave Darren a deposit for a flat in Camberley and bought him a second-hand Porsche 911.

But, in my mother's eyes, that wasn't enough. She would call me all hours, demanding more and more. First of all, I would pay money into their joint account, a grand here, a grand there. But it was getting out of control and making me anxious. When I finally refused, she called me a bitch, a whore, a disgrace to the family. I put the telephone down, went to my bedroom and cried. The following day, called British Telecom and had my number changed. Threw myself back into my work, because it was the only thing that made me happy. I started to command higher fees for ads and TV appearances, turned down lucrative deals from Playboy and Mayfair, as the days of getting my boobs out for the boys were well and truly over, for the time being.

As for my personal life, I had some good girlfriends, but they were party girls and I was getting bored with the parties down Browns, Stringfellows and the Hippodrome, and even my then-boyfriend Marco offered me no real emotional support, just sex, and I was even getting bored with that. So, I decided to dump Marco and take a break, as I knew all the deals and my friends would still be waiting for me. I pissed off to Sardinia on my own for a month, in a villa, not telling anyone where I was staying. It was great to be away from the limelight.

I decided when I got back I would carry on with the endorsements, pitch Priscilla's British Working Boys as a TV show, take acting classes and reconcile with my mother. But sadly, I never got the chance, because when I landed at Gatwick, I was shocked to see my face on the front page of the Daily Mirror on the news stand, with the headline 'Priscilla Pryce Goes on Holiday as Her Mother Dies'.

Trembling and sweating profusely, I picked up the paper to read that my mother had had a heart attack, died and been buried. Next to the photos of my mother's funeral was a photo of me, sunbathing topless by the pool in Sardinia. One, how the fuck did they find me and two, why the fuck didn't the paparazzi tell me that my mother had passed away? I knew straight away I would be the most hated woman in England. So, I went to find the British Airways desk, booked a one-way ticket back to Sardinia. My dream was over.

Once I got back to Sardinia, I called my solicitor and now ex-lover, Ernie Harris, asking him to put my flat on the market and to arrange for my items to be put into storage, as I knew he still had the hots for me, and would do anything for me. Oh, I can be a bitch.

I travelled round Sardinia, Sicily, mainland Italy, then the rest of Western Europe for about two years. Had some wild adventures, from Cagliari to Paris. It was getting too wild, but that's another story. I returned to England in the autumn of 1994, knowing I was yesterday's news, and yearning now for a quiet village life, nice cosy pub, rambles, a homely cottage, a brand-new start. Even though I was only 24, I wanted the easy life, not the high life anymore. I moved to Hamlee, Wiltshire, October 1994—went there once with Marco for a weekend, stayed at The Manor House hotel, fell in love with the place and swore to come back one day.

Hamlee didn't exactly welcome me with open arms. Well, the men, the boys and the younger residents did, but not the womenfolk: jealousy, which I've had most of my life. But I knew I could win them over in time and I wasn't in a rush. I got myself a job in the local newsagents, Tweets. I didn't need the money, thanks to my investments and ISA savings account. I knew Tweets was a hub of the community. I got talking to all the villagers, men and women, listened to their woes and worries. I think it took me about a year, give or take a month, before I became part of the neighbourhood. After that, I felt welcomed, loved and protected.

The Old Inn became my local. Joined in with the gossip and the banter. But I wasn't dating. My sex drive had dropped to zero. I am not going to lie: I've had my fair share of lovers, some good, some bad. But I needed space and time out; I didn't want to complicate my life. Besides, there were no real catches at Hamlee apart from Dr Wilfred Johnathan Bannister: quite dashing, well dressed, always charming, but full of himself, which is a real turn-off. But I did like the local bobby: PC Malcolm York, nicknamed Yorkie, 6'1", handsome, well-built, funny, kind, dark hair, with a beaming smile that always warmed me. Attraction levels were rising and if certain events hadn't have happened, I reckon we would have had a relationship.

I adored my little two-up, two-down cottage down The Street that I bought. It had a simple layout: open the front door and you walked straight into a cosy living room with an open fireplace. But I had central heating—the fireplace was just for show. Next to the living room was an open-plan kitchen. Upstairs, a modern fitted bathroom and my fortress of solitude, my bedroom, installed with cable TV and a king-size bed.

My cottage was a five-minute walk or, in some cases, a staggering distance, from the Old Inn. Quite often, a few of the locals, like Dr Bannister or Yorkie when he was off duty, would come back to mine for a nightcap, but I was never alone with either of them, I made sure of that. Two of my favourite house guests were Louis Brookes and Sofia Emmerson: two lovely local teenagers, both finished their A-levels, working all hours God sent at nearby Castle Combe Circuit, saving up to travel around Australia. Real sweethearts. I was only six years older than them, but I had experienced life and was now living on my own terms. They liked that a lot. I could see them succeeding: they had it, they really did. But life had other plans for them.

One morning, Fred Howell, the pig farmer, found the bodies of my beautiful friends, Louis and Sofia. Louis was found impaled to a fence with a pitch fork in his chest. He had slowly bled to death. Five feet or so away from him, the half-naked body of Sofia laid. She had died from strangulation. I can't go into details, because it still breaks my heart to this day thinking that their last moments on Earth were evil.

I cried all day when I heard the news.

Then the rumour mill started to tread, from local priest, Father Murray, to me being a suspect. We all know when something bad happens, everyone has a theory. But one name that kept cropping up was Barney Dawson, otherwise known as Barney Rubble. Overweight, socially awkward, simple and as strong as an ox. Lived alone in his departed mother's house, her only son and heir. Just before the murders, Barney was everybody's friend, seen as helpful and kind, one of their own. But once the gossip spread, the whole village, apart from me and Yorkie, thought it must be him, especially Dr Bannister.

Barney kept his distance. I didn't blame him, because I was now seeing a vicious side to this village. Sherlock Holmes once said that 'nowhere is more evil than an English village'. So true.

Soon after, the rumour mill clunked over from the village to the tabloids, like my former employers, The Sun, naming Barney Dawson as the murderer, due to him being a simpleton and a reliable source from the village who wished to remain nameless stating that Barney tortures pigs, walks in the woods naked and is obsessed with serial killers. But, as the saying goes in the media, 'Never let the truth get in the way of a good story.'

The next day, the BBC, Sky, ITV and fuck knows who else's broadcasting vans were parked outside Barney's house.

Barney was pulled in three times. I was only questioned once, like most of the village. Barney was always released without charge, but the papers wouldn't let up. I called him a few times on his landline, got his answering machine each time, left a message, but he never called back.

Barney must have thought I was against him because everyone in the village had stopped talking to him. But I wanted to help him in his hour of need. That's why I didn't leave straight after the murder. But I did sleep with one eye open and with a fire poker by my side, as there was a nutter on the loose.

Forgot to say, The Sun had a field day when they found out I was living in Hamlee and wasted no time in publishing photos of me in a baggy jumper, jeans and trainers, hair tied back with a few extra pounds, with the headline, Who's That Fatty? Shit like this can send you over the edge. That's why you know I pissed off to Europe for two years, recharged and came back.

It was no surprise that one morning, Barney was found hanging in his garage. I mean who can take two months of the press outside your home, two months of being excluded by your village, two months of police harassment? Who? No one, that's who.

On the evening of Barney 's suicide, the village threw a huge street party. The press was there, even the bleeding CID, turning a blind eye to a few of the locals rolling a joint or popping pills. Fireworks were being let off in the street,

BBQs set up and a big bonfire lit at the cross roads of The Street. I was expecting at any given moment for the whole village to start singing The Wicked Witch is Dead. It really was like the Hammer House of Horrors.

I wanted to leave that night, because this was total and utter insanity. I planned to pay for a taxi all the way to London, because the idea of dancing round my handbag at the Hippodrome with some fella charged up on Charlie, boasting how rich he is, seemed really appealing. At least it's authentic madness, not evil.

As the fireworks were lighting up the sky, I started to pack downstairs. Called a taxi from Chippenham, agreed a price, and the controller said a car would be with me in 45 minutes. I was buggered if I was going to use the local taxi firm, Rusty's Cabs.

As I was starting to see light at the end of the tunnel, there was a knock on my front door. Abruptly, without thinking, I opened the door. In fact, I was in a mood for an argument as they were celebrating the suicide of a man and not mourning the death of two beautiful teenagers.

There, stood before me, was a very merry Dr Bannister. This brought back memories: a pissed horny man knocking on my door late at night. I closed the door slightly and stood in the gap, a natural stance to show him he wasn't coming in. 'Yes?' I said in an abrupt way.

'Not joining us?'

I shook my head gently in disbelief. 'Doctor, I am busy, so if you don't mind…' I started to move back and slowly close the door. Then it hit me, it really did: the murderer was standing right before me.

Dr Bannister must have read my mind. He put his foot in the door, then pushed me hard. I fell backwards, fortunately onto my sofa. He stepped in, slammed the door shut behind him. I leapt up to face Dr Bannister. I was looking at pure evil.

'Priscilla Pryce: Page Three whore. I've spent years wanking over you, fucking years. When you came here, I thought you and I would be at it, at it, at it, at it, do you hear me?'

'I think the whole village heard you,' were the words that left my mouth.

'It was me, me that made the women round here warm to you. When they visited my surgery, I would say, "Give her a chance." They listened and obeyed.

Now, get upstairs, get your clothes off. I am going to give you a rogering you'll never forget.' As he said this, Dr Bannister started to undo his belt.

I smiled, a fake smile, but he smiled back, believing his 'persuasive' words had aroused me. I walked over put my hands on his shoulders. The foolish and drunk doctor closed his eyes, opened his mouth and moved forward towards me. Dr Bannister didn't see me raise my right knee. With all the strength, I could muster, I drove my knee straight hard into his nuts. Dr Bannister screamed out in pain and hit the floor hard. I jumped over him, ran for my dear life to the front door, pulling it open as I ran into the street crying and screaming.

The villagers were still staring at the sky in delight at the fireworks. Then I saw Yorkie with his Border Collie, Sandy, standing back from the celebrations. He saw me and my fear. I ran straight towards him, he opened his arms, I ran into them and he hugged me. As he was embracing me, I screamed out, 'Dr Bannister killed Louis and Sofia, he killed them… he fucking killed them.' Just like a scene from a Western, the piano player stopped.

I suppose you were hoping he was arrested on the spot, but no, oh no. I was arrested for ABH and prostitution. As I was shrieking his wrongdoings to the universe, he came out of my cottage holding his balls and said, 'She's a hooker. She demanded money from me for sex. When I refused… she attacked me.'

This is England, so who are they going to believe? An ex-Page Three girl or a former public-school pupil? Yorkie had no choice but to arrest me and take me to the local police station. Later, I was transferred to Wiltshire Police Station. For 24 hours, I pleaded my innocence and Dr Bannister's guilt. They found no evidence that I was a prostitute and Dr Bannister dropped the charges, so I was released without charge. But the following day, you guessed it, I was front-page news again: 'Priscilla Pryce Call Girl During Murder Inquiry in Her Village.'

This time, I wasn't going to run away, because like last time with my mother's funeral, the papers twisted the facts to get a story. I was going to front it out, be happy and successful.

And that's exactly what I did. I moved back to London. Marylebone. Wasn't going to stay in a village that housed and supported a psychopath. I lost a stone in weight, returned to modelling. I was still a head-turner and young. I didn't go back to Page Three. Took up Playboy and Mayfair on their offers, and lads mags like Loaded were on the up, so I was pretty much in demand.

I still spoke out that Dr Bannister was the murderer, in the papers, mags, on the radio and TV. Opinion on me was divided, but I didn't care. The Wiltshire police said there was no evidence and that I was deluded. Dr Bannister kept threatening to sue me, but he never did, because he knew I was speaking the truth.

I retired from modelling and the limelight for good in October 2001, when I turned 31, and opened Priscilla's Cuisine in Marylebone High Street. So, I had gone full circle, as catering was my first love.

But during this time, I hadn't forgotten about Barney, Louis and Sofia, and swore one day I will bring them justice.

My prayers were answered in 2005, when I got a telephone call from Wiltshire CID one morning at the restaurant, telling me that Dr Bannister had been charged with the murders of Louis Brookes and Sofia Emmerson, along with the murder of Daphne Moore, a medical student, in Salisbury in 2002.

Dr Bannister was stopped in Salisbury, where he had moved to, for drink-driving. The police took his DNA. This is procedure for any arrest then and now. The Salisbury police put his DNA through their DNA databank and bingo, there was a match for the crime scene where Daphne Moore was murdered in her bedroom. Wiltshire CID got involved and reopened the Louis Brookes and Sofia Emmerson murder case, went through the forensics, and found a DNA match on the pitchfork, along with his fingerprint and a DNA match on an item of Sofia's clothing. They got the bastard and I was right all along.

I was a witness for the prosecution at the trial at Swindon Crown Court April 2006. It felt good that a girl that used to get her boobs out for a living was being listened to and believed, as the jury, after three hours of deliberation, unanimously found Dr Bannister guilty. He was sentenced to life, minimum tariff of 25 years.

Dr Bannister protested his innocence right up until sentencing and beyond, but psychopaths never believe they are in the wrong nor give an explanation. By the way, the police are still looking at murders Dr Bannister may have been involved in.

Wiltshire CID, whether it was their snobbery or a masonic handshake, didn't even question Dr Bannister after Louis's and Sofia's murders. Okay, DNA was a new thing in 1995, so not all police forces were accustomed to collecting and using DNA, but if they had taken his fingerprints, Barney 's and Daphne's lives would have been saved. I didn't celebrate, nor did I do any gloating media appearances. I just returned to my restaurant, sad, but at least there had been justice and closure for Louis, Sofia, Barney and Daphne.

All this isn't just another story: it's a bloody book.

The BBC did a Crimewatch special on Dr Bannister in the winter of 2006, but I refused to be interviewed for the programme. So, the Beeb got their revenge in the reconstruction, by having a woman playing me in a tight white dress, white high heels and a real late 80s hairspray hairstyle, with a drama-school London accent. I pissed myself with laughter, as did Jamie Joe, who had just become my boyfriend.

I met the true love of my life when Jamie came to Priscilla's Cuisine for a meet with some heavy looking fellas one evening. I was in that night, we got chatting. Straight away we both felt something. It was instant attraction. Even better when I found out he owned a French restaurant in Chiswick. Sold Priscilla's Cuisine last year for a nice profit and put all my effort into his, because I love him so much. Why, Jamie, why did you wind that girl up?

But at least you are alive, you loon.

Sorry, I didn't mean to scare you. It is just when the Old Bill told me about Jamie being stabbed and the opening melody to East 17's 'Stay Another Day' came on, I thought it was a sign from Heaven. Well, who wouldn't? And what I meant by seeing Jamie one more time before he comes home to rest is just that: he's been told to rest at home for at least a month. Well, I suppose that will keep him out of trouble for a while.

It's a good job his knife, bloody Slicey or whatever he calls it, was blunt, as that stupid chav bird Trudie Pyke only caused mild flesh wounds. Otherwise, I really would be arranging his funeral, not picking him up from St Peter's, a hospital in Surrey.

When I realised that Jamie had only been injured and was at St Peter's, I dropped the girls off with Oscar and Steph, then drove like a loon on the M25. Bloody lucky I wasn't killed. I could have strangled Jamie when he told me about nicking the girl's crisps for a giggle, knocking out her kid brothers cos they were giving him the evil and nearly killing the cousins cos he fancied a laugh.

The Surrey police want to press charges for receiving and handling stolen goods: that bike is hot. But Jamie will walk that, easy. But the Old Bill is trying to push for theft of the girl's Wotsits—can you believe that? ABH for his attack on the kids, criminal damage, endangering lives of the men in the van, and Shepherd's Bush Green Met police have asked if Jamie Joe knows anything about a painter and decorator being mugged near Wendell Park on the same day.

There are loads of amusing posts and photos on Facebook and Twitter about this day of madness in Hersham. That's where the Surrey Police got most of their information and possibly the odd local snitch or two.

However, I doubt if the Surrey Police will be able to get any charges to stick, as Trudie Pyke is a member of a huge travelling family down that way: the Pykes. All residing in modest houses now, but still living by their own code, one being 'not talking to the police'. The kids on the BMXs said to the Old Bill they were just having a laugh with Jamie. The cousins said it was an accident. Trudie said he never nicked anything, and Jamie said he walked into a knife by accident, twice, which Trudie was holding after finding it on the street, so he's not pressing charges against her. Even the fellow that was nearly lynched for apparently shagging his dog ain't saying a word: just said it was down to it being a high-spirited, hot summer's day.

As for the painter and decorator, Craig Harris, from South Acton, he did go to the Old Bill in the Bush. I am sure Jamie will pay him off—he's done it before. But as for the £500 Jamie apparently took, the cash has never been found, doubt it ever will be. Though I did hit the roof when Jamie told me he turned this chap over because he didn't have a sense of humour. Christ give me strength.

But bless. My baby is alive and well, so I better get the girls their breakfast, scrub up, and go and pick up Jamie. See ya. Have a wonderful day and remember: don't let the bastards grind you down.

Love ya,

Priscilla

xxxx

17

A Laugh a Day with Dino

I bet Oscar or Eddie haven't said too much about me—Dino. No? Well, what a surprise. I'm the quiet and moody type, speak when I need to, and most of the time let my actions do the talking. I am first-generation Italian Londoner and, contrary to belief, not all Italians are loud and animated. My father, Mario, a Sicilian lad who came to the Bush in the 50s with my mother Silvia, well he was as quiet as a mouse. Sometimes, I didn't even know he was in the room. When Italy won the World Cup in 1982, he just clapped at the final whistle, whilst me, my older brother Luca and my mother were tearing up the front room. One of the few times when my old man would show any sign of life was when he was watching The Benny Hill Show or when Jimmy Tarbuck was on the box: he pissed himself with laughter. Oh, yeah—I'll tell you about Tarbuck in a second.

Sadly, my old man passed away in March 2006: lung cancer. He smoked 40 a day, silly sod. So, I never got to share the experience of seeing Italy winning the World Cup a few months later with him. I am sure he would have come out of his shell, because as he was getting older, he was becoming more open and loving. My mother is alive and well, living in Brentford with her sister, my aunt (both widows). And as for Luca, the sensible brother, he's around, but I ain't spoken to him in years: he always talked down to me and gave it the holier than thou towards me with my lifestyle choices. But you know what? I'd rather have been part of The Magnificent Six than get my boring brother's seal of approval. Fuck him. Sorry, he just winds me up still to this day. Talking about The Magnificent Six, I am not a nutter like Jamie Joe, vain like Oscar, mouthy like Honest Ron, sensible like Quicksilver or cocksure like Eddie. I'm an ideas man, that's me.

The first scam we ever done was my idea, at Bentworth Primary School. It was just me, Eddie and Ron. There was a food delivery every Wednesday during morning break at 10am. The driver and his mate (can't remember their names) would go into the school's kitchen to chat up the dinner ladies, get a cup of Rosie and a choc biscuit. One day, I noticed the back doors of the van open. Me, no shit, decided to go and close them. Then I saw a packet of mince, which I thought my old girl would like for her spaghetti Bolognese. I was one of the first kids around the Bush to eat proper Italian food back then, due to me being Italian, of course. The other kids thought spaghetti was something Heinz done in a tin, and their parents thought spaghetti grew on trees, thanks to an April Fools' joke by the BBC in the 50s.

I didn't tell the others. Took the mince home, my mother loved it and asked me to get some more. Back-of-a-lorry stuff was the norm with my family: my mother was a sewing machinist, so we always had plenty of fabric in the house, and the old man was a driver for the brewers, Fuller, Smith and Turner. What? You thought because he was Italian, he was a gardener or owned an ice cream van? Ha. Anyway, the house was never short of booze.

The following week, I told Eddie and Ron, both nicked something for their tea that evening. Eddie came back the next morning, saying his Uncle Wilf will pull up next Wednesday with his mates, Larry, Ernie and Tommy, and clear the van out. This was about 1973, a year before he went down. So, they did, twice, until the driver made his mate wait in the van, whilst he drunk tea with the dinner ladies.

Wilf and his lads sold all the grub around White City where the black market was—and still is—part of everyday life. Me and the boys got a nice cut from Wilf and that, my friends, was the start of The Magnificent Six's criminal enterprise.

Apart from Ron, Eddie and me all have a bit of crime in our blood, Eddie more so, as he's a Savage. Whilst Ron's folks were really law-abiding, God rest their souls, they were good sports, though: turned a blind eye and never said a word.

Word soon spread from the playground to the streets of White City that we were lovable but tough rogues, as we had a member of the Savage family in the gang. So, we had a reputation well before we were teenagers, which was nice. Oscar joined us in late 1974, after standing his ground with me and Ron. As his old man was inside for fraud, he jumped at the chance of being friends with a band of children thieves. And when Quicksilver and Jamie Joe joined us at the Christopher Wren, then we truly did become The Magnificent Six. God bless you, Steph, for calling us that at school. I loved being in a gang from an early age, gave me confidence and belief. I think this is why Luca has never approved of me, because he was never in a gang. He was jealous, oh yes.

So, we would nick and spend our ill-gotten gains in Bransdon Newsagents on sweets, football cards, comics and munching chips outside Pilcher's, which used to piss Terence off no end. We got used to seeing all the stars from the BBC and Thames Television, a few from Thames would drive from Teddington Lock, just to sample his grub, keeping it real in their eyes. Most of the stars, would say hello and give us their autographs, still got loads up in the loft somewhere.

The fucker Savile came to Pilcher's early one Saturday afternoon as we were sitting outside, eating chips and swapping football cards. Eddie always had the cards I needed. Man, was he a hard kid to trade with.

We exchanged glances with Savile. Jesus, he sure did look like The Child Catcher from Chitty Chitty Bang Bang, he really did. Savile invited us to his TV show Clunk-Click with promises of meeting all these stars and all the football cards we wanted. We told him to fuck off. All four of us got a bad vibe straight away. It didn't feel right. Savile, being the predator, sensed we would talk, even fight back. We were tough kids from tough families, who thankfully told us at an early age the world was full of dangerous people. I mean if we had been wrapped up in cotton wool, we could have easily been that cunt's victim.

That was the only time Savile popped down Pilcher's. Even Terence, the owner and our lifetime adversary—I like Terence, we all do, and he likes us, good old banter, he's still there—got a bad feeling from Savile, so Terence, gave us some extra chips for telling him to fuck off.

On a brighter note, one day in the summer holiday of 1975, a brown Rolls Royce pulled up right outside Pilcher's and out stepped Jimmy Tarbuck, bold as brass. I couldn't believe my eyes and my luck, as I knew my dad would love his autograph. I decided to wait until he got served and returned to his motor. As he was just about to open the driver's door, whilst holding a bag of fish and chips under his arm, I walked over and politely asked, 'Please, Mr Tarbuck, could I have your autograph for my dad? He's a big fan.'

Tarbuck didn't even look at me. He just said in a low whisper, 'Piss off, kid.'

I started to cry, which made Eddie, Ron and Oscar come to my aid. As Tarbuck was getting into his Rolls, through snot and tears, I told my friends what had just happened, which made Eddie shout out, 'Stone the motor.'

So, we picked up stones by the kerb, took aim and fired. All the windows smashed, with Tarbuck screaming out, 'You cockney wankers! I'll be back with me mates.' This urged us on more, so we kept stoning the car. Give Tarbuck his due: he didn't bottle it and drive off. In fact, he started his car, mounted the pavement and tried to run us over. Luckily, we saw that and ran home with tears of laughter.

Eddie told us years later he was inspired by the booklet inside The Who's Quadrophenia album, the original one from 1973: his uncle, Rockin' Wilf, bought a copy when it came out. The booklet had photo scenes of Shepherd's Bush mods smashing a motor up, a scene replicated in the 1979 film version of the album, when the mods were fucked over by a drug dealer. What a nice touch: one generation of Shepherd's Bush lads inspiring the next generation to vandalise their enemy's property.

We all thought Tarbuck would let it go. Then one night, a van-load of Scousers turned up at Pilcher's, looking for us. Unlucky for them, but lucky for us, Mad Pat, the original bovver boy and hardened QPR fan, and his mates were there after seeing QPR play a friendly at Loftus Road. This is well before the likes of Sampdoria or Athletic Bilbao would come over to London for a pre-season friendly. Back in the 1970s, it was usually the local pub team. When Mad Pat and his mates heard that these Liverpudlians wanted to slap some local kids, well they got a real hiding, a hospital job and their van was smashed to pieces. But no one, including Terence, saw anything.

Sod's law would have it, the opening game of that season on Saturday 16 August 1975 was QPR to play Liverpool at home. Fucking thousands of them turned up. But that wasn't—and still isn't—unusual, as Liverpool fans

195

always travel in numbers. All of us were there: me, Eddie, Oscar and Ron. Ron's dad took us, he usually did. As much as I love the Hoops, got to say, I love Juventus, too.

So Tarbuck came on the pitch with a tannoy before kick-off. He must have slipped the stewards a few quid to get on the green. We all looked at each other in total disbelief as he stood in the centre circle. Yet Tarbuck was unable to speak, as all the Liverpool fans started to sing, 'There's only one Jimmy Tarbuck', which was met by the QPR fans singing, 'Jimmy Tarbuck is a wanker.' Eventually, both set of supporters quietened down. Then Tarbuck, over the tannoy, said, 'I love London and Liverpool. Two months ago, my car was smashed up in Shepherd's Bush for no reason. My friends came down to talk to the culprits, yet they were severely beaten up. From this attack, we found out that those responsible for the vandalism of my car are affiliated to QPR. I want no trouble, other than for the offenders to apologise and pay for their damage. That is all I ask, and to bring peace between London and Liverpool.'

Before we knew it, Mad Pat, ran onto the pitch, smacked Tarbuck. But he didn't go down. Tarbuck smacked Pat back, then the Old Bill steamed in, followed by the QPR and Liverpool fans invading the pitch. It kicked off big time. Tarbuck must have done a runner, cos we didn't see him after that. Ron's dad, me, Eddie, Ron and Oscar just sat there watching this madness unfold before our eyes. We didn't know whether to laugh or cry. The fighting only stopped cos all the fans and the Old Bill got knackered. How no one was killed is beyond me.

Well, as you can imagine, the kick-off between QPR and Liverpool made the Sunday papers' headlines, which was followed by the BBC's Nationwide report on the Tuesday, with their presenter Bob Wellings walking through White City, making out it was a war-torn council estate. Then the following Monday, a Panorama special was aired, with Jimmy Tarbuck being interviewed, saying all he did was pop in to pick up some fish and chips for his tea, and we stoned his car for no reason. The BBC, the fuckers, secretly filmed us but didn't ask for our version of events. Well, that's the media for you and it hasn't changed one bit. The Panorama special is out there on YouTube: shit quality, but worth a view if you're bored.

But all the negative mainstream media attention helped to give us snotty nosed kids an even tougher reputation around the Bush. I remember Steve Jones, before The Pistols hit the big time the following year, 1976, buying us chips with cans of coke, telling us to keep smashing the stars' motors. 'Anarchy in the Primary School', oh yes. The BBC and Thames Television kept away from Pilcher's for about a year or so, but by 1977, Terence was back in business, as me and the gang were yesterday's news.

The funny thing is that the chanting, not so much the fighting, still goes on to this day. Any time QPR and Liverpool play each other, home or away—which isn't every season, because we yo-yo between the Premiership and the Championship—kids from West London, who have no idea who Jimmy Tarbuck is, will chant in the stands that he is a wanker, whilst Merseyside whippersnappers will chant in his honour. I suppose it's a tradition handed down from father to son.

I know I am not unique, as every man or woman has a ripping yarn or two to spin. I suppose when you get older, there is a danger that you might start to look back, more than forward. Of course, childhood adventures, juvenile antics and 20- to 30-something insanity are wonderful experiences and something to treasure. The Magnificent Six certainly got a master's degree in the school of life. But we all need to move on and see the world differently.

Most of The Magnificent Six have done all right. Quicksilver is in Australia, in advertising. Fuck knows how he done that. I know for the first five years in Oz, it was madness for him.

We had a ruckus in a boozer down the Elephant and Castle with some likely lads in the early 90s. I think Q felt there was more to life than this and fucked off a few months later. Quicksilver has been back a few times. Most of us have endured the 24-hour-or-more flight to visit the land down under, apart from Ron. He's the local smack head now. Ron hasn't just aged, he looks ill, like today could be his last day on Earth. It's a shame to see. No, fuck it, it's heart-breaking. Jamie Joe is clean and sober, still with Pricilla—she's expecting their third child.

As for me, I am doing good. I am happily married to Maureen from Liverpool, believe it or not. Her old man was at the famous QPR Liverpool game with Jimmy Tarbuck. He doesn't like me and the feelings are mutual. I met Maureen as she was waiting for a Tube at Fulham Broadway in 2004. I still live in the manor, Sinclair Road. I've got two beautiful children, a boy and a girl, Sean and Charlotte.

For a living, I am a consultant in the cybersecurity game: you know, making sure no one hacks into my client's servers or data. Started off buying and selling 'back of a lorry' PCs and laptops, along with moody software in the early 90s. It was Eddie's uncle, Rockin' Wilf, who introduced me to some fellas from Tottenham who were looking for someone to shift their nicked IT stuff. Wilf wasn't that interested. I had bought my first laptop, a second-hand Compaq, from my Indian neighbour, Reyansh, in White City. First kid I knew who was into the whole computer thing: he was studying it or something. I got it cheap, got my head around it and, in Wilf's eyes, I was the expert from The Magnificent Six. So, I started flogging the PCs and all that via word of mouth, Loot, Exchange and Mart, ads in shops windows, as a buyer and consultant. It started off as cash in hand. Then Eddie invested in me in late 1993, I went legitimate and it grew from there, Diamond Computers, and still doing it. But moved into cybersecurity around 2008, big money, reseller and consultant. Now called Diamond Cybersecurity.

Thing is, though, I dabble on the other side: you know, hacking, ATM scams and much more. Taught myself. This is one of the reasons why I am flying in the cybersecurity game. Ha! But that's all you need to know: even Maureen, my employees and the lads don't know anything about this, because the less people know about your business, the less likely you are to get caught. I told you I was an ideas man, but Jesus, all The Magnificent Six still fiddle with this and that, even Oscar with his tax returns from his contract telemarketing.

Talking about Oscar, he has written a book at last. Well, two, in fact: one about being a Mod, entitled I am a Mod, and the other about being a Casual, entitled I am a Casual. Not the world's most original titles, but they are doing all right on Amazon, and ex-Mods and Casuals are singing their praises on social media. Oscar self-published his books because he said to us all publishers want are novels about victimhood, not the celebration of life. I don't know: not really that interested, truth be told. O ain't scratching a living from his writing, not yet, anyway. And at last, Oscar and Steph tied the knot last year at The Old Marylebone Town Hall, better late than never. Half The Beatles got married there. I think that's why Oscar and Steph chose it: both bonkers about The Beatles.

I've always had a soft spot for Steph: cracking girl. Those two were made for each other. Quicksilver flew back with his wife, Cindy, and his three loud-mouthed blond Oz bastards, who you wanted to slap every time they spoke. Ron was straight during the ceremony but lost the plot at the reception at The Queen Adelaide. But we all did. Of course, Jamie Joe and Priscilla, Eddie, Louise and their kids—even though the Posh and Becks of White City are going through a divorce—and loads of old faces were in attendance. Even mad fucking Rooster, on parole for the umpteenth time. It was a great day: we drank, laughed, cried, hugged, danced and, of course, it nearly kicked off. Well, it wouldn't be a wedding without a fight. The only one missing was Rockin' Wilf.

No, no, he's not dead. Wilf is alive and well and doing time at HM Prison Leyhill, Tortworth, Gloucestershire: an open prison. Wilf was doing his bird at Wandsworth for about six months, before he was given Category D status. Trust me, that took some doing for him to get transferred. But Wilf shouldn't be in the nick in the first place, as he was wrongly convicted for fraud in July 2016, where he was sentenced to three and a half years. One plus is that Wilf should be out some time in 2018; seldom does anyone do their full sentence.

How did he end up in nick again?

Well Rockin' Wilf was on Channel 5's TV show Can't Pay? We'll Take It Away! Christmas 2015. If you ain't seen it, it's a factual-stroke-reality docu-mentary programme, where bailiffs turn up to a debtor's home or place of work to collect a debt. If the debtor fails to pay the bill, the bastard bailiffs take away the debtor's goods, hence the title. It's a huge hit, as there seems to be a perverse pleasure with the British public in seeing other people suffer.

Two High Court enforcement officers from DCBL Bailiffs & HCE turned up at Rockin' Wilf's flat at Hudson Close early one morning. Apparently, Wilf owed £1,500 to a second-hand car dealer for a bright red 1959 Cadillac Eldorado, which he had bought.

Wilf pleads poverty and starts to cry. I pissed myself with laughter, as I hadn't seen acting so bad since the early days of EastEnders. The bailiffs begin to make an inventory of goods, as the Cadillac was nowhere to be found, that they can seize to clear the debt, which, in Wilf's case, is his original and rare Elvis record collection. Wilf and the bailiffs start to talk fondly about 'the King', leading Wilf to play his records, as he calls his friends to come to his aid. The music gets louder, as caring buddies turn up with a hundred or two in cash. Soon, Wilf, the bailiffs and the chums are dancing to Elvis like there's no tomorrow.

I hadn't seen Wilf for a few years but straightaway, I knew this was bullshit. One, Wilf never buys anything on the never-never. Two, his nephew Eddie is a self-made millionaire twice over, which might be less after his divorce, but Eddie would always bail his uncle out. Ed even offered to buy Wilf a nice one-bedroom flat in Esher, Surrey, but Wilf loves the hustle and bustle of White City, fair enough.

I found Wilf's little TV appearance hilarious. I watched the show by accident—you know the one, chilling out on the sofa with the love of your life. Clearly, the tabloids felt the same as me, as it was plastered all over their papers, websites and social media pages. I am sure you saw it. Anyway, no harm done, just a little bit of laughter across the UK.

However, one eagled-eyed woman—a pensioner in Woking, Ruth Berry—went back to her Sky+ recordings of Channel Five's Benefits Britain, The Nightmare Neighbour Next Door and Nightmare Tenants, Slum Landlords. Low and behold, Wilf had appeared in all three, and in Nightmare Tenants, Slum Landlords, he had appeared as a tenant then a month later as a landlord.

Seemingly, Wilf got approached by a researcher in 2014: Britney Watts, a real Shoreditch media, vapor-smoking, hipster-type for Benefits Britain, when Wilf was walking across Bush Green. She simply asked if he wanted to be on a reality TV show. Wilf said yes, then Britney asked if he was signing on, as she had forgotten to ask that. Wilf said yes again. But he wasn't: Ed has had Wilf on his payroll since 1992. Then, when Wilf turned 60 in April 2008, he gave up the graft, but his loving and loyal nephew has been topping up his bank account ever since, and, off the record, Wilf still does all right from the black market. So, Wilf is mortgage- and debt-free.

The supposedly irate Mrs Berry, along with her grandson Mickey, took screenshots of Wilf in these TV shows and emailed the images to the tabloids.

Within a day, if not less, Wilf had been exposed as 'a crisis actor' across all forms of media. What followed, no one could predict.

Soon the press were emphasising that Wilf was making a fraudulent living from adversity. Well, the bloody government has made us used to living under these circumstances. But the public (well, most of them) thought Wilf was a chancer and had no problem about him appearing in these shows. I thought: give it a week or two and it will blow over.

Then the one-time Detective Constable Wright of the Flying Squad, now the retired Detective Superintendent of the Serious and Organised Crime Command, who arrested Wilf and was attacked by him in 1974, which led to Wilf's wrongful and unjust imprisonment, spoke to one of the papers—I think it was The Mail—about his dealings with Wilf. Wright portrayed Wilf as an evil wrongdoer and by God did all the media lap it up. Fortunately for Wilf, his former adversaries from the police, Detective Sergeant Rodgers and Arthur Legg had passed away, whilst Sergeant McDonald, Mac bloody Mac, was now a homeless man who shouts at clouds around London. So, none were available for a comment.

Then guess who resurfaced. Jimmy bloody Tarbuck, who told The Mail how his car windows were smashed in White City in 1975. Wilf replied rather cheekily and certainly foolishly via email to The Mail that his nephew Eddie was the instigator. Well, that was the catalyst needed for the police to arrest Wilf for organised fraud (the TV appearances), serious organised crime (Eddie, me, Oscar and Ron smashing Tarbuck's car windows) and handling stolen goods, which is always a given in Wilf's case. They couldn't arrest me and the rest for criminal damage, as we were all under the age of ten at the time, therefore too young for criminal responsibility.

The media went into overdrive, with articles in all the papers and the now standard Panorama special. But the one that made me laugh was the ITV two-part crime drama, Rockin' Wilf, London Crime Lord, with Daniel Mays playing the lead. I loved the scene with Mays as Wilf in his cell in 1975, with the close-up, as Mays says, 'Tell the kids I want Tarbuck's car windows smashed: a quick in and out job,' then the camera pans to one of his men in his cell saying, 'Wilf, no, not that,' followed by Mays as Wilf severely beating the man with his belt. As for the child actors that were meant to be us in the 70s, shit, it was like a scene from Oliver! I was expecting the kids to burst into 'Consider yourself at home, consider yourself one of the family.' As ITV's two-part series ended with Wilf's release in the early 80's, and not his recent arrest.

The serious organised crime and handling stolen goods charges were dropped: lack of evidence. But the police, thanks to the Crown Prosecution Service, charged Wilf with fraud, fraud by false representation, fraud by failing to disclose information and fraud by abuse of position.

Wilf pocketed ten grand from his TV appearances, which was traceable as they were BACS payments from Britney Watts, not Channel Five, into his bank account. Eddie, me and the rest of the gang all thought it was a magistrate job, a fine and case closed. No, this went to Southwark Crown Court. So you have gathered Wilf was found guilty unanimously on all charges and you know the sentence. Wilf's defence team argued that ITV's Rockin' Wilf, London Crime Lord was libel and likely to prejudice the jury, but the judge wasn't interested: of course, he wasn't, as this was a set-up, no doubt about it. We are still fighting this.

We all know that TV channels fabricate documentaries, and Wilf goes down for it? Come on! Please! I mean why the fuck didn't the BBC get charged with fraud in the 50s for their 'spaghetti growing on trees' fake report. Fake news is part of everyday life...

I am not a fan of what people call conspiracy theories, but we, as in me and the rest of The Magnificent Six, reckon it was a fix from the get-go. I mean Britney Watts bumps into Wilf, pays a substantial amount of money for him to appear on TV, an eagle-eyed pensioner with hours of recordings and the media becoming judge, jury and executioner for Wilf? A little too easy for me. And how the fuck did ITV manage to get a drama made and aired shortly after Wilf's arrest. No, the establishment hadn't forgiven or forgotten how Wilf had become a working-class hero in the 70s and 80s, after not succumbing to a police set-up.

By the way, Wilf never received a penny in compensation, because he did break that copper's nose, Rodgers, with his teeth in front of the British media in 1974.

The Magnificent Six reunited, thanks to smartphones, in Wilf's hour of need, hoping to prove his innocence and how he was fitted up. Then Wilf called Eddie, asking him and us to cool off for a bit, as he was getting used to life in HM Prison Leyhill, as he is working out, catching up on his reading, eating well, doing a creative writing course, off the booze and the fags.

Even though it's an open prison, there's still an edge in the air: fellas high on Spice, sex offenders, murderers and such like doing the final years of their bird there. In other words, it's not a holiday camp. But Wilf was born into the underbelly of society, so he is used to it, and from what we've gathered, he's well liked there, cos Wilf is certainly a character. Funny to think he is 70 next year. Shit, we are getting old and the policemen are getting younger.

Wilf knows in the eyes of the establishment and to some of the British public, he is nothing but a criminal, but Wilf has always divided opinion, because he also knows there are loads of people across the world who love him and see him as a rebel and a hero. I mean you can't go on Twitter without seeing the hashtags every day: #iamrockinwilf, #freerockinwilf #rockinwilfisinnocent. This is all thanks to Eddie's youngest, Dwayne, born March 2001, a Generation Z kid born into the internet, who is now Rockin' Wilf's official social media manager, while Eddie is now his manager, as Wilf is now a product. Overseeing all merchandise sales, Eddie has just closed a deal with Universal Music to release Rockin' Wilf's Rock 'n' Roll Jukebox. Eddie is also in talks with TV and film companies in England and the USA, as well as trying to sue ITV for Rockin' Wilf, London Crime Lord. Wilf is no fool: he knows the longer he is in stir, the more his value increases. That's why he told Eddie and us to back off with the appeal.

Out of these amazing opportunities, we have discovered the one thing Wilf really wants to do is to write a book. He's asked Oscar to be his co-author. Oscar was over the moon when Wilf asked him during a visit to HM Prison Leyhill. I was there too with Eddie. Oscar asked Wilf if it was a straightforward autobiography? Wilf swiftly said no, it is to be a collection of short stories, about him, us, some of our girlfriends, some of our adversaries and a few more.

Then Eddie asked, 'Got a title yet?' to which Rockin' Wilf smiled and softly replied: 'Tales of Aggro.'

18

Epilogue

Oscar's face breaks into a warm smile as he brings his Skype call with Quicksilver in Australia to a close on his Samsung S8. Oscar loves the technology of smartphones. Yet to this day, Oscar is still annoyed that he thought he was the first out of The Magnificent Six to embrace smartphones.

However, when Oscar purchased a Blackberry 5810 in 2002, he made a point of going to see Dino at his office in Hammersmith. Even though they hadn't spoken for about three years, Oscar never got over the fact that Dino purchased a laptop before him. But when Oscar showed Dino his latest acquisition, not only was Dino able to match it, he bettered it by pulling out his old Blackberry 857 from late 1999, which Dino kept in his bottom desk drawer. Oscar went spare. Concerned yet amused, Dino couldn't believe that even in his late thirties, Oscar was still preoccupied with wanting to be one step ahead with his close friends.

Now, Oscar places his Samsung firmly in his jeans pocket, biting his lip as he heads towards The Queen Adelaide to join Eddie the Casual, Jamie Joe, Honest Ron and Dino.

Even though The Magnificent Six were briefly reunited in person at Oscar's wedding, this is the first time in a long while it's just been them alone, minus Quicksilver. The lads are celebrating, as Wilf is due to be released soon and Ron has been clean for two months now. So, this evening, Ron is on the orange juice.

As Oscar returns to the table in the pub, a happy Eddie asks, 'Anyone fancy chips? My treat?'

'Don't break the bank on our account,' teases Dino.

'You sure, E? I'll lend you a tenner if you want,' adds Jamie Joe.

'Mate, you spoil me, you really do,' jests Ron.

Oscar doesn't say a word: he is just happy to be with his true, loving and loyal friends once again.

As The Magnificent Six—well, five—step into Pilcher's, all five of them smile to see a now grey haired but healthy-looking Terence Pilcher, with his grandson, Liam, helping out behind the counter. Even though these boys, back in the day, gave Terence hell, he always loved them, as they were the life and soul of his business.

'Evening, boys. Takeaway only, as I am not having you upsetting my customers.'

'Piss off, T,' says a joyful Oscar, as everyone in the fish and chip shop starts to laugh.

ZANI on Social Media

If you love Tales of Aggro and ZANI, please follow us on Social Media

ZANI is a passionate and quirky entertaining online magazine covering contemporary, counter and popular culture. A full spectrum of modern life regardless of gender, religion, race, age and lifestyle.

 FOLLOW US ON TWITTER

https://twitter.com/ZANIEzine

 FOLLOW US ON FACEBOOK

https://www.facebook.com/zanionline

 FOLLOW US ON INSTAGRAM

https://www.instagram.com/zanionline/

MATTEO SEDAZZARI

Biography Author of Tales of Aggro and
A Crafty Cigarette - Tales of a Teenage Mod.

Tales of Aggro is Matteo Sedazzari's second novel. His debut novel A Crafty Cigarette - Tales of a Teenage Mod, with the foreword by John Cooper Clarke, sold well, received favourable reviews by the independent press and the public. Sedazzari even attended a handful of radio and TV stations to promote his work.

A Crafty Cigarette was endorsed by author Irvine Welsh, British Actor Phil Davis (Chalky in Quadrophenia) and Ex -Creation Record label owner Alan McGee. Sedazzari was equally delighted that Paul Weller and Rick Buckler, former members of The Jam, allowed photographs of them holding a copy of Crafty Cigarette to be used for marketing purposes. A fitting tribute, as The Jam features heavily throughout the novel.

Matteo Sedazzari prides himself on being a self-taught writer, skills he developed when he produced a fanzine entitled Positive Energy of Madness during the height of Acid House. Positive Energy of Madness dissolved as a fanzine in 1994 and resurfaced as an ezine 2003, which became ZANI, the ezine for counter and pop culture in 2009, promoting online optimism, along with articles, reviews and interviews with the likes of Bobby Womack, Clem Burke of Blondie, Alan McGee, Chas Smash of Madness, Shaun Ryder of Black Grape/ Happy Mondays and many more.

With Sedazzari's confidence growing and his unique modern raw Gonzo style of writing developing, his natural next step was to pen a novel. Inspired by the works of writers like Hunter S Thompson, Harlan Ellison, Arthur Conan Doyle, Mark Twain, Irvine Welsh, DH Lawrence, Alan Sillitoe, Martina Cole, Frank Norman, Joyce Carol Oates, F. Scott Fitzgerald, Iceberg Slim, Patricia Highsmith, Joe R. Lansdale, Daphne du Maurier, Robert Bloch, George Orwell, Harry Grey. The list is endless, as reading is as exciting and enjoyable to him today, as it was when Sedazzari read Wind in the Willows for the first time as a child.

American comics like Batman, Superman and Spider-man, along with Herge's Tintin are a huge influence on Sedazzari's fast-paced style of writing.

Films like Twelve Angry Men, A Kind of Loving, Blackboard Jungle, Z, Babylon, This Sporting Life, Kes, Midnight Cowboy, Scum, Wild Tales, The Boys, Midnight Express, La Commare Secca, Dr Terror's House of Horrors, and many more, have given Sedazzari endless hours of inspiration and happiness.

As for music, anything that is passionate, vibrant and with heart is always on his playlist.

Matteo Sedazzari resides in Surrey, outside of writing, supports Juventus, travels to Italy and Spain likes to dress well, bike rides, being happy and a better human being.

MORE BOOKS FROM ZANI

Available on **www.zani.co.uk** or **Amazon**

The Secret Life of The Novel by Dean Cavanagh

ISBN-10: 1527201538 ISBN-13: 978-1527201538

"A unique metaphysical noir that reads like a map to the subconscious." Irvine Welsh

A militant atheist Scientist working at the CERN laboratory in Switzerland tries to make the flesh into Word whilst a Scotland Yard Detective is sent to Ibiza to investigate a ritual mass murder that never took place.

A Crafty Cigarette - Tales of a Teenage Mod
by Matteo Sedazzari
Foreword by John Cooper Clarke

ISBN-10: 1526203561 ISBN-13: 978-1526203564

"I couldn't put it down because I couldn't put it down."
John Cooper Clarke

A mischievous youth prone to naughtiness, he takes to mod like a moth to a flame, which in turn gives him a voice, confidence and a fresh new outlook towards life, his family, his school friends, girls and the world in general.

Feltham Made Me
An oral history novel by Paolo Sedazzari
Foreword by Mark Savage

ISBN-10: 152721060X ISBN-13: 978-1527210608

Feltham Made Me is the story of three friends whose characters were forged on the playing fields of Feltham School. In this tough, testing environment you need friends, and the closest and deepest friendships you will ever form are very often those made in our formative years at school, as we grew up and learn about the world together.

THE SINGLE

Recorded in Surrey during the long hot summer of 2018,
ZANI have created a sound that pays homage to their musical
inspirations, The Jam, The Who, The Smiths, Madness, The Kinks,
the list is endless and a remix that possesses the soulful vibe of funk
and Balearic beat. Bands and music genres that always get the pulse
racing and the feet dancing.

The songs, Tales of Aggro and A Crafty Cigarette, are two novels
published by ZANI.

Novels that have won the support of Irvine Welsh, 'A real slice of life
told in the vernacular of the streets', and John Cooper Clarke,
'I couldn't put this book down...because I couldn't put it down'.
Endorsements that appear on the front covers of Tales of Aggro
and A Crafty Cigarette respectively.

ZANI has taken the raw, upbeat and authentic narrative of these
novels about growing up, fashion, music, counter and pop culture and
turned them into music with attitude, just like the books.

Happy Listening!

ENDORSEMENTS

'Tales of Aggro is a kind of time machine that takes one back to the days of 'Scrubbers', 'Scum' and 'Get Carter'. Very redolent of those atmospherics.'
Jonathan Holloway – Theatre Director and Playwright

'A real slice of life told in the vernacular of the streets'
Author Irvine Welsh

'It's A Treat to Read, Just Like A Crafty Cigarette'
Punk Legend Poet - John Cooper Clarke

'Enjoyed Matteo Sedazzari's previous book Crafty Cigarette and this continues a similar narrative. Excellent 10-10'
- Danny Rampling (DJ – Founder of the Legendary Shoom)

'Tales of Aggro is lively and funny'
-Phil Davis (British Actor - Quadrophenia, Silk, The Firm)

'Tales of Aggro highlights Sedazzari's knack for creating and building such stimulating characters, but more so his ability in how he has them interact and bounce off each other that just seems to draw you in every time'.
Louder Than War –

'Tales of Aggro has got the feel of 'Green Street' and a touch of 'Lock Stock and Two Smoking Barrels'. This is fiction for realists.'
Vive Le Rock –

'A captivating fictional novel that works real characters from the real world, into fictional events that never really took place, yet in Tales of Aggro are surrounded with an aura of pseudo-authenticity.'
Scootering Magazine

'Laugh out loud funny, exciting and above all, written with real warmth and passion for London and the Character's making their way through this tale and life itself.'
– Gents of London

Printed in Great Britain
by Amazon